To Shona
I hope you en
book as much as I enjoyed
writing it ♡

The Truth Lies Within the Walls
of Woodland House

Elizabeth Ellen Hutchison

The Truth Lies Within the Walls of Woodland House

Olympia Publishers
London

www.olympiapublishers.com

OLYMPIA PAPERBACK EDITION

A CIP catalogue record for this title is
available from the British Library.

ISBN: 978-1-80074-227-7

Some references to historical events, real people, or real places are used fictitiously. Other names, characters, places and events are products of the author s imagination, and any resemblance to actual events, places or persons, living or dead, is entirely coincidental.

First Published in 2021

Olympia Publishers
Tallis House
2 Tallis Street
London
EC4Y 0AB

Printed in Great Britain

Dedication

I wish to dedicate this book to my oldest friend, Graham Laird, who sadly passed away on 31st August 2017. Graham loved Plockton and had always hoped to retire there with the love of his life, Angie. I miss you, my friend, however I take comfort knowing that you live on through your art. Graham Laird Art

Acknowledgements

Thank you to my husband John, my beautiful children and grandchildren, as well as all family and friends who supported and believed in me. I would also like to thank my late mum, Betty Pender, for making me the woman I am today. Gone but never forgotten. Love you always, Mum.

Woodland House

I wake to find myself alone in a strange house, with nothing but the gentle tapping of the rain on the roof above me. I feel comforted, I feel safe.

I'm on the floor of an old musty smelling house and I have no idea what day it is; or even what year. Who am I? Why does nothing seem familiar to me? Everything in here is old and covered in dust. I'm pretty certain no one has been here in a very long time. I search my mind for even the smallest clue as to who I am and why I'm here but nothing, nothing but darkness.

I look in the mirror, I vaguely recognise the female looking back at me, however, the harder I try to remember the more my head hurts. I look for any sign of injury to my head; no bruising, no blood, no bump, nothing. Despite having no signs of any trauma, it feels like I have been repeatedly beaten about the back of my head, in fact I hurt all over. I reach up to touch the back of my head to see if perhaps there is an injury or trauma there but nothing, all seems normal. I am so confused, what's going on? Why can't I remember who I am? I look around me searching for anything that looks familiar, anything to give me a clue as to why I'm here alone and feeling so desperately confused.

I hear a loud noise behind me, it seems to be coming from outside the room. I open the door to see the outside door about two metres in front of me. I quickly realise the noise is the letterbox rattling in the wind. The rain outside is now falling heavier than before and the wind is howling through the house. I walk towards the front door expecting it to be locked, however,

9

to my surprise it opens. No sooner do I open the door when I quickly close it again to avoid being soaked by the driving rain. The weather outside is treacherous.

I decide to explore the house on the hope that things will become clearer for me. I walk up the wooden staircase to the right of the front door. This leads me to a rather large landing with four closed doors. I open the first door directly to my left at the top of the stairs. As I enter the room there is a strong, stale smell, like wet soil, earthy. Despite this I have a nice comforting feeling run through me as I enter the room. There is very little furniture; a double bed running directly down the middle of the room with a small bedside table at either side. The only other thing in the room is a small wardrobe on the back wall. I walk towards the wardrobe and as I do I get a strange feeling in the pit of my stomach. I open the wardrobe slowly, trembling as I do for fear of what I might find. Inside the wardrobe there is a rack with items of woman's clothing; not like the clothes I am wearing. The clothes in this wardrobe are old fashioned. I instantly feel the need to pull the clothing close to me. Whose clothing is this and why does it feel so familiar? As I look through the wardrobe, I recognise all the clothing, but it's far from anything I would wear. As I turn and look around the room, I notice that like downstairs, everything is old and dirty.

I close the wardrobe door and turn to walk out of the room when something catches my eye. It's a photo on the bedside table at the right-hand side of the bed. As I walk towards the photo and look carefully at it, I see a woman wearing one of the dresses I have just seen hanging in the wardrobe. Next to her is a child, a small child, about two or three years old, the child is wearing a dress that matched the woman's. The photo is black and white and extremely faded. I'm even more confused than before as I look down at what I'm wearing, a pair of faded denim jeans and an oversized sweatshirt with white sneakers. Clearly not from the same decade as the clothes in the wardrobe. I look closer at the photo and find myself staring at the woman, I can see a resemblance to the refection I saw in the mirror downstairs! Perhaps she's a relative of mine? I need to know what's going on... I need to know who I am.

I move across the landing to the next room however the door is locked, I wonder why, however I quickly move on to the next door. This leads me into a bathroom, which is also really old and dirty. It consists of a toilet with hanging cistern and a long chain, porcelain wall mounted sink, and a bathtub with a wall mounted shower attachment. There is a shower curtain hanging loose and the walls are tiled in small black and white hex tiles. I've no idea why but I get a strong urge to step into the shower. I notice the toiletries, one old toothbrush one faded dirty towel and an old bar of soap, none of which look as if they are being used. A strange feeling of déjà vu comes over me. The feeling that this is not the first time I've stood in this bathroom, a feeling of belonging. I don't understand but I feel tears burning my eyes and rolling freely down over my cheeks. Why am I crying?

On leaving the bathroom I move across the landing to the last of the four doors. I try to open the door but this room is locked, just like the last room. I wiggle the handle for a few seconds and eventually the door opens. I look down to find the handle still in my hand with the rest of the handle/lock lying on the floor at my feet; I have broken the lock. I instantly feel a sense of shame as I've clearly entered a room that has been locked for many years. I immediately turn to leave the room but I can't move. I have the strongest feeling that the answers to who I am lie within. I need to know who I am. I need to know who owns this house and why I feel so drawn to this room. I slowly enter the room, torn between the guilt of entering a room that has been locked for a reason for many years and the need to find out why I'm so drawn to it, why I believe this room could have answers that I need. Once in the room it is more than apparent that no one has been in this room for a very long time as the room is thick with dust and there are spiders' webs hanging from the light shade and the curtain pole, even more so than in the other rooms. There is a four-poster bed with curtains hanging loosely from it that match the top bed spread and the window curtains. They had been very beautiful once, however, they are now extremely faded and threadbare. In the room, there is the most beautiful dressing table with a huge mirror and a stool that is covered with the same material as the curtains and bed spread. On the dresser, there are many bottles of different creams and perfumes. I pick up an old bottle of perfume and I immediately recognise the smell, it' is so familiar and makes me feel all warm inside bringing me an overwhelming feeling of comfort. There is also a beautiful hair brush with remnants of someone's hair still entwined within it. Something compels me to pick up the hairbrush and as I do, I cannot stop myself from touching the hair and smelling it. I get the most vivid vision of the woman from the photograph in the other bedroom sitting at the dressing table smiling into the mirror as she brushes her beautiful long hair. The resemblance to my reflection from the mirror is overwhelming. Despite being rather ashamed of rummaging through the belongings of someone I don't know I just couldn't help myself. I look in the small double wardrobe, it's full of the most beautiful men's and 'women's clothing. I was drawn in particular to a man's shirt that hung neatly pressed despite being covered in dust and spider's' webs. It was blue check and for some reason felt really familiar. I took it from the coat hanger and held it up to my cheek taking in a deep breath as I did so. There was a faint smell that was familiar and comforting; once again I found myself with tears streaming down my face, but why? Why do I feel so comforted by old clothing belonging to a complete stranger! There is definitely something familiar about this house and everything in it. I'm really confused as I have no idea where I am or who lives here so why do I feel so relaxed and comfortable in this house? Everything feels so strange and yet so familiar at the same time. My head is spinning I need to figure out where I am and where I belong. I must be someone's daughter; am I a sister, a wife, a mother? Who am I?

I move out of the bedroom and make my way back down to the living area. The rain is still very heavy outside and the wind is howling around the house. It's starting to get dark outside; I have no idea what time it is or how long I have been here. I sit down on the sofa and look around the room, I notice there is no TV. I lie back on the sofa as I feel exhausted and before I know it, I must have fallen asleep. I'm not sure how long I had been asleep when I was jolted awake with the noise of someone moving around the house. The hair on the back of my neck stands on end and I can feel the fear from the tips of my toes to the top of my head. Should I hide; am I in danger? I quickly jump up and hide behind the sofa. I can hear the footsteps getting closer, my heart is thumping so hard I feel like it's about to jump out of my chest. Suddenly I hear a very faint female voice saying, "don't be afraid little one I won't hurt you." I have no idea who this is, but something inside tells me that this voice is familiar and whoever it belongs to means me no harm. Perhaps she holds the answers to who I am and how I ended up here. I stand slowly, I look around me in the direction the voice came from. I was not prepared for the person standing in the doorway… she was very small and looked very old and dirty, when she opened her mouth to talk, I could see that most of her teeth were missing and those still there were brown and chipped. Her hair was very long greyish white with some red still visible. It was obvious this woman hadn't taken care of her hygiene for a very long time. She asked if I was hungry. The last thing on my mind was food, I had no idea who I was or where I was. I asked if this was her house and she said it was. I asked her if she knew my name and where I had come from, however, she was as much in the dark as I was. She said her name was Emily, she had been out in the woodlands surrounding the house having her daily walk when she came across me lying on the ground. At first, she thought I was dead, however, as she approached me, she could see I was breathing. She bent down and touched my face to see if I would open my eyes, however I didn't budge. This was not something Emily had ever imagined would happen, not here in the depth of the woodlands. She had been walking in these woodlands for many years and had never seen a single soul. In fact, the only time Emily had ever seen another human being over the last god knows how many years was on the odd occasion she walked in to Plockton to pick up supplies. Emily knew she couldn't just ignore this girl lying out here in the woodlands, there was a storm brewing and despite not wanting human company something inside Emily was compelling her to help this girl. Emily ran back to the house where she had an old boating trolley that she used for supplies when she did venture into town. The trolley wasn't that big, but neither was this young girl. Emily returned ten minutes later with the old boating trolley. It took every ounce of strength that Emily had in her to roll this young girl on to the trolley. Emily once again tried to wake the girl however nothing.

Emily was used to pulling the trolley back from Plockton full of supplies however never had she attempted to pull it with a human lying on it. Emily knew this wasn't going to be easy, however, she was determined to get this girl back to the house. 2 hours of pulling, stopping, resting and pulling again Emily finally arrived back at the house. She had a make shift ramp that she used to pull the trolley full of supplies up the two steps in front of the house. Emily ran to the shed, grabbed the ramp and placed it on the steps. She opened the front door and jammed it open with an old door stop that had been lying around for years. Emily accessed the ramp and the trolley with the girl on it and decided it would probably be best to try and push the trolley up the ramp rather than pulling it. It took a few attempts and a lot of energy however finally Emily managed to get the trolley and the girl in to the house.

Plockton General Store

Emily approached the general store pulling her trolley, just as she had many times over the years. She would go into Plockton for supplies; however, this time was different.

Everyone in Plockton new Emily, despite the fact she never spoke to anyone. All the locals knew her past and the story behind her having become a recluse. Older members of the community had passed the story down to generations below them so everyone in Plockton knew who she was. No one tried to approach Emily as she hadn't spoken for years. She would enter the general store pick up all the supplies she needed, pull the trolley over to the counter, pay for the supplies and leave with not so much as a hello to the store assistant Edna despite having known her all her life. This was the same story every eight weeks at the exact same time of day. The locals knew not to try to approach her or speak to her as she wouldn't even meet the eyes of those around her. It was clear to see how uncomfortable it was for her to be in Plockton around people. If it hadn't been that she needed supplies to survive I'm not sure she would ever have gone into Plockton. As soon as she had what she needed she would leave the general store and head back to Woodland House. Other than that, the only time she would leave the house was at noon every day when she would walk through the woodlands to get some fresh air. She never ventured far and was out for precisely thirty minutes a day, no more, no less, rain or shine.

Edna, the assistant in the general store looked up as Emily walked through the door. Edna was surprised to see Emily as it had only been a few weeks since she had been in the store last. This was extremely out of character for Emily as not only had it not been eight weeks since her last visit, but it was two p.m. in the afternoon and not her usual time of eight a.m.

Edna watched closely as Emily wandered around the store picking up things she had never picked up before and putting them in her trolley. She wandered around the store for about twenty minutes, picking things up and putting them back. She looked really flustered, however, Edna was fully aware that to try to talk to her would be a waste of time as Emily would just ignore her. No one had heard her speak since before the shocking news of her daughter, Amelia's, death in 1933 and the subsequent suicide of her husband Peters the following year. Fifty years had passed and not a word had she spoken.

Emily finally approached the counter with goods on her trolley that Edna had never seen her purchase. Meat, salad, cheese, fresh bread, tomatoes, pasta, toothpaste, a toothbrush, shampoo and a few other bits and bobs. Clearly Emily had never eaten a proper meal in years nor had she cleaned her teeth or washed her hair. This was more than apparent as Emily had very few teeth left in her mouth and her hair was so long and straggly with matted clumps proving she had never attempted to brush her hair never mind wash it. Edna remembers Emily as a young woman as she was so envious of her, all the girls in town were, including Emily's own sister Molly. Emily had the most beautiful long wavy red hair that she brushed three or four times a day. It was so long and shiny everyone in Plockton commented on it. Emily was the only one of her siblings to have red hair; Molly had brown hair and the twins were blond. Looking at Emily today you would never guess that this was the same woman. It was actually heart breaking to see how she had just let go of everything in her life and merely existed as opposed to living. How could someone so beautiful end up like this? It was such a tragic story that I guess no one would ever understand unless they had lived it first-hand.

Edna picked up each item from Emily's trolley one by one and bagged them as she went. The total amount was more than Emily had spent in years. Edna couldn't help but wonder why the change in routine after all these years... Why the purchase of shampoo, deodorant and toothpaste now when almost fifty years had passed without her purchasing any of those items. It bothered Edna, however, she knew there was no answer to her questions as they would fall on deaf ears so packed up the supplies and put them back on Emily's trolley without question. Emily handed over the money without looking up, took her change and left.

Edna had worked at the Plockton General store since leaving school back in June 1922. The store was owned by her parents and grandparents before them. Edna had never left Plockton, she saw no need to travel when she lived in such a beautiful place.

Edna had been friends with Emily's elder sister Molly all throughout her school years and for a few years after school until Molly left Plockton. Molly left to venture to other parts of Scotland less rural with her boyfriend at the time Paul McKay. Molly ended up living in Glasgow with Paul and never returned to Plockton. Edna had dated one of the Laird twins, Tom, for a few months in 1914 prior to him enlisting in the army with his brother Dan. Unfortunately, both twins never returned from the war as they were both killed in action. Edna never recovered from the news of Tom's death as she had loved him for as long as she could remember. Edna never married; she dated a few local boys, however, it just never seemed to work out for her. Still single she was happy living in Plockton in her family home working in the family business. Her parents had both passed away over the last three years and as Edna was an only child, she was the only family member left so Edna now owned the house and the General Store. Aged seventy-six Edna never missed a day at the store, she was there at seven a.m. sharp every morning and remained there until six p.m. every night, seven days a week. Edna loved her life and despite working lots of hours seemed to be very content and had no health issues. Perhaps, due to never having had the stress of a husband and children… Who knows! There was only one thing Edna would like to achieve before the end of her life and that was to break through the barriers that Emily had built up around her. To understand Emily and to help her move forward, to be able to live the rest of her life the best she can. Edna knew in her heart this would never happen, however, she never stopped hoping that one-day things would change. Emily having broken her routine today after so many years had Edna thinking that perhaps it wasn't impossible after all, breaking through Emily's barriers. She was, however, aware that if it was possible, it would take time and she would need to approach Emily cautiously. For that reason, she made a conscious choice not to try and speak to Emily on this occasion.

Emily left the store without so much as a glance behind her, even for a second. Not that Edna had expected anything different, however, given that the whole visit was out of character I guess Edna had hoped that Emily might have at least looked at her. A few of the locals had seen Emily enter the store and like Edna had wondered why she had returned to the village so soon after her last visit. It also didn't go unnoticed that Emily was in the store for quite a considerable time and had purchased quite a lot more supplies than normal.

Being a small village word quickly got around that Emily

Wilson had been back into the village much sooner than normal. No one knew why, but like any small village the rumours started and before long there were three or four different stories going around the village as to what was going on up at Woodland House.

Ruth

My name is Ruth Elizabeth Bald, born 31st May 1960 to Maureen and Martin Bald. I was brought up in a housing estate in Edinburgh in a two-bed flat in bad need of repair. Everything smelt of damp and the wallpaper was hanging off the walls. In my bedroom the window leaked and every time there was heavy rain, I would find a puddle on the floor by my bed. The room was so small, all I had was a single bed and a small chest of drawers. As for toys, well, let's just say I had a stuffed dog with one eye and a doll that had been passed to us from a neighbour.

My father Martin David Bald worked in the whiskey bond in Leith. He had worked there for many years. I've no idea how he managed to keep the job as he seemed to come home drunk every night, I'm sure he drank more than he bottled. He wasn't a loving father, in fact, I really don't think I ever heard him say he loved me or my mother for that matter. He would come home from work, eat dinner, then fall asleep on the couch in front of our small black and white television. If ever my mother tried to change the channel he would jump up and shout "I'm watching that." It wasn't a happy home but it's all I knew. My father came from a single parent home where he was the youngest of four boys all of whom were nothing like my father. My uncles lived far away from us so we never really saw them unless they happened to be at my nanas on the odd occasion when we were there.

My mother, Maureen Agatha Bald (Nee Hamilton), worked as a cleaner. She was a very bitter woman who seemed to resent everything in life including me. She had left home, aged sixteen, and never saw her parents or siblings again. I have tried many times to ask about them, however, I would get shut down before I even got to finish my question. All I know is that they hated my father, and she chose him over them. Looking at their relationship I have no idea why… All I can imagine is that they must have been horrendous parents for her to have chosen dad.

I never knew my paternal grandfather as he was killed in the war. My nana however was the most loving person in my life. I loved when I got to go visit her, albeit not very often. She walked with two walking sticks due to complications during the birth of my father's younger sister Ruth, who unfortunately died at birth. This never held her back, she was an amazing woman who just embraced life, I adored her as she always made me feel special. Nana had a box of different sized buttons, all various colours. I would spend hours at her house putting the buttons into piles of like for like, and never got fed up. When I wasn't doing that, I would be sitting by nana listening to stories of her childhood.

My childhood wasn't the best; I got teased at primary school for always being dirty and never having any nice clothes. Everything I owned was second hand and had been worn by one child too many before finally becoming mine. My school uniform was too big for me but my mother said I would grow into it. I'm not sure I ever did! When finally, it was time for me to go to high school my nana bought my uniform for me. It was the first time in my life I had anything brand new that was just for me. I felt like I was floating on air my first day as I was kitted out like every other new starter. I never wanted to feel like the poor dirty kid ever again so I made it my mission to get a Saturday job so that I could start to buy my own toiletries and clothes. It didn't take me long to find a job, there were a lot of local clothing shops near my home and I went from shop to shop until finally I hit the jackpot. Not only did they employ me to work on a Saturday, they also wanted me to work on a Sunday at Ingliston Market. I was only thirteen when I started work, however I worked hard and never missed a shift. Soon I had saved enough money to buy myself some nice clothes, which I purchased from my work as they gave me a staff discount.

In February, 1979, I met Keith Vesillio at a party I attended with some friends. Keith was really tall with dark hair, dark skin and the biggest brown eyes I had ever seen; he was just gorgeous. I couldn't believe my luck when he approached me and asked me to dance. At first, I couldn't speak as I was so nervous but he just stood there until finally I agreed to dance with him. That night Keith kissed me and asked me to be his girlfriend. I couldn't believe that a guy like him wanted to go out with a girl like me. It felt so comfortable and I felt so alive for the first time in my life. As the weeks rolled by I just felt happier and happier, however, I knew that eventually I would have to introduce Keith to my parents. I was convinced that once he met them and saw my home he wouldn't want to stick around. I couldn't have predicted how things would turn out. My mother fell in love with Keith almost instantly and she couldn't have been any nicer. This confused me as my mother was never nice to me, however, I was just happy that she was so nice to Keith. My father on the other hand barely said hello. The following week I took Keith to meet nana. I knew instantly that she approved and couldn't have been happier than I was at that exact moment standing with the two people I loved most in the world, my adorable nana and the love of my life, Keith. Could life get any better!

Keith took me to meet his parents Anna and Tony on a

Saturday afternoon straight after he picked me up from work. They could smell the aroma of his mother's cooking as they approached the front door. Keith's mother loved to cook, and she was extremely good at it, as Ruth was about to find out. Ruth also met Keith's nonna as she lived with the Vasillios since her husband passed away, eight years ago. Ruth was extremely nervous when she first entered their home, however, she needn't have been as the Vasillios loved her, especially nonna.

On the 10th July 1982, just over three years since Ruth & Keith met, Keith proposed. He had planned it for months and had picked out a ring and written a speech so everything would be perfect. He picked Ruth up from work and took her to their favourite spot in the Queens Park, got down on one knee and read out his pre-written speech. Ruth was so excited she, for once in her life, was speechless. When, finally she found her voice, all she could say was, yes, yes, yes, I will. Her first thought was how happy her Nana would be, she just couldn't wait to tell her and show her the ring Keith had picked out by himself. Her next thought was how excited her colleagues and friends would be for her. She then thought about the excitement she knew would be shared between them all when they sat Keith's parents and Nonna down to tell them. She was just so excited it didn't even cross her mind how her parents would react to the news; to be honest it didn't matter what they thought she really didn't care. Keith was so happy that he was finally going to marry the most amazing woman he had ever met and to top it all his family loved her too. They decided to go straight to Keith's parents to tell them the good news first as they both knew it would be received with enthusiasm and love; especially from Nonna. They drove straight to Keith's parents' house from the Queens Park, stopping briefly to pick up a bottle of 'Champagne', okay, cheap fizz! As they approached the Vassillios' she felt guilty that her first thought was to tell the Vassillios her exciting news. She not only felt that she wanted to tell them first, she had a need to tell them first.

Anna was in the kitchen cooking as was normal at seven pm of an evening. Tony was sitting on his chair watching the television as was his normal, waiting on Anna to call him for dinner. Nonna was feeding Teeto, the family cat, out in the conservatory when she heard Keith and Ruth come through the front door. No one stopped what they were doing as to them this was just a normal evening. Little did they know that they were about to find out some amazing news that would truly bring them great happiness.

Keith walked into the kitchen first, followed by Ruth looking rather sheepish. They asked Anna to stop what she was doing and come into the living-room and to bring Nonna with her as they had some news. Anna's stomach was full of butterflies as she pulled nonna from the conservatory into the living room. Nonna suspected what was about to happen but wouldn't allow herself to get over excited just in case she was mistaken. Anna sat on the sofa pulling nonna down by her side; Tony looked at them as they sat wondering why they had all come into the living-room. "Is there a problem?" said Tony.

Keith looked at his father and said, "No Dad there is no problem; in fact, I'm pretty sure what we are about to tell you will make you all very happy."

Anna couldn't hold back any longer, "Oh my goodness you're pregnant Ruth, aren't you?" Ruth blushed and didn't quite know how to react.

Keith looked at his mother and said "No, Ma, Ruth is not pregnant... However, she is engaged..." Nonna squealed with delight as Anna rushed over to Ruth and pulled her close to her telling her over and over how happy she was to be gaining such a wonderful daughter.

Tony stood up and reached for his son's' hand with a huge smile on his face. "Congratulations, boy," he said as he looked his son in the eye. His next words shocked Ruth, but not Keith as his father was always a very generous man. "The weddings on me," he blurted out without even consulting his wife. Ruth couldn't believe her ears as this was not what she expected to hear. Tony saw the shock on Ruth's face and mistook this for embarrassment/anger so quickly said, "Unless your parents wish to pay, of course."

Ruth couldn't speak for a few moments as the thought of her parents even congratulating her was far from what would happen never mind offering to pay for the wedding. Ruth finally found her voice and started to speak however she was so overwhelmed that she found herself tongue tied and couldn't string a proper sentence together. Keith replied on her behalf and said, "Pa, we would love to accept your offer." Tony was really happy and grabbed his son into a bear hug then pulled Ruth forward to join in a group hug. Meanwhile Nonna and Anna had already started planning the wedding. Ruth couldn't have been happier, this was by far, the happiest day of her life. Keith poured five glasses of "'Champagne'," and asked everyone to raise their glass to toast the soon to be newest in a long line of Mrs Vasillios. After the toast Keith announced that they would have to go as they still had to tell Ruth's parents and Nana. Anne was upset as she wanted them to stay for dinner, however, understood the importance of telling Ruth's family about their engagement. Ruth on the other hand would have been happy to stay for dinner had it not been that she was extremely excited to go and see her Nana to give her the good news. She wasn't excited to tell her parents as she knew the response would be nothing like the one from the Vasillio family, nor that from nana.

Ruth and Keith kissed the family goodbye and left to go tell Ruth's nana the good news before heading on to tell her parents. As they approached nana's house Ruth noticed a police car parked outside. She quickly dismissed it assuming it was for someone else in the street, nana would have no reason for police to visit her. As she walked up the path, she noticed that the police were in fact in nana's house. She started to imagine all sorts as she ran towards the door. Keith was following behind not quite knowing what to think. As they entered the house, they heard nana scream. Ruth pushed passed the policewoman who stood in the doorway of nana's living room and ran over to Nana who was hunched over whaling like an injured animal. "Nana, Nana, Nana what's happened?" asked Ruth, however her nana couldn't even look up never mind explain to Ruth what was going on.

The policewoman in the doorway looked directly at Keith and said, "I think you'd better both take a seat." The policewoman looked at Ruth and said, "Are you Ruth Bald?"

Ruth answered "Yes, I am Ruth Bald; what's going on?"

"|Can you please sit down, Miss Bald!" Ruth sat down on the sofa next to Keith. Nana was still sobbing into her hands; Ruth's heart was beating very fast. "I'm sorry to have to inform you that there has been an accident. Your father was driving and he lost control of the vehicle which then veered across the road and went head on into an oncoming car. Both cars were badly damaged and I'm afraid all passengers were pronounced dead at the scene. Your parents were both in the car; I'm so sorry, Miss Bald."

Ruth sat in silence as the policewoman continued with all the details of the accident and what would happen next. When the policewoman was finished Ruth stood up, shook her hand, and said she would be happy to identify her parent's bodies once she had tended to her nana who obviously had just lost her son. The policewoman was a little shocked at Ruth's reaction to the news; she had just lost both her parents and yet there seemed to be no emotion other than the need to comfort her nana. The policewoman handed Ruth her card and said she would be in contact once the bodies were at the morgue in order to arrange a day and time for identification. "Thank you," said Ruth, as she showed the two police officers out. Ruth returned quickly to the living room and immediately ran over to her nana and sat by her side pulling her into her to comfort her. Keith sat in silence; he too was shocked at the lack of emotion from Ruth. To him Ruth was so loving and caring and he had witnessed that with her nana and indeed his family too. That said he knew that Ruth did not have a close relationship with either of her parents, however, he never for one second would have expected Ruth to seem so removed from the emotion of the events of the car crash and subsequent death of both her parents. He was shocked and at the same time worried that Ruth was holding everything in for her nana's sake. She was bound to break down when they got home...

"We are going to stay here for a few days with Nana," said Ruth. "She's had a terrible shock, and I don't want to leave her alone; she has just lost her son after all." Keith stared at Ruth for a few moments but there truly was no sign of any grief from her, no emotion at all other than the need to comfort her nana. It seemed odd that Ruth needed no comfort despite just hearing the awful news that both her parents had died in a road traffic accident. It was almost as if two people she didn't know had just died and she was focused on making sure the family got all the

28

comfort they needed. I'm not going to lie, it shocked me how aloof she was; I didn't recognise Ruth at all. Perhaps it was shock, and she had just gone on auto pilot to make sure nana was all right. After all her nana was the one person in her life who had loved her unconditionally and who she had loved the same in return.

Nana looked up with tears still streaming down her face. Her clothes were tear stained and she looked so tiny and vulnerable as she looked up at Ruth and me. "You must both go home she said, you have to process this terrible news and deal with your emotions. Staying here won't help any of us darling. Ruth, I need to be alone to deal with this awful news as losing a child is the worst thing a mother can experience. I need to focus on myself and how I am going to cope without my boy. I will be no good to you if I can't get myself to a stronger place to enable me to cope. You need to go home and allow yourself to take on board the fact that you have lost both of your parents today my darling. I know they were far from perfect and you didn't have the best life with them, however, they were still your parents. You need to find a way to move forward and forgive them all their sins and grieve for them properly otherwise you will not be able to move forward with your life."

I agreed whole heartedly with Ruth's nana as I was extremely worried that she would throw all her strength into comforting her nana and that she would eventually fall to pieces. Surely, she must be holding back for her nana's sake! No one can lose both their parents and feel nothing! Or perhaps I don't know Ruth as deeply as I thought I did. Ruth cuddles her nana and insists that we stay to look after her. However, her Nana is very set in her ways and tells Ruth that the best thing Ruth and I could do for her was to leave her be and allow her to process her feelings in her own way. Ruth was reluctant to leave however I persuaded her that leaving her nana to do things her own way was the most respectful and loving thing to do as it is exactly what she requested and needed. Ruth finally agreed to leave on the understanding that we would return the next day. Ruth's nana agreed that we could come back, however, not the next day, she requested that we give her a couple of days and that when we did return, we would leave when asked and didn't try to convince her that she needed them there. Ruth agreed and we left her nana to process her loss and deal with her emotions in a way that only she could. We got back to Ruth's flat without a word passing from either of them. I was certain that Ruth would break down as soon as we got into the flat, however I couldn't have been more wrong. "Do you want a drink, Keith?" were the first words from her mouth.

"I think we need to talk about what's happened, darling. Come and sit with me, I'm here for you to support you in any way I can."

"I don't need support Keith. I just need to get on with things. My parents never showed me any form of love, so their death doesn't change anything. I've always been alone except when at nana's, until I met you that is. It's not as if I've lost anything, my life will be no different, in actual fact life will be so much easier now, as I don't have to pretend to be part of a family I never belonged in. I can focus on my future with you and making sure nana has everything she needs from me. I don't expect you to understand, Keith, as you have a very loving family, your parents have shown me more love and respect in the short time I've known them that either of my parents showed me my whole life."

"You're right, Ruth, I don't understand, however, I hear you loud and clear and love you enough to respect your wishes as you have respected your nanas. I will only discuss your parents if and when you feel the need. Other than that, I will be here for you on all levels as before. I do feel, however, that we should put off our engagement for the time being."

"No way," said Ruth, "I'm not letting them ruin any more of my life. I've never felt as happy as I did when you proposed, so no, Keith, we are not putting our future on hold no matter what. Let's face it, it's not as if we have plans to marry next week!"

"Okay, my love, whatever you feel is appropriate."

I stayed with Ruth that evening as I often did and not another word was spoken with regards to her parents' accident. The following morning, I woke to find Ruth had gone; there was a note to say she had gone to work and would call me later. I shouldn't have been shocked as her behaviour was no different from what I should have expected given her reaction to the whole situation the evening before. I called his boss and explained the situation; he was a great guy and told me to take the rest of the week off. I kind of felt bad as Ruth was working while I took time off, but I just wanted to be around just in case Ruth needed me, despite insisting she wouldn't. I took a shower then headed over to tell my parents and nonna the news about Ruth's parents. I pulled up outside their house at ten thirty knowing they would be up and around and breakfast would be over as they always got up at seven thirty and ate breakfast at eight thirty. I sat in the car for a few seconds contemplating how I explain Ruth being at work. My family were extremely close and I just knew in my heart that they would not understand Ruth's lack of grief. I didn't want my parents or nonna's view of Ruth to change as they adored her. I was extremely worried that this would change everything.

I was just getting out of the car when I noticed nonna in the garden, she often spent time there pottering about pulling weeds and making sure everything looked perfect. As soon as she saw me, she shouted, "Ciao bambino mio." Nonna didn't realise how loud she was as she was hard of hearing, however, she refused to wear any form of hearing aid. I walked up the path and embraced Nonna as I always did, she knew however that something was wrong "Qual e il problema bambino?"

"Please Nonna just go inside, and I will explain."

Nonna walked into the house and I followed behind. My mother was in the kitchen making homemade pasta and my father was sitting in front of the television watching sport as always. I asked my mother to come into the sitting room then asked my father to please turn the television off for a moment as I had something important to tell them. I could see the worry in all of their faces, and it immediately came to me that they would be assuming something had happened to Ruth. I quickly explained that Ruth was fine to put their minds at ease. I asked them to sit down while I explained everything to them. Explaining about the police being at Ruth's nana's when we arrived and the whole story about the road accident and Ruth's parents being dead was straight forward enough, however when I stopped talking, they all looked at me in shock.

"Where is Ruth?" my mother asked.

My stomach knotted at that moment as I knew what I was about to say would not sit well with any of them. "Ruth is at work" I said feeling the tension in the room and the disbelief on all three faces in front of me. Che Cosa? said my mother and nonna at the same time. My father just stared at me looking for an explanation. I wanted so badly to explain to my parents why Ruth was acting the way she was, however, truth be known I'm not really sure I understand myself.

My mother sat staring at me as if she needed me to help her to understand how my beautiful Ruth, the girl they had known and loved for so long was acting so aloof. "I'm not sure I can help you to understand the way Ruth has reacted to her parent's death other than to tell you that her family was far from the perfect family."

"No family is perfect," said Nonna.

"Yes, I know, however, Ruth's family are not, or should I say were not like our family."

"What do you mean" asked my father.

"Well Ruth's father was an alcoholic who barely acknowledged anyone else's existence and her mother made it more than clear that she had no time for Ruth."

"It was like Ruth was more of a burden than a gift to her parents."

My mother and nonna both spoke at once; "surely not," said my mother.

"Come puo un genitore non pensare al proprio figlio come a un dono?" said Nonna.

I looked at the three of them with tears in my eyes and said, "She had a terrible childhood, had it not been for her nana I'm not sure Ruth would still be here."

Nonna gasped in total shock, "La povero bambina."

"I know it's difficult to see the Ruth that we know and love act in a way that we could never have anticipated, however truth be told it's Ruth's life, it's her story to tell. She must be respected and if one day she chooses to tell you all about her past then fine, if not then that should also be fine. All I ask is that you do not judge Ruth on the way she is choosing to react to the death of both her parents. Just always think of her as the Ruth we see in front of us. The Ruth who laughs with us and eats with us; that's my Ruth, our Ruth, the girl I'm going to marry." I knew that both my parents and nonna understood what I was trying to say, however, I could also tell that no matter what I said they would worry that one day Ruth would crack as her grief would have to manifest in some way. That would always be their opinion and who am I to disagree when in actual fact I worried about the same thing happening. All I could do was be there and show her how important she is to so many people who love her. Ride the storm if it comes and help her pull through to the other side.

Emily

Emily Jane Laird, born 6th June 1910 to Angela and Graham Laird. I was the youngest of four; I had two brothers, Dan and Tom, and a sister, Molly. I was brought up in the Highlands of Scotland in a small Village called Plockton, population 378. My father was a fisherman before and after the war. My mother was a stay-at-home mum who grew all her own vegetables and had chickens which laid fresh eggs. Unlike some families during the war, we never went hungry. Mum was an amazing cook and could turn the smallest amounts of food into enough to feed us all. She was an extremely loving person not only with us, her family, but with everyone in the village. I can't think of one person that mum didn't like or that didn't like her.

In 1914–1918, during the 1st World War, while all the men enlisted, the women of the village would pull together while the men were away. They would rotate who watched the children while the others kept the fishing boats running, bringing home lots of herring. Herring fishing was the key to local prosperity in Plockton; this had to be maintained war or not. I was very young at the time of WW1 so have no real memories.

In May 1928, just before my 18th birthday I met Peter Wilson, born 14th June 1909. Peter had come to Plockton looking for a summer job on the fishing boats. He met with my father who was happy to give Peter a job as not only was he young and strong but he was a fresh face to Plockton. Peter had nowhere to live so my father brought him home knowing that my mother would happily take him in. Peter shared a room with my brothers,

Dan and Tom sleeping in a sleeping bag on the bedroom floor. Peter and I got on extremely well and quickly fell in love. My parents couldn't have been happier when Peter proposed to me in November of 1928 only six months after arriving in Plockton. We married on the 14th of March the following year in our local church with just a few close friends and our family attending. Peter had lost his father in the war and his mother Cathy couldn't afford to travel to Plockton for our wedding as she had Peter's younger siblings to look after; George, sixteen and Catherine, fourteen.

On the 31st May 1930 Peter and I welcomed our first child into our family. Amelia Catherine Wilson, she was the most adorable child you could ever imagine. She was born with a head full of carrot red hair and the most beautiful skin I had ever seen. She screamed the moment she arrived, however, that was the first and last time I ever heard her scream. Amelia was such an easy child; she fed, slept, had a nappy change and then started all over. She was just so cute when she was tired, she would snuggle into me and suck her pinkie, not her thumb like any other child, her pinkie. Life could not have been any better for us, we had a loving family around us as we lived in a small concrete building in the back of my parent's property for the first couple of years of our marriage.

In January 1932, we heard of a house in bad need of repair about half an hour away from my parent's house going for a very reasonable price. My father was determined we would have this house as it had so much potential and he wanted us to have a bigger home as we had discussed having more children. We went to see the house and, despite it being really run down and in the middle of nowhere, Peter and I fell in love with it instantly. Before we knew it, the house belonged to us and Peter and my father spent every weekend up there repairing the roof and making our house into a home we could live in and happily extend our family. In January 1933, almost exactly a year after purchasing our home, it was ready for us to move into. By this time, I was two months pregnant with our second child and felt like my life was just perfect. We moved into our home and couldn't have been happier. Amelia was almost three and was the most adorable child. She was so happy at the prospect of a new baby in the house but was determined it had to be a girl or it was to go back. Peter continued to work on the fishing boats in Plockton with my father and left extremely early every morning and was home about seven p.m. One evening, about two months after we moved in, Peter was home early which was very rare. He took the opportunity to read Amelia a bed time story and tuck her up in bed. While Peter tended to Amelia, I decided to take some time to just relax as I rarely had the opportunity these days to have more than five minutes to myself. As I sat down to pick up my knitting, I felt a tightening in my abdomen. The pain become very intense very quickly and soon I was on the floor screaming. Peter came running and found me on the floor surrounded in blood. It was clear that I was losing the baby as when Peter knelt down by my side, I had terrible pain and a pressure followed by a feeling of passing something. When Peter looked there was a small sac in my underwear with a tiny foetus inside. Both Peter and I cried for what seemed like hours before Peter helped me to the bathroom to clean me up and then put me to bed. There was no point going to see a doctor, as there was nothing he could do for us; our baby was gone. I just couldn't stop thinking of how to tell Amelia that she was no longer going to be a big sister and that the baby was gone. How do you explain that to such a young child? Peter and I decided to leave it for a few days to tell Amelia as we both needed to come to terms with the loss before trying to explain it to her?

Two days after the loss of our baby we decided to sit and talk to Amelia. She wasn't quite three yet so we had to try and explain it to her as simply as possible. We sat her down and explained that mummy and daddy were sad and had been crying the last few days because our baby has gone to heaven and is now an angel and won't be coming to live with us. I'm not sure how much she understood as she seemed to just want to go play with her toys. We let her go play as we thought it best to just let her be herself, and if she needed more answers then in her own time would ask. That day never came, Amelia was such a happy child and she just thrived despite our devastating news.

Soon it was May 30th the day before Amelia's third birthday. We had bought her a little trike to ride around on in the garden. It wasn't brand new as we had to be careful with our money especially as we had decided to keep trying to extend our little family. Pink was Amelia's favourite colour so Peter had purchased some pink sparkly paint which he used to paint the little trike. We both knew that Amelia would be so happy with her present and wouldn't even notice that it wasn't brand new. Peter bathed Amelia and took her to bed to read her a bedtime story while I headed to the kitchen to start the birthday cake. Tomorrow was going to be perfect!

We had to wake Amelia the next morning at eight thirty, otherwise she would sleep for at least another hour. I just couldn't wait to see her excitement when she saw her trike! Peter carried Amelia through to the lounge; she whooped with excitement as they entered the lounge as she could see pink sparkles through the glass door panel. When Peter put Amelia down, she ran straight over to the trike and without hesitation was on it and driving round and round singing happily as she cycled. I couldn't have felt any more content than I did at that moment. Peter and I were blessed to have such a wonderful little girl, she really was our world.

Peter's mother came to visit that summer with his sister, Catherine, now 18. George, Peter's brother had met and married an American and moved over there. It was the first time Cathy and Catherine would meet Amelia and my parents. It was also my first time meeting them given they hadn't made it to our wedding. Amelia took to them so easily which to us was no surprise as Amelia loved life and was a very sociable little girl. My parents also got on well with Cathy, as did I. She was such a lovely woman and everything Peter had told me about her was true, she really was adorable. His sister Catherine was quiet and it took Amelia a couple of days before she finally felt comfortable. Catherine looked so much like Peter, it was crazy. How could a girl look so much like a boy and yet still be beautiful...? And beautiful she was. They stayed for a week before heading home to Herefordshire. It was sad to say goodbye, however, they promised to visit again soon and we also said we would try to visit them.

Soon it was July, then August and September, but still no sign of another pregnancy. Every month I cried as I told Peter that there was no baby again this time. I had learnt to live with losing the baby and would now have to come to terms with the fact that we may never have another child. What's meant to be is meant to be Peter would say! I'm sure you're right I would respond while secretly thinking it's never going to happen; how can that be meant! We have Amelia my parents would say every time I said not again this month. I know I should be grateful as Amelia really was an amazing child but why did that mean I had to settle for just her. I would smile at my parents and nod in response while inside I was screaming at them to stop being so insensitive to my needs; I need another baby, why can't any of you understand this?

Soon it was winter and still no baby. Peter didn't seem concerned as between work and family life he had everything he ever wanted. Another child would of course be welcomed by him but if it didn't happen, it wouldn't be the end of the world. Me on the other hand, well, I seemed to feel less and less of a woman as I failed month after month to conceive. Peter didn't seem to notice how much my inability to conceive was affecting me.

Early November my parents came for Sunday dinner as was often the case in the winter months. I loved to cook a roast and enjoyed cooking for my family; roast dinner with all the trimmings. Summer months we spent most weekends at my parents' house as dad was the BBQ King. So once winter arrived Peter and I would welcome my parents for the weekend. I would enjoy chatting with mum while cooking Sunday Roast. Peter and dad would always sit in the garden when it was dry despite the cold as they both loved the outdoors. If it was raining, or snowing, they would sit in our old shed that we kept Amelia's toys in. They had two little stools that they loved to sit on and chat about the future of fishing while smoking cigars. On this day the weather was actually beautiful, cold with crisp blue skies and not a cloud in site. Dad and Peter as always were sitting on their stools, half in and half out of the shed. Amelia squeezed past every 5 seconds to change the toy she was playing with but neither Peter nor my dad would ever get annoyed with her as they both adored her and loved to see her playing happily. It was a normal Sunday afternoon with mum and me in the kitchen preparing the vegetables as the roast cooked slowly in the oven.

Everything felt perfect; for the first time, in I don't know how long, I found myself talking about all sorts of things with my mum and pregnancy or lack thereof didn't even come into the conversation once. I felt happy, content even and I really can't remember how long it has been since I felt this way.

Soon dinner was ready, I called on dad and Peter to come in. Amelia ran past them with the biggest smile on her face as she loved having Sunday dinner with her grandparents. Go wash your hands young lady my mother said to Amelia. Without question, off she went into the bathroom to wash her hands. She really was such an easy child.

After dinner my mother and I took Amelia upstairs for her bath while dad and Peter had a smoke and yet another of their man to man chats that they liked to have after dinner. I love the relationship between Peter and my father; they are just so close, friends, as well as work colleagues and family. They just have so much in common and have very similar work ethics and life values.

Amelia squealed with delight as my mother added bubbles to her bath water, she loved her bath but even more so on the odd occasion my mother brought some bath bubbles for her. Amelia played in her bath until the water ran cold then begged for some more hot water so she could play a little longer. I could never say no to my little girl as she so very rarely asked for anything. So, more hot water it was, and another twenty minutes of bath time fun.

Once Amelia was tucked up in bed, she asked for Peter to come up and give her a goodnight kiss as he did every night. I called on Peter and as soon as he was sitting with Amelia my mother and I left them to say their goodnights to one and other. Peter came back down stairs about ten minutes later and said that

Amelia had complained of a pain in her head. This was very unlike her as she was never ill, so I went upstairs to check on her, however, when I entered her room, she was fast asleep. I bent over, kissed her on the forehead and left her room, closing the door behind me.

Peter and I sat with my parents talking about life in general with no mention of pregnancy or anything that could potentially upset me. I was so thankful that the conversation flowed without so much as a moments silence where my mother could potential bring up the pregnancy or lack thereof. We had a lovely evening chatting and soon it was extremely late and time for us all to call it a night.

When my parents stayed over, they always knew that Amelia would run into their room in the morning and jump on them as she loved to see the surprised look on their faces as they woke to her enthusiastic jumping all over them. This morning however my mother woke and was surprised that Amelia had not been in to wake them. I was in the kitchen drinking my morning coffee leaving Peter to sleep late. I had assumed Amelia was with my parents, however, my mother walked into the kitchen, and to my surprise she was alone. "Where is Amelia?" my mother asked, "I assumed she was with you and Dad, however she must be in with Peter this morning. It's so unlike her not to jump on me and Dad. I missed waking up to her beautiful little face, even if it is while she jumps all over us."

I poured my mother a cup of coffee and within a few minutes Amelia walked into the kitchen crying that she had a sore head. I was really surprised as it was just so unlike her. She clambered up onto my knee and I swaddled her like I did when she was a baby. This always made her feel secure and would settle her on the odd occasion she didn't feel great or if she had fallen over.

Within a few minutes Amelia was asleep in my arms. This concerned me as she was not one for sleeping during the day once she was up and about; that was her until bedtime. She is clearly under the weather I said to my mother. If she's no better when she wakes up, I will take her into the village to see Dr Henderson.

Amelia slept on and off most of the day and didn't even make a fuss when my parents left which was extremely unlike her as she loved having her grandparents around. Before I knew it, she was back in bed and the day had passed without her eating or drinking very much.

"I'm worried about Amelia, Peter, she's just not been her happy playful self today. I really think we need to take her to see Dr Henderson in the morning as I don't like the fact that she was complaining about a sore head. Little ones shouldn't suffer from head pain," I said to Peter.

Peter agreed that he would not go into work in the morning until we had taken Amelia to see Dr Henderson.

Amelia woke early the next morning and came running into our room as if nothing had happened the day before.

Peter looked at me with a huge smile on his face and said "I guess we were worried for nothing!"

I wasn't sure as the day before had been so out of character that I said to Peter that I would feel happier if we took her to see Dr Henderson anyway. Peter agreed and we got up had breakfast as a family then headed into Plockton to see Dr Henderson.

Dr Henderson was surprised to see us as despite knowing my family very well he had very rarely had us in his practice. "Good morning Emily, Peter, so nice to see you both and oh my how big is this little princess getting!" Amelia instantly hid behind Peter as she was rather shy with people she didn't really know very well. I explained to Dr Henderson what had happened the day before and the evening before that. "Okay little Amelia how about we get you up on this big bed and I have a quick look at you to see if we can work out why you have been having a sore head." Amelia reluctantly climbed up on to the surgery bed with Peter's help. Dr Henderson examined her thoroughly, making Amelia laugh as he did so. He had an amazing way with people and was especially good with kids.

"The good news is that I can't see anything that immediately jumps out at me to say Amelia has anything serious. I'm happy that she seems well in herself despite having experienced some head pain over the last couple of days. It may well have been over excitement or exertion, however, just to be sure I will run a couple of blood tests.

"Now then young princess how about we make a trade? I will give you this pink lollipop if you give me just a little of your blood." Amelia looked at Dr Henderson strangely as she longed for the pink lolly however didn't like the idea of him taking some of her blood.

Dr Henderson promised Amelia that it wouldn't hurt and that the pink lolly would be worth it. As promised Dr Henderson took a small amount of blood from Amelia as gently as possible with Peter distracting her with one of her favourite stories that he would tell her of a bed time. She wasn't too happy with the pin prick however was soon smiling with the promised pink lolly in her hand.

We left the doctor's surgery feeling a lot happier that Amelia had been seen by Dr Henderson whose' initial reaction was that she was fine and felt better that he had taken a belt and braces approach by doing some blood tests just to be sure.

Once back home Peter said his goodbyes to us and left for work. Peter loved his job and had never missed a day. He had only been late once before and that's because Amelia decided to come into the world very early in the morning. He knew he would need to ask one of the local guys to take him out to the fishing boat as my father and the crew would have left hours ago. In a small place like Plockton we were all more like family than just neighbours, so Peter knew this wouldn't be an issue.

Amelia played in her room as I went about my daily housework; just another normal day in our household. Before I knew it Peter was home and we had dinner then Amelia was bathed then put to bed just like any other night. Peter and I sat and discussed his day and how fishing was a real passion for him not just a job. I loved to listen to him describe his day with such enthusiasm; I could actually picture every moment. I really don't think at that time that anything could have made my life any more perfect than it was. Another baby would be nice, however, Peter and I had Amelia and she was our everything. Days passed and life went on as normal, Amelia had no more headaches, Peter was having a great fishing season and I was content with life.

Eight days after we had been to see Dr Henderson, I was walking past the general store in Plockton, with Amelia, when I happened to bump into Dr Henderson. "I'm glad I bumped into you Emily," he said, "I have the results of Amelia's blood tests."

My heart sank for a brief moment as I had put the headaches and the blood tests to the back of my mind. In the few moments that it took for me to stop and listen it felt like hours had passed.

Dr Henderson looked at me, he must have seen the panic in my eyes as he smiled and said, "I'm glad to say that as I suspected, everything came back perfectly normal."

I couldn't contain myself, I flung my arms around him and kissed him on the cheek. Dr Henderson went quite red in the face as he wasn't used to women throwing their arms around him and kissing him. I blushed with embarrassment as I saw how uncomfortable he looked, however, the news he had given me was worth the moment's discomfort. Dr Henderson smiled, wished us good luck, and scurried away quickly to avoid further embarrassment.

That evening Peter didn't get home until late as they had an exceptionally big catch. By the time he came home Amelia was already fast asleep in bed. He walked through the door and didn't even get a moment to catch breath and say hi before I was upon him. I flung myself into his arms and began to tell him the good news given to me earlier that day by Dr Henderson. Peter, like me, was over the moon to learn that Amelia had been given the all clear. We could relax and enjoy our family unit as all was well.

The Breakdown

18th September 1983, exactly one year and ten weeks since the death of Ruth's parents. She was attending a wedding dress fitting with her nana, Keith's mum and nonna when she finally broke down. Up until this moment she had never shed a tear for her parents nor spoken about them with anyone.

After one and a half hours and numerous dresses tried on Ruth finally picked up a beautiful ivory dress with a lace bodice and instantly knew this was the dress she had to have. She went into the changing room helped by one of the assistants, she came out looking like a princess. Her nana looked at her with tears in her eyes and said "I just wish my boy was here to see his beautiful baby girl in this astonishing dress, you are breathtaking Ruth, you really are." Nonna, and Anna, Keith's mother, both burst into tears at the sight of Ruth in this stunning dress. Ruth looked around her at the three of them, and without warning, fell to the floor in floods of tears. Fourteen months' worth of pent-up grief finally released; Ruth sobbed uncontrollably. The shop assistant had no idea what had happened and was rushing about like a mad woman asking what she should do. Her concern was not for Ruth as she had no idea why Ruth was acting like this. All she could think about was the expensive wedding dress that Ruth had on which had not been paid for, in a heap on the floor. Keith's nonna, and mother, Anna, didn't quite know how to react, they both looked at Ruth's nana for guidance. Nana quickly moved towards Ruth, she couldn't get down beside her as she knew she wouldn't be able to get back up due to her disability. She motioned to Anna to help Ruth up, once on her feet her nana dropped both walking sticks and pulled her close to her. Let it out darling, let go of your emotions, cry until there are no tears left. Ruth's small frame shook uncontrollably with every sob. After what seemed like hours Ruth finally stopped shaking and her sobs turned to a faint cry. Nana looked up and asked Anna to help get Ruth into the changing room. Anna did so without hesitation. Once in the changing room Ruth finally stopped crying, and with Anna's help she removed the wedding dress and put on her own clothes. Anna handed the dress out to the assistant and asked her to put it aside for Ruth and to give her the bill. Instantly nana interrupted, she had promised to pay for Ruth's wedding dress from the day she was born and that's exactly what she would do. Nana knew that her son and daughter-in-law had not been good parents to Ruth and had always tried to do her best by her. She thanked Anna for her generosity, however, insisted that she was paying for the dress. Anna and Tony were paying for the wedding and that was more than generous.

While Ruth changed back into her clothes with the help of Anna, nonna called Keith to come and pick them up. As soon as Keith heard that Ruth had broken down, he was in the car and on the way without a moment's hesitation. His love for her was like no other and the thought of her being upset was tearing him apart, he needed to be there with her, embrace her and assure her that they would get through this together.

Keith pulled up outside the wedding dress shop just as Anna was opening the door to let Ruth out to get some fresh air with nonna holding on to her. Ruth's nana was paying for the dress and discussing the next step with the assistant. There was plenty of time as the wedding wasn't for another seven months. Nana said they would call to arrange the next dress fitting when Ruth felt strong enough.

Keith couldn't get out the car quick enough when he saw Ruth. He ran towards her and scooped her into his arms. Ruth once again started to sob uncontrollably as soon as she felt the warmth of Keith's arms around her. Keith asked his mother, Anna, to drive so that he could sit in the back to comfort Ruth. Anna and nonna got into the front of the car as Keith helped Ruth into the back. He shuffled in behind her and once again pulled her into his arms. They waited for nana to finish up in the bridal shop then headed for home.

Anna had already called Tony to meet them at Ruth's flat so that he could drive nana home and then take her and nonna back to theirs. That way Keith could concentrate on Ruth, he needed to comfort her without having to worry about anything else. Tony was already there waiting as Anna pulled up outside Ruth's. Ruth didn't even look at Tony as Keith helped her from the car, she didn't even say goodbye to her nana which was very strange as Ruth always gave her Nana a kiss and cuddle when they parted ways. Keith focused on Ruth and left Tony to deal with the others. His priority was Ruth and making sure he got her into the house as quickly as possible. Anna handed her son his car keys and quickly pecked him on the cheek, gave him a loving glance, and left. As soon as they entered the flat Ruth collapsed in a heap on the floor, her sobs uncontrollable, Keith got down beside her and just held her. He didn't speak, he decided it would be best to go with her lead. Let her cry until she was ready to talk then allow her the space to say everything she needed to, uninterrupted. He knew that their relationship was solid enough to stay silent and know that she understood his silence. After what seemed like an eternity, probably realistically ten to fifteen minutes, Ruth sat up straight and began to talk. Once she started there was no stopping her, out it all came, how much her parents had let her down and yet how she still loved them as they had given her life, albeit not a great one. She went into details about her childhood that Keith had never heard. Staying silent while she offloaded was extremely hard as some of the things that she said disturbed Keith and he instinctively wanted to respond. He knew however that she needed to get everything off her chest to allow her to move forward. His love for her was so strong and his feeling of hatred towards her parents was causing him great pain, no wonder she hadn't broke down when they heard the news of their accident and subsequent deaths. In a lot of ways, it was probably a relief that they were gone and she wouldn't have to deal with them any longer. All Keith could think about was how different her life had been to his and how he wanted to make sure that her life going forward would be the best he could possibly make it for her. She was an amazing woman and deserved to be treated with the greatest of love and respect. Keith was so thankful that while growing up she at least had her nana who he knew loved her dearly. God knows if she would ever have survived without her love and kindness.

"I can't ever remember being told I was loved from either of them," said Ruth. "They always told me I was stupid and I was a burden to them. If it wasn't for nana, they would have put me in care as I was just so much trouble. I really never understood why I was such a burden as I never asked for anything. I was always at school, or in my room, if not outside with the one friend I did have, Julz. Everyone made fun of me at school because I had old clothes that were either too big or too small and I stunk as my parents never bathed me. Julz was the only person in the school who didn't say nasty things to me. She would sit with me and tell me not to listen to the bullies."

Keith wondered why he had never heard of, nor met, this friend Julz. He didn't want to interrupt Ruth by asking questions that may stop her when he knew she needed to keep talking, so he sat back and just listened.

"Julz stayed by my side all the way through primary school and would always be there to make me feel better when my parents had been nasty to me. Her mother would give me a treat of some sweets or ice-cream when we played in their garden. I would often dream of being Julzes sister and having her parents as my own. When we went to high school things changed for me as nana bought my uniform and I was working weekends so could afford to buy toiletries and made sure I washed daily. Julz had given me the confidence to stand tall and believe I was just as good as the next person despite my parent's continual verbal abuse."

"In 1975 I would often go with Julz to visit my nana as we were old enough to go alone. One day in November on our way to visit my nana a truck skidded on some ice and spun round and mounted the pavement. I managed to jump far enough out of the way, however, Julz was hit full on. My beautiful best friend was killed instantly. I was broken I just couldn't get my head around the fact that she was gone. The one friend I had and she was no longer there, she was gone forever."

It was now clear why Ruth had never introduced her to Keith, however, he couldn't help but wonder why she had never mentioned her.

"I just couldn't bring myself to accept that she was gone and for a long time I just didn't want to go to school or work or even get out of bed. My parents had no sympathy for me whatsoever, they would push me out the door every morning for school, and at weekends force me to work, as they wanted the money I gave them every week from my wage. It became easier to pretend that Julz never existed, how could I miss someone that was never there so I pushed her memory to the back of my mind and I've never spoken about her since. Another reason to hate my parents."

Ruth began to sob uncontrollably again, obviously grieving her best friend as she had never been given the chance to do so back when Julz was killed. Keith comforted her as she sobbed knowing that getting all of this off her chest could only be a good thing.

Ruth finally stopped crying and poured her heart out about her conflicting feelings towards her parents, how much she hated them because despite everything she still loved them. It was hard for Keith to grasp as his childhood had been so amazing. He had, of course, suffered losses in his life but he was always surrounded by love growing up and he still was today, that would never change. He listened for as long as Ruth needed then finally when she had calmed down and stopped talking, he turned her to face him and promised from that day forward she would feel nothing but love, from him and his family, as they adored her. She of course had the love of her nana, however, Keith needed her to know that she was surrounded by people who love her, and she would never feel lost or alone ever again.

Keith stood up and walked into the kitchen, pulled a bottle of wine out the wine rack along with two glasses from the cupboard and headed back into the living-room. Ruth was now sitting on the sofa and smiled at Keith as he walked in the room with the wine. He knew that today was going to be the first day of their future without any ghosts in the closet. Today was day one of the rest of their life together.

They sat all night talking over Ruth's past and how her

opening up and finally accepting everything that had happened in her life was the first step to her recovery. Keith promised her that there was nothing that could possibly stop him from loving her. She was everything he had ever dreamed of and despite having had a very stressful childhood had turned into an amazing young woman.

Keith asked Ruth if she thought that going to counselling would help her. She did not refuse and said that between Keith, her nana and Keith's family, she would get over her past and begin a fresh new start. She wanted to go with Keith as a couple and sit together with his family so that she could open up to them. Ruth felt that this would enable her to accept, process and move on from her past. Keith's family were about to become her family and now that Ruth had broken through her barrier, she wanted a clean, fresh start for them all. In order for this to happen Ruth needed Keith's parents to know everything about her past and why she had reacted to her parents' death by blocking it out.

The following day, Keith called his mother to let her know that Ruth was all right and that they had talked most of the night, into the small hours. He asked if they could go to hers for dinner on the weekend as he wanted to sit as a family and discuss Ruth's breakdown. His mother was so quick to say that there was no need and as much as Keith agreed with her, he explained that Ruth needed to discuss things with them as a way of putting her past to sleep and moving on with their future, with a clean slate. Keith's mother understood and asked if he thought Ruth would like her nana to be there so that she would feel a little more comfortable. Keith said he would ask Ruth, however thought it was a lovely idea and was sure Ruth would say yes.

Keith hung up the phone and went into the kitchen where he prepared coffee for them both. He took the coffee into the bedroom as Ruth was still in bed. She had slept on and off all night. Obviously everything they had discussed had been going around and around in her head, keeping her from sleeping properly. Keith had intended for her to stay in bed as long as she needed to, however, he had heard her moving around while he was on the phone so knew she was awake. Ruth sat up and welcomed the hot cup of coffee; something she wouldn't miss no matter how late she was for work or an appointment. Even if it meant taking it to go Ruth had to have her coffee every morning.

Keith sat on the edge of the bed and kissed her gently on the forehead. She looked up and gave him the biggest smile he had seen from her since his proposal. He knew at that moment that they would be okay; they would get through all of this together and life would be good. Ruth would become his wife and they would be happy.

The rest of the week Ruth stayed home from work and spent time focusing on the wedding and all the little incidental things that, as a man, Keith had no interest in. He was happy she was taking time off work, as he knew in his heart she needed to be free from any form of routine and structure; she needed time just to relax and focus on whatever made her happy. Space to digest everything she had offloaded and time alone to accept that life as she knew it was firmly in the past and her future held nothing but happiness, and the odd argument of course; Keith was just a man after all and it was his duty to piss her off.

Soon it was Saturday and Keith and Ruth were getting ready to head off to his parents for dinner. Keith had spoken to Ruth about her nana joining them and she was happy with that as it meant she only had to tell her story once more, then she could move on and begin to focus on her future with Keith. They picked up Ruth's nana at six thirty p.m. then stopped en-route to Keith's parents to pick up some wine.

They arrived at Keith's parents' house at seven p.m. as agreed. His dad was in his usual position perched in front of the television as his mum and nonna prepared dinner. As soon as they walked in, his dad jumped up to attend to Ruth's nana. He was a true gent, if nothing else.

"Please Mrs Bald, come and sit over here." He quickly turned the television off and made sure that Ruth's nana was comfortable.

"Please call me Lyn," she said. "We are family after all."

"Lyn it is, and I would be honoured if you would call me Tony."

Keith's mum and nonna came through to say hi and ask if anyone would like a drink. They were already on first name terms with Lyn as they had spent some time together planning the wedding and of course had been together at the dress fitting when Ruth had broken down.

Keith took the wine into the kitchen and poured a glass for everyone; well, except his dad, who always preferred a beer. The dinner smelt amazing. Keith just couldn't help myself; he lifted off a saucepan that contained nonna's homemade meatballs and quickly dipped a piece of bread into the sauce while his mum and nonna had their backs turned.

Keith's mum caught him just as he popped the bread in his mouth. "Some things never change Keith, always dipping bread into the dinner pot."

Keith smiled, picked up two glasses of wine and proceeded to take them into the lounge for Ruth and Lyn. Keith's mum followed with his dad's beer and told everyone dinner would be on the table in ten minutes.

The dinner, as always, was just delicious; no one cooked

quite like Keith's nonna and mum.

After dinner, Lyn offered to help clear up, however Anna wouldn't hear off it. "Sit and relax, Lyn. Keith will pour you another glass of wine while I stack the dishwasher."

Keith poured a glass of wine for both Lyn and nonna, who sat chatting while he and Ruth helped Anna clear the table. Tony had popped outside for a quick smoke. Anna was right, some things never change…

Finally, everything was cleared away and everyone sat together in the lounge. They all knew that the conversation about to take place was going to be extremely difficult, not only for Ruth but for all of them. It wasn't going to be easy for Lyn to hear Ruth say things about her son, despite the fact that she knew it to be the truth, nor for Keith's family, who had always been very close and loving, to hear of the heart-breaking upbringing that Ruth had endured. Despite this, they were all prepared to listen and allow Ruth to do all she needed to get everything off her chest now that her barriers were down.

Once Ruth began to talk it was as if a dam had burst; there was no stopping for breath. Ruth knew if she stopped, she may never start again, and she so badly wanted to get everything out in the open to allow her to accept it as having been her life but also to acknowledge that it didn't have to shape her future. Keith could see how uncomfortable Lyn was while Ruth described her childhood, however she was also very proud of the way in which Ruth described her as being the one constant loving family member that she truly believed to be the reason she was still alive and well today. It wasn't easy for his parents and nonna to hear the story of Ruth's childhood as it was so alien to them. However, they listened without judgement and allowed Ruth the safe environment to talk in as much depth as she needed in order for her to be able to move on with all the skeletons out of the closet and put to rest once and for all.

Ruth had tears streaming down her face as she told the story of her childhood. To be honest, they all did.

The conversation that evening had been cathartic for all as it helped everyone understand each other on a much deeper level than before. It also allowed them to look forward to a future as a family, including Lyn. Keith's parents and nonna embraced Lyn into their family despite everything that Ruth had told them about her father, nana's son. A mother cannot be held responsible for her child's shortcomings, especially when she had shown him nothing but love. Ruth adored her nana and had a lot to thank her for.

A few weeks passed and Ruth and Keith were both back at work. Life seemed to be going pretty well considering everything that had been brought into the open and discussed about Ruth's childhood. Keith had worried that bringing it all back to her and talking so deeply about everything in detail would bring back so many bad memories that she would find it difficult to move on. It seemed he was wrong; the discussions had obviously been just the therapy that Ruth needed to free herself of her past. She seemed so much happier than she had been in a long time and was thriving at work. In turn, Keith felt so much happier and more relaxed about their future, so much so that he felt confident that he could bring up the conversation of their wedding and hopefully they could move forward and agree an exact date and not just a rough month. Hopefully they could finally get something booked.

That evening when Ruth returned from work, Keith was ready and waiting for her with a home cooked meal (okay nonna cooked it for him) and a nice bottle of Ruth's favourite white wine, Moscato; a sweet white Italian.

Immediately Ruth smiled, "Okay, what's going on, have you been promoted or something"

"No," said Keith, "please come and sit down, I need to speak to you."

Ruth sat down without uttering another word as she could see he was nervous.

"You know how proud I am that you have broken through your barriers and spoken openly about your childhood and the struggles you faced while growing up. So much so that you even trusted my family, your new family with your deepest, darkest secrets. I know that it was not easy for you to bring everything up from your past given it had been so difficult for you. Also knowing how it would make Lyn feel knowing that your father was her son and despite his faults she loved him dearly. Despite everything you have come so far and have put your whole life out there to be acknowledged, accepted and moved on from. I won't lie, I was worried that the bottom would fall out of our world at some point soon after you had been so candid with everyone. However, as time has passed you seem to be going from strength to strength and I just need you to know how much I love and respect you for everything. The you that was, the you now, and the you that will be in the future, as my wife."

Ruth looked at Keith with tears in her eyes, she just kept smiling but didn't utter a word. He was a little unsure if he should proceed or not, however decided to throw caution to the wind and blurted out… "On that note, I thought that perhaps tonight would be a good time to discuss our wedding and perhaps set a date?"

Ruth flung herself into his arms and said, "Thank god, I was beginning to think you had changed your mind given you haven't mentioned the wedding in such a long time."

"No way," Keith said, "I just wanted to give you time and space to process everything you had brought back up from your past. I wanted to make sure there was no aftermath and that you were strong enough and happy enough to move forward."

Ruth looked at Keith lovingly. "I can't think of anything I would rather do tonight than discuss and agree a date for our special day, the day I become Ruth Vasillio. I love you so much Keith, you are my world, my everything and I just can't wait to be your wife."

Keith gave out a huge sigh, he had never been so relieved as he was at that moment in time when he realised that not only had he not lost the love of his life to her past but she had become so strong and was more than happy to crack on with the wedding. "Onwards and upwards," he said. "Let's drink to that."

After a lovely meal and the full bottle of white, Ruth and Keith ended up on the floor making love with more passion than they had shown each other in months. Just being inside her made Keith realise how lucky they had been to find each other. They were the perfect fit, the perfect match in every way.

After making love, they lay on the rug wrapped in each other's arms, just taking time to reflect on their happiness. No need for words, the silence spoke volumes.

The Mystery Girl

Emily returned to Woodland House pulling her old fishing trolly behind her. She wasn't sure if the mystery girl she had discovered and taken back to her home would be awake, or even if she would still be there. As Emily walked through the door, she heard what must have been the mystery girl, who we will call Jane, for now, moving around. As she entered the living room, it was clear that the girl had woken up and had been scared. She obviously had no idea where she was and on hearing Emily enter the house had move quickly to hide.

"Don't be afraid little one, I won't hurt you," said Emily standing in the doorway of the living-room. She could sense the girl was in the room however wasn't sure where. Emily looked around and finally the mystery girl appeared from behind the sofa. "Are you hungry?" she asked the girl.

Ignoring Emily's question, the girl asked, "Is this your house? Do you know who I am, and where I come from?"

Emily looked at the girl with sadness in her eyes. "Yes, this is my house, however, I have no idea who you are or where you come from"

"I came across you in the woodlands while out for a stroll. I bent over you as I thought at first you were dead, however you were still breathing but did not respond to my touch." I ran back to the house for my old trolley and brought you back here on it. I've just been into Plockton to the general store to buy some bits and pieces as I never normally have guests and there was nothing here that I could give you to eat."

The girl looked at Emily and asked her name, "I am Emily Wilson" she replied. Little did they know that this day would be the beginning of a long journey for them both.

"Is it okay if I call you Jane," said Emily "given that neither of us know who you are."

"I guess so, Jane is as good a name as any." Emily hadn't spoken to anyone in years, her voice was extremely croaky, and her throat hurt. Still for some reason she felt the need, wanted to speak to this girl, Jane. There was something about her that made Emily want to speak for the first time in such a long time. For some reason, she felt at peace around Jane.

"Do you live here alone?" asked Jane. Emily felt mixed emotions as it had been fifty years since she had been living alone, fifty years of not talking to another soul. She wasn't sure what to say to Jane as she didn't want to go into details about the life she had chosen to live since losing Amelia, then Peter. Nor did she want to discuss the life she had had previously with Amelia and Peter. If she couldn't bring herself to speak to her parents all those years ago, why would she want to talk about them with a complete stranger! Emily looked at Jane and simply nodded in response. Jane saw a sadness come across Emily's face and was aware that she seemed reluctant to talk about herself. Jane decided it was more important to try and discover who she was rather than risk upsetting Emily by asking too many questions that she was clearly uncomfortable answering.

Emily looked out the window, "The wind has really picked up and the rain is very heavy. Given that neither of us know who you are or where you belong, I think it would be sensible for you to stay here for a while. Assuming you are all right with that?"

"That's very kind of you," said Jane. "If the weather is better tomorrow perhaps you could take me back to where you found me, and we can try and work out how I got there."

"No problem," said Emily as she moved out of the living-room heading towards the kitchen. "Would you like a coffee?" she asked as she entered the kitchen. "I'm not sure if I like coffee, however, I'll give it a try." Emily filled the old kettle from the sink and placed the coffee and sugar from the supplies she had just brought back from the General Store on the kitchen worktop. It had been so long since Emily had had a coffee, she couldn't remember how she liked it. Emily placed two empty cups on the worktop, she opened the coffee and put a teaspoon in each cup. She thought it would be best if they both tried the coffee before adding sugar as it could always be added later but couldn't be taken out. The kettle boiled and Emily filled the two cups leaving a small space for milk. She tasted the first cup and it was very bitter so she began by adding one sugar and found that two made it taste perfect for her. Jane on the other hand liked the bitter taste so opted for no sugar. They sat in silence sipping their coffee listening to the wind howling outside and the rain battering off the windows. Both women seemed to be comforted by the sounds of the stormy weather outside.

Emily said that Jane was welcome to sleep in her room upstairs and that she would sleep on the sofa. Jane was confused as she knew there was at least one other bedroom upstairs if not two. At that point, she was overcome with guilt as she remembered breaking the lock on one of the upstairs rooms.

"Emily, I have something to tell you," said Jane. "When I first woke, I had no idea where I was. I was very confused and totally disorientated. I looked at myself in the mirror and although I look familiar, I really have no recollection of who I am or where I've come from. I had no idea if this was my home or not. I thought if I looked around, I would perhaps remember something. I went upstairs and the first room I came across was directly to my left. I went inside and looked around, but I didn't really recognise anything, that said, I can't explain why but I felt some form of comfort looking at the woman's clothing in the wardrobe. I must apologise as this is obviously your bedroom and I feel awful knowing that I have gone through your things." Emily looked at Jane with a smile on her face, it was the first time in a very, very long time that Emily had smiled. She had forgotten what it felt like to converse with another person and to feel relaxed enough to smile.

"Don't stress yourself about it little one, you had no idea that this wasn't your home. I would have done the same thing had I been in your shoes."

Jane looked across at Emily, however, she looked as if she was about to cry, despite Emily smiling back at her. "I have more to tell you," she said. "I tried to open another door; however, it was securely locked. I then went into the bathroom and again I can't explain why but I felt a strange sense of belonging. I looked around however once again there was nothing of any significance to me. I then moved along the landing to another door that was locked, however when I shook the handle, I'm so sorry but the lock broke and fell to the floor. I was left with the handle in my hand." Before Jane had the opportunity to say anything else, Emily had run out of the kitchen and flew up the stairs.

As soon as Emily reached the top of the stairs, she could see that the room she had shared with Peter, the room she had locked leaving it exactly as it was the last time Peter slept there, fifty plus years ago, was in fact open. Her hands flew up to her face as she sank to the floor letting out a wail. Jane ran up the stairs to see Emily crouched on the floor outside the open room, crying.

"I'm so sorry, Emily, I feel awful, I didn't mean for the lock to break, but when it did, I just couldn't help myself, I was compelled to enter the room. I have no idea why and I realise now that it was wrong however at the time I just had to go into that room. I didn't stop to think, I just walked in. It felt so normal, as if I had been there, walked through that door many times before. I'm so sorry I've clearly opened up a room that had obviously been closed for a long time. For some reason, you didn't want it opened or anyone to go inside and I have done both. I have disrespected your home and I feel awful."

Jane stood there for what seemed like ages while Emily sobbed quietly into her hands. Jane didn't know what else to say, so decided to remain silent. Finally, Emily stopped sobbing, stood up and moved past Jane, heading back downstairs to the kitchen. Jane followed her downstairs, however decided to stay quiet and wait for Emily to speak.

They sat in silence for over an hour, when finally Emily spoke, "Please do not go near any of the rooms upstairs apart from my room where you will be sleeping, and the toilet."

Jane apologised once again and said, "It goes without saying that now I know this house is not mine, I will only go into rooms that I have been given permission to enter by you. "I am deeply sorry Emily, my intention was never to upset you, or anyone for that matter. I was merely curious as to where I was and to see if the surrounding would perhaps shed some light on that for me. I would never look around someone else's property without their permission and I certainly wouldn't go into a room that had clearly been locked.

"Do you think you can forgive me?" Emily realised that she had been a bit hard on Jane, it wasn't her fault that she ended up in a strange house all alone. Emily hadn't stopped for a second to think about Jane having amnesia or just waking up in a strange home. Emily wished now that she had hung around until Jane had come around before leaving to pick up supplies. However, what was done was done and there was no changing that. Emily looked at Jane and said, "Please don't worry. I know you didn't intend to upset me. Let's just get some sleep and tomorrow we can begin trying to figure out who you are and where you belong."

"Sounds great" said Jane as she smiled at Emily.

Neither of them could sleep that night. Jane couldn't sleep because she was obviously concerned just in case there was a family out there looking for her. Emily lay on the sofa but couldn't sleep, all she could see every time she shut her eyes was the room upstairs that she had shared with Peter and all the hurt and pain she had felt back then came rushing back to her. She didn't realise how much that room being locked had stopped her from actually being able to acknowledge, accept and move on from everything she had gone through in those terrible times when both Amelia and Peter had been taken from her. Perhaps locking the rooms and trying to forget about her life had been a mistake. Maybe, just maybe her parents had been right all those years ago, perhaps she should have dealt with her emotions differently. Too late to think about that now as fifty years had passed. It was too late to change the past, however, tomorrow would be a new day and maybe, just maybe, Emily would make some important changes now that she had broken her silence. Maybe it wouldn't even take that long!

Planning the Honeymoon

Ruth and Keith had planned their honeymoon based on what they liked to do. Anna and Tony wanted them to go to Italy so Ruth could see where Keith was from. Although Keith thought it was a lovely idea this was something they would perhaps consider in a few years. He wanted to take Ruth to Italy and to travel around so she could understand the culture as well as taking in the beauty of his mother land. He didn't want to do it on a budget and that's exactly what they would have to base their honeymoon on, a small budget given that they were paying for it themselves. Lyn had bought the wedding dress after all and Tony and Anna, helped by nonna had paid for the wedding and reception. The honeymoon was down to Ruth and Keith to pay for and despite both working full time they didn't have huge salaries.

As soon as they set their wedding date, they opened a bank account for the honeymoon fund. They put away as much as they could every month however they had a mortgage and bills to pay first. Keith had moved in to Ruth's flat and they had been splitting all the bills down the middle with the intention of opening a joint bank account and having the mortgage put into both names once they were married.

Three weeks before the wedding they sat in their flat discussing the honeymoon. They had managed to save a good few hundred pounds; enough to get them a lovely break in the UK. Ruth and Keith both agreed that they would like to remain in Scotland, somewhere North. Keith had popped into a travel agent on his way home from work that day and had brought home a few holiday brochures for different locations in the North of Scotland.

After dinner, they sat looking over all the brochures at all the amazing different places open to them for their honeymoon. Ruth immediately fell in love with Plockton as soon as she saw the pictures and read all about the history; her mind was made up. Keith wanted Ruth to have everything she desired therefore it was a given, Plockton it would be. The next day Keith would make it his mission to finalise all the details with the travel agent and pay for their honeymoon.

Ruth and Keith were so excited about the prospect of going on honeymoon to Plockton in the north of Scotland they just couldn't wait. "Three weeks and counting" Ruth said to Keith as they cuddled in bed that night. "I just can't wait to be Mrs Vasillio and to set out on our first adventure as husband and wife." Keith smiled at Ruth as he pulled her into his arms and kissed her passionately. Ruth just melted into Keith's arms and responded to his kiss like she had never kissed him before. More passion and longing than she had ever felt before ran through her like a lightning bolt. Keith was so full of desire and passion for Ruth, he pulled her on top of himself and entered her with a deep desire to be as one. They made love that night like they had never done before. They had always been gentle and passionate with each other but that night was full of lust and the passion was overtaken by that and they had the most amazing sex. It went on and on well into the night until they both rolled over satisfied and exhausted.

The next day Keith finished work early so that he could go to the travel agents and finalise their perfect honeymoon. He couldn't wait to get home to tell Ruth it was a done deal. They would leave for Plockton the day after their wedding and would have a week in a luxury cottage with a log fire just the two of them. It was going to be the perfect start to their marriage.

As soon as Keith told Ruth everything was sorted, she jumped up and down with such excitement knowing that soon not only would she be Keith's wife, but they were going away together to start married life in a beautiful setting in the North of Scotland. She had made a pot of mince for dinner, however, dinner would have to wait as the longing she had to once again have Keith inside her took over. She pulled Keith into the bedroom and pushed him onto the bed while she pulled her clothes off. Keith was excited by this side of Ruth, she seemed to have another side to her sexually, a side of her sexuality that he had not seen before last night, he liked it. He stripped naked before she had the chance to change her mind. He pulled her naked body on to the bed and once again they had the most amazing sex, even better than the night before. They spent the rest of the night in bed exploring each other in a way they had never done before. Dinner was the last thing on their mind. The next meal they would have would definitely be breakfast, certainly not dinner anyway as they were way too wrapped up in this newfound sexual need to leave any part of their bodies unexplored. Finally, tiredness took over and they both fell asleep, extremely satisfied and happy.

The next day Ruth couldn't wait to tell her nana of their plans. She called her as soon as she got up and didn't let poor Lyn get a word in. Ruth was just so excited at the prospect of getting married and then going away with Keith to Plockton for a whole week. "I can hear from your voice that you are really excited darling," said Lyn. "I've heard that the North of Scotland is very beautiful and Plockton sounds idyllic, if it wasn't your honeymoon, I would come with you" Lyn said jokingly.

Ruth stopped speaking for a moment, she clearly missed the joking tone in Lyn's voice. Ruth pictured her nana's face, all alone in her house and immediately felt guilty of her own happiness. "Come with us Nana," she said before giving it a second thought.

"I love you Ruth and I appreciate your kind gesture however darling, no grandmother wants to go on honeymoon with their grandchild!" Ruth and nana both laughed, and carried on the conversation putting the offer for Lyn to go on honeymoon out of their minds. After a few minutes Ruth had to hang up as she wanted to call Anna before heading off to work. During her conversation with Anna, she could hear nonna in the background squealing with excitement every time Anna repeated what Ruth was saying. It was clear that they had accepted that Italy would have to go on the back burner and were just so excited that the kids had booked and were looking forward to exploring Plockton.

Ruth arrived at work with three minutes to spare, very unlike her as she normally arrived half an hour early. She was so excited about her upcoming wedding and honeymoon that she had lost track of time while speaking on the phone all morning. She was still at work on time and that's all that matters. Ruth worked harder than ever that day as she was so happy and content with her life. Working hard made time pass quickly and that's exactly what Ruth wanted. She wanted the next three weeks to go by as quickly as possible so she could get to be Mrs Keith Vasillio and go on honeymoon to Plockton.

November 1933

It was the end of November and Emily and Peter were out in the woodland surrounding their home. They were with little Amelia, taking a walk as they often did, and the sun shone despite the low temperature. They liked Amelia to have as much outside time as possible especially in the winter as there can be long spells when no one can get out. It had been snowing the night before and the snow lay on the ground about two inches thick. Amelia squealed with joy as she ran alongside her parents kicking the snow with her little red wellington boots. It was by far Emily's favourite time of the year. She loved the snow, always had, as far back as she could remember, as did Amelia. Peter wasn't a great lover of winter however enjoyed watching his girls enjoying the snow and loved that as a family they had beautiful woodlands surrounding their home to explore on nice winter days like today. Peter had loved Plockton since the day he first arrived and had never looked back. In January 1933 when Emily, Peter and Amelia moved into their forever home Peter finally felt that he belonged. For the first time since he was a very young boy, he actually felt like everything was as it should be. He had a loving wife and daughter, great in-laws, a job that he loved and now his forever home with his own little family. Life was complete. In the woodlands surrounding their home there was many little walks that as a family they could explore and enjoy. About a 20–30-minute walk from their house there was a really large tree, much bigger than the rest that stood out not only because of its size but the beauty of this tree was remarkable. Peter had picked this tree as his favourite and as a family they would picnic under this tree in the summer. In winter, however, it was usually surrounded with snow or the rain was too heavy and wind too blustery to even visit the tree. Today however the sun shone brightly despite the snow and the low temperatures so Peter was adamant that they should walk as far as the big tree before heading back towards the house. Given that Emily and Amelia loved being out in the snow there was no argument from them. As they approached the tree Amelia spotted a tiny rabbit hoping around, she ran after it squealing with delight, not understanding that her squeal was scarring the poor little rabbit so much that is scurried away as fast as it could. Amelia stopped in her tracks and began to cry; she had so wanted to play with the bunny rabbit. Peter crouched down beside her to explain that as much as she wanted to play with the rabbit it was a wild rabbit and it would be scared of people. Within a few seconds Amelia was back to her usual happy self, running in circles around the tree occasionally hopping like a rabbit. Emily and Peter laughed at the sight of their beautiful daughter running and hopping around the tree. They both loved Amelia, the way she embraced life and just wanted more of everything that was nature, the trees, the flowers, the bushes, the animals, the snow, the rain, everything made her happy. She was the centre of their universe and an absolute joy to have around. They had been blessed with Amelia as she was so alive and happy all the time. It was a rare occasion that Amelia cried for any longer than a few seconds as there was always something that would distract her and make her smile and laugh. Small flurries of snow began to fall, Amelia opened her mouth as she ran around the tree trying to catch them on her tongue. Peter called to Amelia, "We better head back before the snow becomes heavy." She ran and threw herself into Peter's arms with a smile that just melted his heart. Emily walked alongside them as they set off home. Amelia was running in front of her parents as she had on many walks before when suddenly she dropped to the ground. At first Peter and Emily thought she was just playing and had thrown herself onto the cold snow, however there was no high-pitched laugh. At this point Peter knew something was wrong, he ran towards his daughter with Emily close behind. As he approached, he could see that Amelia wasn't moving, fear ran through his whole body. As soon as he reached Amelia, he knew something was terribly wrong as she was so still. He bent over and picked her up; there was a pulse however it was very weak. Without a word passing between them Emily and Peter ran through the woodlands back to their home. Graham, Emily's father had left his car at the house as Peter had been doing some repairs to the interior for him. Emily ran into the house to get the keys while Peter put Amelia in the back seat of the car. They drove to Doctor Mackinnon Memorial Hospital as fast as they possible could with Emily in the back seat holding Amelia. The hospital was approximately 30 minutes away however Peter was pushing the car to its maximum speed hoping to shorten the journey time as much as possible. On arrival at the hospital Peter stopped in front of the emergency doors as Emily ran through the doors screaming for help. A doctor quickly came out and Peter helped him put Amelia straight onto a hospital gurney. The doctor proceeded to take Amelia straight into an examination room with Peter and Emily close behind. The doctor immediately started CPR as Amelia had stopped breathing, however, despite the best efforts of the medical team Amelia passed away. There was nothing more they could do for her, she was gone. Peter just stood there in shock; how is this possible, how can my baby be gone… Emily fell to the floor both hands across her mouth as she screamed. Emily could hear an animal wailing as if in the most excruciating pain; it took a few moments for her to realise that what she was hearing wasn't an animal it was actually her. Peter immediately got down beside Emily and cradled her in his arms as they both sobbed uncontrollably for their child. The doctor helped them both up and escorted Peter and Emily into a private room to allow them the privacy to process the fact that their baby girl was dead. The doctors had no explanation for Emily and Peter as to why their little girl had suddenly died. Dr Henderson asked Peter for as much information as possible prior to them arriving at the hospital, however, there really wasn't anything to tell him as Amelia had been her happy joyful self, right to the last minute when she collapsed. There had been no fall, she hadn't banged her head, nothing, she merely collapsed.

The doctor left Peter and Emily in the private room for what seemed like hours. On his return, he found Emily had cried herself to sleep in Peters arms. He felt terrible that he had to wake her, bring her back to the reality of what had happened to her child, however it was important that both parents understood what needed to happen next. He informed Peter and Emily that in order to give a reason for Amelia's death he would have to perform an autopsy.

The thought of their precious Amelia being cut open was too much for both Peter and Emily to take in. They needed time to process the fact that they were going home without their beautiful baby girl.

Dr Henderson continued to speak as it was important that the autopsy was carried out as soon as possible to determine the cause of death. He handed Peter a document that needed to be signed by at least one parent to allow them to proceed with the autopsy. As Peter put his hand forward to take the document

Emily grabbed it and tore it into a million tiny pieces. You are not cutting my baby girl open, you can't, she is perfect in every way and you want to open her up, why? She's dead what does it matter how... She's not coming back, leave my baby alone please I beg of you. Let her go out of this world as perfect as she came in. The doctor looked at Peter with sympathy however Peter understood that Dr Henderson was merely doing his job and had to do the autopsy as he needed to have a cause of death for Amelia's death certificate, which would be needed to put her to rest. Peter motioned for the doctor to step out of the room, he followed closely behind and agreed to sign the form. Dr Henderson had another form ready as this was not something new to him, he had experienced too many people go through the same process over the last twenty years as an ER doctor, no one likes the thought of their loved one being cut open especially a child.

Peter signed the form and gave it back to Dr Henderson. With a heavy heart, he entered the private room where Emily sat alone and led her by the hand out to the car. Peter and Emily drove home in silence.

Peter and Emily entered their home with not a word spoken between them. Peter went straight up to Amelia's bedroom while Emily sat in the darkness of their living-room.

Peter sat on Amelia's bed. I've lost my beautiful Amelia; how will I ever get through this pain? My beautiful baby dead in front of me... I don't want to be alive any more, not without my amazing Amelia. How do I even begin to deal with this pain? The loss, the yearning to have her back and the million questions as to why. I know Emily is going through the same and I know I must go on for her as she needs me to be strong for both of us, but how?

Emily sat alone in the dark; there are no words to explain the emptiness or the holes left behind. The laughter and happiness of our home, our family unit gone forever. Why Amelia? Why not me? Why is all I'm left with, why, just why?

There will never come a day, hour, minute or second that we will stop loving or thinking about Amelia, Peter thought, she was just so alive and brought so much love and laughter to our family unit. How will we survive? Can we get through this together? I need to try, I need to be strong for Emily as I know she will need me more than ever now. I must go and see Emily, but I can't, I just can't bring myself to leave this room. I can still smell my beautiful little girl, I can picture her smiling up at me while I read her a bedtime story. I miss my baby so badly and she's only been gone a few hours. How do I go on from this? I know I must try as Emily needs me.

I must have cried myself to sleep as I wake to the light shining in Amelia's bedroom window. What time is it? Where is Emily? I pull myself up from Amelia's bed and head down to the kitchen as I can hear Emily moving around. I walk into the kitchen to see Emily still in the clothes she had worn yesterday. All the cupboard had been emptied and she was scrubbing down all the insides of them. I asked her what she was doing however she didn't even acknowledge that I was in the room she just continued to scrub clean the cupboards. I tried several times to speak to her but she was in some form of trance cleaning as if her life depended on it. I decided it was best to let her be for now, she clearly needed to process our daughter's death in her own way.

I knew the news of Amelia's death would travel very quickly around Plockton as that is what life was like when you lived in such a small place. I worried about how Emily's parents would react to the news however I just didn't have the strength to go and tell them what had happened, anyway what would I say as we have no idea why Amelia is dead, why she collapsed and stopped breathing. I knew that Dr Henderson would go to see Angela and Graham as he had been a lifelong friend of theirs and would want to be the one to break the news of their granddaughters death. Oh my god, my mother and Catherine, who would tell them? Peter thought suddenly. I would have to ask Angela to call my mother as I just can't. What would I say? How could I possible explain what happened when I have no idea myself.

Emily's parents arrived about an hour later. Angela fell into my arms sobbing as she entered the house with Graham right behind her looking so pale. Clearly, I had been correct in my assumption and Dr Henderson had gone to break the news to them. I had no word of comfort for Angela and Graham as I was still trying to process the news myself. I had to grieve and help Emily to grieve before I could even contemplate acknowledging anyone else. I am just not strong enough to cope with everyone's grief.

Emily remained in the kitchen cleaning out each cupboard over and over again. "I don't know what to do," I said to her parents. "She hasn't spoken a word since we left the hospital." Angela walked over to Emily and tried to talk to her, she asked her to come sit down so they could talk. Emily however acted as if no one was there, it's as if she was deep in a trance and was unaware of anything or anyone around her.

"Has she been here all night, Peter?" she asked.

"I think so as she is still wearing the same clothes she had on yesterday. I went straight to Amelia's room and I must have fallen asleep as when I woke it was morning and I could hear Emily moving around down here."

"Go get Dr Henderson," Angela said to her husband, "Emily

is clearly in shock and needs a sedative to make her sleep, she can't carry on like this." Graham did as his wife asked and went to fetch the Doctor. When they returned, Emily was still moving from cupboard to cupboard emptying, cleaning, refilling.

Dr Henderson spoke in a gentle voice, "Emily, can you please stop what you are doing and come sit with me for a few minutes." Emily ignored his request and continued to clean. Dr Henderson put his hand on Emily's arm and what happened next shocked us all. Emily turned on him grabbed his hand and bit deeply into his arm. She then proceeded to scream hysterically while waving her hands around knocking all the contents from the cupboard she had been cleaning on to the floor. Dr Henderson's arm was bleeding badly as she had sunk her teeth in as far as she could. None of us knew what to do, Angela grabbed Dr Henderson's bag in search of a bandage as he put pressure on the wound to stop the bleeding. Graham started to pick up all the goods on the floor and I stood there with my mouth wide open in shock. In all the year's I had been married to Emily, I had never seen her like this. She was like a mad woman. I did not want to approach her given what had happened when the Doctor did, so decided it was best to just leave her to calm down.

Finally, after what seemed like hours, Emily dropped to the floor in a heap and sobbed quietly until she fell asleep. In the meantime, Angela had found a bandage in the doctor's bag and helped him dress his wound. Once he was able, he pulled out a syringe from his bag along with a vile of some sort of sedative which he continued to administer into Emily as she lay on the floor. I then picked her up and took her upstairs to our bedroom. Little did I know that my wife would never speak another word from that moment on.

Time passed and Emily still didn't speak, she had locked

herself inside her head with her grief and wouldn't allow anyone in, not even me. I tried everything I possibly could but she refused to even get out of bed most days. Her parents would come around often to try to encourage her to get up and eat. Some days it worked other days it didn't. On the odd occasion when she would get out of bed, I would raise my hopes thinking that was the day that I would get my Emily back, however, she would eat a little, drink some water and go back to bed with not so much as a glance in my direction. Every day got harder and harder as she seemed to slip further and further away from me. I had lost my beautiful Amelia and my Emily on the same day and there was nothing I could do about it, I was helpless.

The Wedding November 1984

Ruth and Peter agreed on a winter wedding as they both loved the winter so much. They settled on Saturday 24th November 1984. Anna & nonna were so excited that Ruth and Keith had set a date. Finally, the preparations could begin. Ruth would have been happy with a small private wedding however Anna would not hear of it, not in a million years. She wanted the best wedding that money could buy for her perfect son and his amazing wife-to-be. So, on and on the lists went, one after another after another.

As time flew by and it came closer and closer to her wedding day Ruth realised that she didn't have a maid of honour. Keith didn't have a lot of friends so it was a given that his work colleague, and friend, Harris would be his best man. Who could Ruth ask? She didn't really have friends and despite being popular at work she couldn't really class any of her colleagues as a close friend.

Ruth decided to go see Lyn after work to discuss her dilemma, who better to talk to than nana. Ruth arrived at Lyn's house at 5:30pm. Lyn wasn't expecting Ruth so had just sat down to eat her dinner when Ruth rang the bell. Lyn answered the door with her slippers on and an old cardigan that she just wouldn't part with despite Ruth trying several times to throw it away.

"Hi, Nana," she said kissing Lyn on the cheek, "I've not come for dinner so don't panic; I'm merely here as I need to ask you something."

"Come away in Darling," Lyn said as she walked slowly back into her kitchen where she had been sitting eating her dinner. Ruth followed closely behind and for the first time ever noticed how frail her grandmother had become.

Ruth had intended to ask her grandmother to give her away despite Tony's heavy hinting that he would be more than happy to do the honours. However, on reflection she decided against asking Lyn as she really hadn't noticed how frail her nana actually was. Ruth felt that to ask her to give her away would be too much to ask. She knew her nana well enough to know that she would of course say yes as she wouldn't want to let Ruth down, but Ruth knew in her heart it would be far too much to ask of her. Instead, Ruth proceeded to ask her nana to be a witness at her wedding. She explained that she didn't have any true friends to ask to be a maid of honour, and given that it's not necessary, all she needed was a witness to sign the register and she hoped that nana would agree to do so. Lyn was both delighted and disappointed. Delighted to be asked however disappointed that her beautiful granddaughter did not have so much as one good friend to ask to be her maid of honour. Lyn smiled at her granddaughter and said that she would be delighted as long as she could sit down to sign the register.

"Perfect," said Ruth hugging her nana, well, that's that then. Now, to tell Tony that he would in fact be taken up on his offer of giving Ruth away.

Ruth and Keith had arranged to go for dinner with his parents on the weekend. Ruth decided she wouldn't tell Keith of her plan to ask Tony to give her away, she decided it would be nicer to surprise everyone at once while they sat at the dinner table. They arrived at the Vasillio's at six thirty p.m. on the Saturday evening as planned. Nonna, as always, was cooking with Anna while Tony watched football. As Keith and Ruth entered the Vasillio's home they both shouted hello at once. This made nonna jump as the echo of both voices was pretty loud. Nonna dropped the lid of the saucepan she was holding, "Che paura sanguinosa!" she screamed "perché stai gridsndo?"

"Mi dispiace cosi tanto, Nonna," said Keith as he entered the kitchen and grabbed nonna in a huge bear hug.

"Okay, okay, abbastanza, abbastanza, mettimi giù. Tesoro ho bisogno di cucinare," said Nonna.

Keith let her down gently and kissed her on the top of her head. "Can I pour some wine for my beautiful ladies?" he said as he moved across the kitchen to his mother's' wine rack. All three declined and said they would wait for dinner.

Keith and Ruth took off their jackets and proceeded to set the table, this had been Keith's job since he was a small boy. Ruth loved to help as it made her really feel like part of the Vasillio family. Dinner was ready at seven p.m. Everyone washed their hands and sat down at the table ready to be served. Keith poured the wine as Anna plated up the food. The meal was delicious, so much so, that Ruth didn't want to waste one second of savouring the flavours of her food by talking so decided to keep quiet until the main course was over. Once dessert was on the table and they were once again seated at the table ready to eat, Ruth announced that she had something she wanted to say. "Well, it's actually a question that I would like to ask Tony" she said as she looked around the table at the Vasillio's. "Tony, will you do me the honour of giving me away at our wedding?"

Tony jumped up off his chair, ran around the table pulling Ruth's chair out and lifting her into his big strong arms, he swung her round shouting "Si Si certo che lo faro ne sarei onorato." Despite not speaking Italian, Ruth knew by the word 'Si' and his actions that Tony was happy to accept the role of giving her away. The rest of the evening was full of laughter and discussions about the wedding.

It was three weeks before the wedding when nana went with Ruth for her final dress fitting. Her dress was the most beautiful gown she had ever seen in her life and she just couldn't believe it was hers. Nana had always done her best by Ruth however this was on another level. It must have taken every penny that nana had to purchase this beautiful gown. As she stood there getting the last tiny alterations done to the dress, she had a fixed smile on her face that could light up the world. Nana just kept saying "Ruth, Ruth my beautiful Ruth I am so happy that you have found love in your life. You deserve happiness more than anyone I know." I'm not sure Ruth even heard a word her nana was saying as she seemed to be in a trance enjoying the moment of feeling like a princess while everyone fussed around her sorting out her dress for what would be the most important day of her life.

Finally, the day arrived, it was eight a.m. on 24th November 1984. The day Ruth had waited for all of her life. Ruth had stayed with her nana the night before as she didn't want any of the Vasillio's to see her prior to the wedding. She had arranged for Tony to come with the wedding car to pick her up at two p.m. to take her to the church. Nana would go in a taxi to pick up Anna and nonna and meet them at the church in time for the wedding at two thirty p.m. Keith would obviously make his own way to the church with Harris.

Tony arrived with the car at exactly two o'clock. Nana let him in as Ruth put the finishing touches of her make-up on. Nana told Tony to sit while he waited for Ruth to come through from nana's bedroom where she had dressed. Nana went into the room to speak with Ruth before leaving for the church in a taxi. When Ruth turned to face her Lyn almost collapsed with emotion. Her baby granddaughter was the most beautiful bride she had ever seen. She approached Ruth with open arms taking her into her breast and savouring the last few moments of her granddaughter being her little girl and carrying her name. Soon she would be a vasillio, a wife and hopefully someday, a mother. Before Lyn left, she handed Ruth a small package. Ruth looked up at her smiling and asked what it was. "Open it" she said, "don't just stand there smiling." Ruth's hands shook as she attempted to open the small package. She had no idea why she felt really nervous despite having no idea what she was about to open. Ruth finally managed to pull the package apart to reveal a tiny white gold pin in the shape of an Angel. Ruth looked up at her nana and said, "I love it, it's just so beautiful Nana."

Lyn took the tiny pin and attached it to the bodice of Ruth's dress. "Your grandfather had this made for me when my daughter Ruth, your aunt was taken from us. I want her with you on your wedding day and every day thereafter. She would have adored you just as much as I do my darling." Ruth didn't know what to say, tears fell from her eyes down onto her dress. "Now, now" said Lyn, "no tears, this is a happy day. Only happiness moving forward, no looking back, only to the future." Lyn embraced her Granddaughter for the last time as a single woman and left to go pick up Anna and nonna. "See you at the church my darling" she said as she left Ruth fixing her makeup. Ruth didn't think she'd ever been happier. The pin just felt right and she was ready, ready to go and start her new life.

"Ruth, the car is here," shouted Tony. "I'll be there in a minute" she replied. Ruth walked out of the bedroom a few minutes later looking spectacular. Tony took one look at her and his hand flew up to his mouth "oh mio non ho mai visto una sposa cosi bella," he said as he walked toward her with open arms. Ruth had no idea what he had said however knew it was heart felt and sincere.

Tony put out his arm for Ruth to take and said, "Shall we?" Ruth smiled, linked arms with Tony, and they walked out to the wedding car that was waiting outside. The neighbours were all out clapping and cheering. Ruth was a little embarrassed, however loved every moment, she had never felt so special in her entire life. The photographer took some photos of Ruth and Tony walking to the wedding car and more as Ruth climbed in. He then jumped in his own car to ensure he was ready and waiting at the church when they arrived.

At two thirty p.m. Keith was at the church standing at the alter with Harris by his side waiting on the arrival of Ruth. The church was full of well-wishers, neighbours, colleagues of both Keith and Ruth and of course Keith's family who had travelled from Italy for this special day. Anna looked around her and smiled as she bent over and whispered to Lyn, "what a magnificent day for a wedding."

Lyn looked at Anna with tears streaming down her face, "I never thought this day would come." Since Ruth was born, I have wanted her to find someone who would love her the way she deserves to be loved; your son has brought her so much joy and happiness. I just can't express how happy it makes me to see the way he loves her with such passion and depth. I just, I just can't thank you all enough for welcoming Ruth into your family with such warmth, also for throwing such a beautiful wedding for them both."

It was two forty-five p.m. and still Keith waited, Ruth had not arrived. Keith was sweating and kept asking Harris if he thought Ruth had changed her mind. Just as he was about to ask Lyn if she knew what was happening the organist began to play 'Here comes the bride'. Ruth had arrived. With Tony by her side

Ruth walked down the aisle towards Keith, shaking, for fear that she would trip. Everyone in the church gasped as she walked past, she was just astonishingly beautiful. Harris looked round to see Tony and Ruth walking towards them, he gasped at Ruth's beauty. "Wow" he whispered under his breath. By this time Keith was shaking, he just couldn't wait to marry Ruth, this was all he had ever wanted from the moment he set eyes on her.

Tony and Ruth reached the altar, Tony let go of Ruth's arm once she was standing next to Keith and he took a seat beside Anna. Keith looked across at his bride-to-be, he gasped at her beauty. Keith had never seen Ruth look so radiant. They both stood there shaking as the priest began to talk. He first led everyone in the signing of the cross. He then greeted the congregation and lead with a prayer naming both Ruth and Keith, asking for god's blessing; after which he proceeded with the vows. Finally, the priest announced, "I now pronounce you man and wife, you may kiss the bride." Keith turned to face Ruth, he lifted her veil and kissed her; they both smiled at each other with tears in their eyes. The congregation cheered as they walked down the aisle towards the church entrance. They were Mr & Mrs Keith Vasillio at last.

The Funeral

The tiny white coffin lying in the sitting room on the large dining table should not be there. Today Peter and Emily would lay their baby girl to rest. Emily had been given yet another sedative to calm her as she wasn't coping with Amelia's death. As soon as the sedative wore off, she would become violent and destroy everything around her. She hadn't uttered a word to anyone including Peter since Amelia was pronounced dead. Peter hoped that once the funeral was over Emily would begin to grieve properly and begin to calm down and eventually come off the sedatives.

Amelia was to be buried in Plockton Burial Ground within Plockton Church in Inness Street beside all her relatives from Emily's side of the family. Angela had contacted Cathy, Peter's mother, to let her know the arrangements for the funeral just in case she wanted to attend. However, she politely declined, she said she just couldn't cope with a child's funeral let alone her grandchild. As much as Angela 'couldn't understand how Cathy could say she wasn't going to attend she had no option other than to relay that information back to Peter. Peter just shrugged his shoulders and walked away when told that his mother and sister wouldn't be coming to Plockton for Amelia's funeral. To be honest, Peter was walking about in a state of shock anyway so who turned up and who didn't wouldn't make any difference to him or Emily.

The hearse and funeral car pulled up outside. Peter and Graham carried the small white coffin out to the hearse and laid it in gently with the beautiful wreath of small pink roses in the shape of a heart laid on top, pink was Amelia's favourite colour. Angela led Emily out to the car along with Dr Henderson. Peter and Graham joined the others in the funeral car and proceeded to follow the hearse to the Plockton Church where they would hold a service in Amelia's memory.

The church was full, everyone from Plockton had shown up to pay their respects to Peter and Emily. Peter's friend and work colleague Rod played the piano and had offered to play some light music while they walked Amelia into the church for her final farewell. Once again Peter and Graham lifted the tiny white coffin and walked into the church followed closely behind by Emily, Angela and Dr Henderson. The congregation were shocked to see Emily so frail, it was obvious that she was sedated as there was no expression on her face. She looked as if she was sleep walking.

"Poor Emily, no mother should have to experience this," said Edna, one of the local women, as Emily walked past, supported by her mother.

Peter and Graham put Amelia's coffin on the stand at the front of the church and proceeded to take a seat next to Emily and her mother. Everyone was seated and the priest began to speak.

O Merciful father, whose face of the angels of thy little ones do always behold in heaven; Grant us steadfastly to believe that thy child Amelia hath been taken into the safe keeping of thine eternal love; through Jesus Christ our Lord. Amen

People sobbed quietly as the priest continued to talk about Amelia's short life and how she had brought greatness to the world with her laughter and her love of life. He spoke about the history of her family within the community and the respect shown over the years to her ancestor's. Of how she would be greeted by her loved ones and taken under their wing and cherished until it was her parents' time to join her. Amelia was laid to rest, after the service, in the grounds of the church, while the sun shone brightly above.

Peter had not organised for people to come back to the house after the funeral as he knew Emily wasn't up to it, if he was honest, neither was he. It took him every ounce of his strength just to get through the ceremony without breaking down. Peter took Emily straight over to the car as soon as the burial was over. Angela and Graham headed back to the car after they said their thanks and their goodbyes to those who had taken time to pay their respects at the grave side.

Once back at the house Emily headed straight upstairs to her bedroom without so much as a backwards glance at her parents or Peter. Peter tried to speak to her as she moved slowly up the stairs, however she didn't acknowledge him in any way, she continued silently up to her room.

Peter broke down as soon as he sat down, the pressure of the last week finally taking over. He sobbed quietly as Angela bent down and cradled him in her arms. Graham poured a whiskey for himself, and one for Peter. He waited until Peter had calmed a little then handed him the glass.

Angela poured herself a small glass of wine and sat by her husband's side. "What are we going to do about Emily?" she said as Peter and Graham sat sipping their whiskey.

"I can't seem to get through to her Angela, I've tried everything, but she won't even look at me. You know yourself that had you not dressed her she would not have gone to the funeral today. She never gets out of bed nor eats or drinks anything I take to her. She won't look at me, let alone talk to me, and if I try to mention Amelia she starts screaming like a wounded animal and I have to give her a sedative to calm her down. Dr Henderson left me a bottle, however, he has said that he cannot give her any more after they are finished as it would not be ethical. So, if you have any answers Angela then please tell me and I will do whatever it takes."

Angela, like Peter didn't have the answers, all they could do was love and support Emily and hope that soon she would become stronger and be able to accept and move on from the death of her baby girl.

It was ten days after the funeral when Dr Henderson turned up at the house. In his hand, he had a brown envelope containing information regarding Amelia's death. He knocked on the door and within a few moments Peter was standing in front of him with the door open. "Come in Dr Henderson, take a seat. I will get you a cup of tea, or would you prefer coffee?"

"A glass of water will be fine, Peter, thank you." Peter returned from the kitchen a few moments later with a glass of cold water for the Dr and a glass of orange juice for himself.

Peter sat across from Dr Henderson, "so what can I do for you Dr?" he said."

Dr Henderson asked if Emily could join them as he had the autopsy results and wanted to discuss them with both parents. Peter said he would ask her to come down but wasn't confident that she would. Peter climbed the stairs to the bedroom where Emily remained curled up in the foetal position just staring out the window.

"Emily," said Peter, "Dr Henderson is here, he has Amelia's autopsy results and wants to discuss them with both of us."

As Peter had predicted, Emily totally ignored his words and continued to stare blankly out of the window. Peter waited a few moments just in case it took a few seconds for what he had said to sink in however Emily didn't so much as acknowledge his presence in the room let along digest what he had said.

As Peter re-entered the living room he looked across at Dr Henderson and said, "I'm sorry, but Emily won't be joining us, she's not up to it."

Dr Henderson understood what Peter meant by that as he had witnessed for himself exactly how Emily was choosing to live her life since the death of Amelia. "I guess you can pass on all the information when you feel it's appropriate Peter. When I leave here would you like me to contact Angela and Graham or would you prefer to discuss the matter with them?"

"I would be extremely grateful if you could please contact them on my behalf." responded Peter.

"Indeed," said Dr Henderson as he proceeded to open the brown envelope. Dr Henderson began to speak, "Contained within this letter are the results from the autopsy performed on Amelia. It transpires that she had a brain aneurism. A brain aneurism is a bulge that occurs in a blood vessel within the brain. Many can exist for years without symptoms. If the brain aneurysm ruptures or leaks, there will be a bleeding in the brain. This is called a subarachnoid haemorrhage. This is life threatening if not treated immediately. It is rare to find a cerebral aneurysm in a child however they do occur. A complete blood count such as that performed on Amelia's blood can predict Calcification Grade of Abdominal Aortic Aneurysm but unfortunately not a brain aneurism. Also, as I said it is very rare for children to have such an aneurysm although not unheard of. For this reason, we had no idea when Amelia presented with headaches that it was more than likely the start of the aneurysm leaking. By the time Amelia collapsed the aneurysm had burst which we had no way of knowing. This is why Amelia died on arrival at the hospital, it was too late by that time to do anything even if we had known. I'm so deeply sorry Peter as I know this will be a lot for you to take in. It's not going to be easy for you to try to explain this to Emily as there is no easy way of saying it. I would however stress that these types of Aneurysms are extremely rare in children and are usually caused by a knock to the head or after surgery. As Amelia had not had any form of surgery, I would ask you to think back to the time prior to her headache, was there any fall or knock to the head that may be significant?"

Peter sat in silence as Dr Henderson described the finding of the autopsy. All he could think about was why? Why his child, his perfect little girl? Why not him or someone else's child.

Peter was brought back to the moment with Dr Henderson asking the question about Amelia falling or perhaps knocking her head in any way. "I can't recall her having fallen over or banging her head at any time, well, nothing that would be significant enough to cause her to die."

"Unfortunately, Peter, it's not quite that simple, Amelia could have been born with the aneurysm, it could have resulted from an inborn abnormality in her artery wall and gone unnoticed. Then a fall or knock to the head could have caused the leak which in turn resulted in a rupture."

Peter's mind was racing all over trying to take all this information on board and trying to remember anything that could be significant. "Amelia was always active, running around in the garden and woodlands climbing trees and all sorts. She had no fear, however I really cannot recall a time when she either fell over or knocked her head on anything. That said, Amelia was a very robust child. She rarely cried so she may very well have fallen or banged her head when playing and not cried or come looking for comfort. I really can't believe though that a fall or bang that wasn't serious enough to warrant tears could cause a rupture in her brain."

Dr Henderson looked at Peter with great sympathy in his eyes. "I'm sorry Peter but it is possible that a small knock could cause an existing aneurysm to leak. If the leak continues unnoticed then the potential of a rupture becomes almost inevitable."

Dr Henderson shook Peter's hand, "I wish I could be here giving you different news, Peter, I really do."

"It makes no difference," said Peter, "No matter what the paper in your hand says, it doesn't change the fact that Amelia is gone forever; we can't change that. How she died doesn't really help, it doesn't change anything."

Dr Henderson said once again how sorry he was for Peter and Emily's loss and promised to go and explain to Angela and Graham the findings of the autopsy. He shook Peter's hand and patted him on the back as he left. Peter didn't know if telling Emily would help in any way so decided there was no rush. He went upstairs and into Amelia's bedroom. Hours passed and Peter was still sitting on Amelia's bed pondering on the past and trying to figure out if he had failed his daughter in any way. Perhaps I shouldn't have encouraged her to be so boisterous. If only I hadn't allowed her to climb so much. If only I hadn't worked so much, I could have been around more and maybe she would still be here with us. His head was swimming with what if's.

The Reception

The wedding venue was kept a secret from Keith and Ruth; they had no idea where it would be as it was a gift to them from Keith's parents and they wanted it to be a surprise.

At long last I am Mrs Keith Vassilio. I cannot even begin to describe the feelings inside of me today. I have waited my whole life for this day and finally it's here and the hardest part is over. The service was perfect, no one could fault it and the butterflies I felt this morning are finally gone. It's time now to move on to our reception. I am worried however that people may not enjoy the reception mainly due to the lack of family and friends from my side. Most of our guests are Keith's family (my family now, I guess), his friends and our colleagues. A lot of whom I have not even spoken to before. I want everyone to leave having had the best time. I want them to want to get to know me better and want to spend time with me. What if they don't like me? What if they can see the real me? The poor girl, the girl no one wanted or loved, the girl everyone bullied at school.

It's as if Anna was reading Ruth's mind. "Ruth, you are stunningly beautiful inside and out," she whispered to me as I climbed into the wedding car next to my husband. "I am so very proud, to be able to call you my daughter." In that very moment, Ruth realised that the real her, is the person she is today, not that scared child from years ago. She is gone, along with all the bullying and hatred bestowed upon her. She no longer exists. I, Mrs Ruth Vassillio, wife of Mr Keith Vassillio, am about to have the most amazing wedding reception with my new family and friends along with colleagues of both of us.

When the car pulled up outside The Thistle Hotel at the West End of Edinburgh my jaw dropped. I looked at Keith and could see that, like me, he was flabbergasted. We knew Keith's parents didn't have a lot of money and had not expected to be having our reception in such a beautiful location. The wedding venue was spectacular, small and compact however decorated to the highest standard with no expense spared. My initial thought was that Tony and Anna must have spent a fortune and I hoped that we hadn't caused them to go into debt to give us such a wonderful reception. Keith must have seen by the look on my face the worry that was going through my mind. "Relax," said Keith, "my father and Marco, the hotel manager, have been friends since childhood. Marco must have given my parents a very good discount otherwise we would not be here. My parents would never take on more than they can afford Ruth, you know that." In my heart, I knew what Keith said must be true and decided to enjoy this magical day and build a thousand memories to share with our future children instead of worrying how much everything cost.

As we walked through the doors, we could hear everyone already inside awaiting our arrival. Before I even had time to take in my surroundings, we were being ushered into the reception hall. "Please be upstanding for your hosts Mr & Mrs Vasillio." I don't really remember much in the few minutes after that as everyone cheered and we were surrounded with people touching us and wishing us all the best. Eventually, after what seemed like forever we were seated at the top table with Nana, Tony, Anna, nonna and Harris.

The speeches began with Tony, then Harris, and finally on to Keith. Tony's speech was the longest, gosh that man can talk! It went from English to Italian and back to English with everyone laughing each time he changed language. I really don't think he even realised what he was doing, well until Anna told him to bloody well choose a language and stick to it. By this time everyone Italian or English had got the message loud and clear, Tony was a very happy man. Harris, well let's just say his speech took all of sixty seconds and began with an expletive and ended with one. Not a speech nonna enjoyed, let's just leave it at that. Last, but in no way least, came my husband's speech. Keith had written his speech at least a dozen times before finally deciding to just wing it; and wing it he did. I've never felt so proud of him as I did right then, he didn't need a piece of paper he spoke from his heart. On behalf of us both, Keith thanked everyone for their part to play in making our wedding day one to remember.

The wedding breakfast was delicious, we started with bruschetta pugliese with diced tomato, garlic and herbs followed by pan seared veal layered with prosciutto de parma, roasted potatoes and sautéed broccoli finished with a cheese board and coffee as well as our wedding cake. Not that I ate much, I was too excited. However, Keith, Harris and Tony managed to eat enough for the whole top table so I don't think anyone really noticed how little I managed to eat.

Once the meal was over and the tables cleared the dancing began. The first dance was led by Keith and me followed by Tony and nana, Anna and Harris, then nonna with Keith's ninety-six-year-old great uncle Alfonzo. I've never seen such an old man dance the way Alfonzo danced. He was so graceful on his feet he put us all to shame.

The whole evening flew by and the band that Tony had commissioned were out of this world. There was nothing they couldn't play from old to current day hits. I am confident that everyone had an amazing evening as the buzz in the reception room was constant. Every time I looked at someone they would be laughing, drinking and having fun and looked genuinely happy to be there. I spent most of the evening being introduced to Keith's extended family; my family. I can honestly say that there was not one person at our wedding with whom I didn't have a brief conversation. By the end of the night, I felt as if I had known every one there all my life. Keith's family are just wonderful and so easy to get along with. They all made me feel so comfortable and relaxed. I never dreamt that I would find love, never mind a whole family who wanted to share in our happiness.

Looking back, I wish I had taken more time to actually enjoy my wedding day. Don't get me wrong it was amazing, every part from beginning to end, however I feel I could have taken more time to just take it all in and enjoy every second of the experience as I'll never get to do it again. It's a once in a lifetime event and I truly believe that none of us actually take enough time to soak it all in. We are too busy making sure everyone else is having a great time.

Breaking Point

The last year had been the hardest of Peter's life. Since losing Amelia he had become extremely introverted. He had stopped going to work in the hope that being around the house would encourage Emily to get up and hopefully one day begin to accept that Amelia was gone and try to move on. He wanted to be there on that day as he was certain in his heart that it would come.

Emily's parents would help out by taking them shopping. Angela would clean the house and read to Emily, hoping, like Peter, that one-day things would change. Graham would tend to the garden on his days off and talk to Peter about work hoping to encourage him to return, "Maybe if you come back to work Peter and put some normality back into your life things will begin to slowly change. Emily will see that you are moving forward and perhaps that will give her the strength to do the same."

Peter looked at Graham and gave the same answer he had given for the last twelve months, "maybe next week."

It was the day before the first anniversary of Amelia's death when Angela and Graham turned up with an overnight bag. "We are going to stay tonight Peter if that's all right with you as we are worried how Emily will react tomorrow and feel that we need to be here to support you both."

"Fine by me," said Peter "it makes no difference either way as Emily won't come out of her room anyway."

Angela knew what Peter was saying was fact however she looked at him and said "I would sleep easier knowing that I'm under the same roof as my daughter just in case she needs me."

"Whatever," said Peter as he walked out of the backdoor and into the garden for a smoke.

That night Angela cooked a homemade steak pie. She managed to encourage Emily out of her room for the first time in over a month. This made Peter feel even more hopeless as he hadn't managed to encourage her to get out of bed let alone leave the room. They sat together at the table eating dinner, or should I say pushing it about their plates as no one was actually eating. No one spoke, no one ate, so Angela decided to clear the dishes away. As she did so Emily removed herself from the dining room table and went back upstairs to her bed. Peter and Graham went outside for a smoke leaving Angela to clean up.

The mood in the house was extremely low that evening, with good reason. Angela and Graham retired to their room at ten p.m. leaving Peter alone with his thoughts. Peter opened a bottle of whiskey and poured a large glass, then another and another until the bottle was completely empty. Over the last year Peter's relationship with Emily had gone from being perfect to being non-existent. No matter what he did or said Emily remained silent, stuck inside her head all alone grieving for her child. Peter felt like a complete failure, he couldn't save Amelia on that terrible day a year ago nor could he bring his wife out of her own prison where she had been since Amelia's death.

Peter took a photo of Amelia from the fireplace and sat and stared at his beautiful little princess smiling back at him. The photo had been taken about six months before Amelia died. It was Peter's favourite picture of Amelia, he could remember the day it was taken. It was a Sunday morning and Amelia had woken him up just like she did every Sunday, jumping up and down on him squealing "it's time to wake up Daddy, it's time to wake up." Emily had rolled over as Sunday was her day of rest, and Peter's day to get up and deal with Amelia. Peter didn't mind as he adored spending one on one time with his baby girl. They had eggs for breakfast and then dressed and went out into the garden where the photo had been taken. The sun shone and the birds chirped in the tress, it was a beautiful June morning, perfect in every way.

Peter stood up with Amelia's picture in his hand and walked to the back door, without a second thought he opened the door and walked out into the garden. He walked over to his work shed where he would often spend time on his days off prior to Amelia's death, however he hadn't been there in over twelve months. Peter unlocked the door, walked in, went straight to the back of his shed where he found a long rope that he had kept, like loads of other bits and pieces, just in case he ever needed them. He picked up the rope and his small ladder and walked back out into the garden. Peter walked over to the big oak tree at the bottom of the garden and without hesitation set up the ladder, climbed up and tied the rope over a thick branch about 10 feet off the ground. He made sure the rope was tightly secured then tied a noose in the end and popped it over his head. Without a second thought, with Amelia's photo in his hand, he kicked the ladder away.

Graham woke early the next morning about six a.m. Pretty late in fact for him as having been a fisherman all his life his day had always started much earlier than that. He headed down to the kitchen to make some coffee for him and Angela. He entered the kitchen and immediately noticed that the back door was open. He assumed Peter was up and was in the garden. He walked outside to ask Peter if he wanted coffee, however what he saw would live with him for the rest of his life. Graham saw his son-in-law hanging from the oak tree at the bottom of the garden. He immediately ran to try and cut Peter down however as he grew closer it was more than apparent that Peter was dead. Graham instinctively picked up the small ladder and tried to ease Peter down off the noose. He didn't want Angela or worst still Emily seeing him hanging there. He lay Peter on the ground and removed the noose from his neck. It was then that he noticed Amelia's photograph lying on the grass next to Peter. It had obviously fallen out of Peter's hand as soon as Peter had kicked the step ladder away and the rope had tightened around his neck. Graham noticed the shed door was open and hoped there would be something in there to cover Peter to ensure that no one would see his lifeless body. He noticed just inside the door there was a large tarpaulin which he grabbed and quickly ran over to cover Peter's body.

Graham went back into the kitchen and instantly called Dr Henderson; he didn't know what else to do. As soon as Dr Henderson answered the phone, he knew something was terribly wrong as Graham's breathing was fast and he couldn't really understand what he was saying at first. "Dr Henderson come quickly its Peter my son-in-law, he's hung himself." Just at that moment Angela walked into the kitchen, all she heard was the last words out of Grahams mouth "My son-in-law has hung himself," she instantly started to scream. Graham dropped the phone and reached out just in time to catch his wife before she hit the ground. The shock had caused her to faint. Graham gently lay her on the floor before picking the phone back up, however the line was dead. Dr Henderson was already on his way.

Angela quickly came around, Graham helped her into the living room where she sat holding her face in her hands; a thousand questions running through her mind. "What happened? What do you mean Peter hung himself?" Graham looked at his wife and began to explain the events of the morning.

Suddenly Angela looked up and said, "Oh my god, Emily, we need to tell Emily." Someone would need to go and tell Emily what had happened and neither one of her parents wanted to be that person however they knew that it would be better to come from one of them as opposed to someone else. They decided that Angela would go and let Emily know what had happened while Graham waited for Dr Henderson to arrive. He didn't want Angela to see Peter's dead body. Angela had just gone upstairs when there was a knock at the door, both police and Dr Henderson had arrived at the same time. As soon as Dr Henderson hung up the phone, he had jumped in his car heading to Peter and Emily's house. On the way he stopped at the local police station and asked for assistance as he was led to believe there had been a suicide.

Angela continued to approach Emily as she lay in her bed. While reaching down to touch her daughter she realised that Emily was already awake. "Emily, my darling, something awful has happened." It took every ounce of her strength for Angela to continue without breaking down. "Emily, Peter is dead." Emily didn't so much as look up at her mother, a tear slid down her face as she continued to stare straight ahead. "Emily I'm so deeply sorry, I just don't know what to say or do. Dad found Peter in the garden and it looks like he has hung himself." Emily continued to stare straight ahead and didn't make any attempt to get out of bed nor show any real reaction to what her mother had just told her. Despite Angela persistently pleading with her daughter to get up and go downstairs Emily didn't move.

There was a knock at the door and Graham walked in followed by a police officer who wanted to speak to Emily and Angela. Angela explained that she had been telling Emily what had happened and had been pleading with her to get up however not only would she not get up she hadn't even acknowledged if she understood what her mother had been saying to her. The police officer attempted to talk to Emily however he too had no success. "I think Dr Henderson needs to come and see Emily," said Graham. "She has been in this state since Amelia died a year ago and despite all our efforts has not moved forward in any way. This can only set her further back and we have no idea how to deal with her." At that moment Angela realised what day it was, she looked at Graham and said "Oh my god Graham, it's exactly a year today since our beautiful Amelia died. My poor Emily, my little girl how much more must she have to endure!"

The Doctor had pronounced Peter dead on arrival. The police had given permission to have the body removed from the garden as there were no suspicious circumstances. As Graham had already identified the body as being his son-in-law Peter, there was no need for any further delay in moving Peter's body to the morgue.

Dr Henderson had a brief discussion with the police regarding Emily's state of mind since the death of her daughter. He tried to explain that her lack of emotion to the news of Peter's suicide was not because she didn't care but because she was unable to allow herself the luxury of feeling emotions. In his professional opinion, she remained in her own world surrounded by a safety net which she had put up to protect herself from the pain of losing her child. He had no way of predicting if she would eventually come out of her own private world or remain there forever. "The mind is a very complex thing" he said as he continued to try to explain to the police exactly why Emily remained silent.

Everyone left the room leaving only Angela there just in case Emily needed her. Angela was deeply concerned for her daughter.

Today was one year since Amelia had passed and now Peter was gone. How would her daughter ever cope with life again after this?

The police left after the body had been removed from the garden leaving Graham alone with Dr Henderson. "Can I offer you a whisky Doctor?" said Graham.

"I could certainly do with one if you will join me," he replied. Dr Henderson and Graham sat for a while drinking whiskey and discussing what they should do regarding Emily and her lack of emotion and communication over the last twelve months, also how Peter's suicide was likely to set her further back.

Dr Henderson suggested more sedatives however Graham was reluctant to go back down that root as Emily had been off them for ten months and he didn't feel they had made any difference to her anyway. Dr Henderson was honest with Graham and admitted that Emily's case was unique and he had never come across anything like this in his career. He had read about such things as people retreating into themselves however had never witnessed it and was really unsure as to what the next step would be. He continued to say, "When people grieve it is difficult to know what to say or do as everyone is different. The bereaved struggle with many intense and painful emotions, including depression, anger, guilt and profound sadness. Often, they can feel isolated and alone in their grief. The only advice I can give is for you and Angela to be patient and just be here for her. You don't have the answers so don't try and look for them, just be ready and waiting for when Emily finally breaks down and opens up to you. Unfortunately, we have no way of knowing how long that will take." Once they had both finished their glass of whiskey Graham thanked Dr Henderson for his continued support to his family and bid him good evening.

The Doctor had only been gone about twenty minutes when Graham heard an almighty crash coming from upstairs. He ran upstairs to find Angela lying on the floor and the bedside table was upside down next to her. "What happened?" he cried," as he looked at his daughter who was standing above her mother holding the bedside lamp in her hand as if she was ready to strike her mother with it. Emily immediately started to scream and dropped the table lamp as she ran around and around the room hitting herself on the head. Angela quickly got to her feet and ran out of the room as she was terrified of what Emily would do next. Graham tried to talk to Emily however the more he tried to talk the louder she would scream and the harder she would hit herself. Graham thought it would be best to leave her alone to calm down so he too left the room closing the door behind him. He stood outside the closed door for a few minutes, finally all went silent, Emily was finally calm, but for how long?

Angela waited downstairs in the kitchen for Graham to join her. "What are we going to do Graham?" she asked.

"I really don't know darling I don't have the answers, Dr Henderson reckons all we can do is wait and make sure we are here for Emily when she finally accepts that she needs to move forward with her life, be here for her and take her lead, that's all we can do."

Angela looked at Graham with tears in her eyes, "She's our daughter, we need to do something, we need to help her understand that she needs to grieve for both Amelia and Peter, but how, when she won't even look at us? "I feel like I've failed my child." Graham looked at his wife, he couldn't stand to see both his daughter and his wife suffer and not be able to do anything. He opened his arms and Angela fell into them hanging on to him as if her life depended on it while she sobbed.

After a while Graham led Angela upstairs to go to bed. They listened at Emily's door, all was silent, so they continued on to the spare room where they slept, while they were at Woodland House. Angela cleaned her teeth and then slipped off her clothes and put on her nightgown. Meanwhile Graham had jumped in the shower as he felt he really needed to wash away what had been one of the most troubled days he had ever experienced. Finding Peter hanging in the garden had really affected Graham especially given that he had touched his son-in-law's dead body. He just knew he wouldn't sleep well that night, or perhaps any night in the near future.

Suddenly it came to Angela that no one had contacted Cathy regarding Peter's suicide. "Graham," she said as she covered her mouth with her hands.

"What's the matter?" asked Graham.

"No one has contacted Cathy. "Oh, my goodness, we have been so wrapped up with everything going on here that we have not even contacted poor Cathy about her son." Angela knew in her heart that they had to call Cathy there and then. They couldn't leave it a moment longer as Cathy needed to know what had happened as soon as possible and not a day or so after. Graham said he would call as he knew that Angela would breakdown and not be capable of telling Cathy what had happened. One mother telling another that her son had killed himself, nope it was down to him to call and break the news.

Graham called Cathy and explained the best he could about what had taken place that day. He was reluctant to go into too much detail regarding Emily, however I'm not sure Cathy was listening much past "Peter hung himself in the garden this morning." There really was no need to explain anything any further. Catherine took the phone from her mother who at this point was hysterical. She explained that she would call back in the morning to speak to Graham a little more as at that moment she had to concentrate on her mother. Graham fully understood, said his apologies and hung up.

The next morning Catherine called as promised, Graham explained everything to her including how Emily had reacted to Peter's suicide. Catherine said that her mother and she would come to Plockton for the funeral. "Could you please keep us updated as to when it will be?" Graham agreed to call with information regarding the funeral as soon as he knew anything then once again expressed his sorrow to Catherine and hung up the phone.

The Note

The next morning when Angela and Graham woke, they quickly discovered that Emily was gone. On the kitchen table was a note that she had left for them.

My dear parents,

I don't expect you to understand however my life is over. My Amelia was the most amazing little girl, she was everything I had ever wanted in a child. She was funny and cute and laughed all the time and had the biggest heart and loved everything about life. She had that stupid little habit of sucking her pinkie from as far back as I can remember. Not her thumb like any other baby, her pinkie. I'm sure you both remember. I failed her, I didn't notice that she had something inside her head just waiting to burst. I should have known. I should have made the doctors do more when she complained of a sore head as my Amelia never complained, you both know that. I didn't do anything and in turn my baby died. I've tried to understand why, but I just can't. How could something so terrible happen to my precious little girl. I will never accept that she is gone as in order to do so I would need to understand and that is beyond me. Peter knew I could never move on, he knew my life was over as was his. His way of coping was different from mine and now he has also gone so obviously his way didn't work either. All I know is that there is no way for me to continue living my life without them. Please do not try to find me as I don't want to be found. I want to live the rest of my life alone trying to figure out why, why this has happened. I know it will take an eternity and I will go to my death still asking why. For this reason, I must do this alone. If you love me, you will respect my wishes and allow me to live my life my way.

I love you both, please remember that.

Emily

Emily crept downstairs and popped the note on the kitchen table before going out into the back garden. She moved across the garden quickly as she didn't want to be seen by anyone. She entered the garden shed and went straight to where she knew Peter had hidden the keys for the bedrooms as he didn't want Amelia to accidently lock herself in. She grabbed the keys and ran back into the house moving up the stairs as quietly as she could, not wanting to be disturbed. She firstly moved towards Amelia's room, which hadn't been touched since she died as Peter often sat in their when he wanted to remember his daughter and Emily just couldn't bring herself to enter the room after that dreaded night when they came home from the hospital without their child. Emily popped the key in the lock and turned making sure that no one would be able to clear her baby's things away as she wanted them left exactly how Amelia had left them. Next, she moved over to the room she had shared with Peter and securely locked their door. She never wanted to enter that room again, she never wanted to smell Peters scent or look at his things but she also wanted to make sure everything remained untouched. She moved slowly down stairs and out into the evening leaving her house and her parents behind her.

Emily had no idea where she was going but go she must. She walked into the woodlands the opposite way you would go if going into Plockton. She walked and walked for what seemed to her like minutes but it must have been hours as the sun soon started to rise. Emily knew she must have walked quite far as she didn't recognise any of the surroundings. She had walked in these woodlands every day and had done since she was a child. This alone told Emily that she had gone further into the woodlands than she had ever been before.

Emily suddenly felt tired, it had been a long night. She looked around to see if there was somewhere she could lie down just for a while to get her strength back. To her right there was an old abandoned hut. It was small but looked big enough for Emily to go for a lie down and feel safe. As she approached, she soon realised that the hut was actually bigger than it looked and despite having been abandoned for many years looked stable enough. She tried to open the door, however, it was stuck. She pulled and pulled until finally it gave way and the door swung open. Emily entered the hut and was shocked to see there was an old bed and some old rags as well as some very old rusty tools. This place had obviously belonged to someone who hadn't been there in a very long time. Emily began to wonder if it had belonged to the previous owners of her house as that had also been run down. Anyway, regardless, she had somewhere to lay her head and would worry about everything else later. As soon as Emily's head hit the bed, she fell asleep, her body needed sleep more than she had realised.

Emily woke to the sound of wood pigeons calling back and forth to one another. Initially she had no idea where she was, however, when she sat up, she soon remembered. The small hut she had taken shelter in wasn't actually that bad considering. She knew she could stay here and be safe just until she knew she could go home. She wanted to be in her home but she didn't want her parents there with her and knew that they wouldn't understand. This was the only way she could get them to go home. Emily had packed a small bag full of food to keep her going for a while. There was a small water stream not far from the cabin. She had seen it yesterday, so knew she had fresh water to drink. She would be okay here, she felt at ease for the first time in a long time.

As time passed Emily began to think it was time to go home. She was running out of supplies so thought she would sneak back to her house that night to if her parents were still there. If so, she could at least sneak in and get more supplies. She had no idea how long she had been sleeping in the cabin however knew it had been a few weeks at least.

As darkness fell Emily prepared to make her way back to the house. Despite being further into the woodlands than she had been before she was certain she could find her way back. Once she got passed the stream, she knew it was only a short distance after that before she would recognise landmarks. As predicted Emily found her way back to the house despite the darkness. She noticed immediately that the house was empty and her father's car had gone. Emily felt a sense of relief as she really didn't want to go back to the hut.

Emily entered her house through the back door just to make sure that her mother hadn't stayed behind. She crept in slowly and made her way round the house checking ever room as she went. She was relieved to find no one there, she could now relax. Emily locked both back and front doors leaving the key in both so that no one could enter the property. She knew her parents would attempt to come back to see if she had returned. She knew them so well, not more than a few days had passed when Graham's car pulled up outside. Graham and Angela got out of the car and attempted to open the front door. When it became apparent that they couldn't get in they went around to the back door and tried to enter that way, same issue, door wouldn't unlock. At that moment Graham realised that Emily must be inside and must have locked both doors leaving the keys in the lock. "She's in there," he said to Angela who at this point was starting to stress.

"What? You think Emily is back?"

"Yes, she has obviously locked both doors from the inside leaving the key in the lock so that we can't enter."

At that moment Angela started to shout out "Emily darling, it's mum, please open the door sweetheart. I just want to know that you are okay." Emily hid behind the sofa and held her breath. She didn't want to see or talk to anyone, especially her parents. She hid there until darkness fell and she was sure her parents had gone home.

Emily unlocked the door to her bedroom and gathered up a few pieces of clothing along with the photo of her and Amelia from the side of her bed. She left the room and vowed never to enter that room ever again. Emily also kept Amelia's room locked, she just couldn't bring herself to enter her baby's room and wanted to make sure that no one else could. She was happy to sleep in the guest room where her parents would normally sleep. She put the small amount of clothing that she had gathered together into the small wardrobe and placed the photo of her and Amelia on the bedside table.

Emily sat on the edge of the bed and thought about how she had let her baby girl down by not protecting her. She also felt like she had let Peter down by being unable to accept Amelia's death and understand that he too was grieving. Maybe she could have saved Amelia if she had kept a closer eye on her. Maybe she could have saved Peter had she tried to understand, he too was grieving for their child. However, she hadn't managed to protect either, which in her mind meant that she had failed as a mother and a wife. She would never again hurt another person. For this reason, Emily would never, could never, allow her parents back into her life. She refused to be responsible if they too took their life or fell ill and she hadn't noticed. She had to stay away from everyone as no good could come from her allowing people into her life. She would live alone in silence until it was her time to go and meet Peter and Amelia.

Plockton (The Honeymoon)

Ruth and Keith had packed in advance of their wedding allowing them to relax and have a hearty breakfast before setting off on their honeymoon the next day. Everything was going to be perfect, no stress just lots of fun and a load of memories made. Keith had planned the most scenic route to allow the adventure to start as soon as they hit the road. The journey would take approximately four and a half to five hours, so Keith wanted to make sure that it was a journey to remember.

Ruth made sure they had plenty of snacks and juice packed for the journey. She wasn't the best traveller so wanted to make sure she had plenty of boiled sweets to try to avoid motion sickness. Little did she know that the journey would be so spectacularly beautiful that as soon as they got out of town, she would be so wrapped up in the beauty of her homeland to give motion sickness even a moment's thought.

They left at ten a.m., they wanted to make sure they arrived in Plockton about three p.m. while it was still light given that they had never been before. The plan was to only stop for toilet breaks as they wanted to maximize their time in Plockton. As soon as they left Edinburgh and hit the country Ruth squealed with excitement, she had never done a road trip before and had only ever seen pictures of Scotland's beauty. To see it with her own eyes was in fact one of the most amazing experiences of her life. "Keith," she squealed, "oh my god look at all those sheep, and over there, cows!" Keith just laughed, he loved her enthusiasm and her love for all of Mother Nature. He obviously had to keep his eyes on the road so couldn't enjoy the journey in the same way Ruth could. He did however try to take in as much as possible without compromising their safety.

Ruth had no idea that she lived in such a beautiful country. At this moment she found it difficult to understand why anyone would choose to go to another country on holiday when there was so much beauty for them to explore right here in Scotland. Keith loved the way that Ruth was taking in every inch of the journey as if it were her last day on earth. Her enthusiasm and excitement was intoxicating, all he wanted was to make Ruth happy, today being the first day of the rest of their life together he had started the way he meant to end.

They arrived in Plockton at two fifty p.m., plenty time before darkness would fall so they could easily find the cottage they had rented for the week. As they pulled into the main street, they saw a General Store, Ruth looked at Keith and said, "If you pull over, I will go into the store and ask the assistant if they know the way to the cottage, this will save us driving round in circles."

Keith smiled at Ruth as he pulled over, he had been going to suggest the same thing. What is it they say, "Great minds think alike?"

"More like, "'fools seldom differ!'" was Ruth's reply as she jumped out of the car.

Ruth walked into the Plockton General Store, Edna the assistant looked up from the magazine she had been reading. "Hello young lady, welcome to Plockton, how can I help you?" Ruth smiled at the woman behind the counter. "We have booked a week in a cottage somewhere here in Plockton for our honeymoon and I was wondering if you could direct us to save us driving in circles?"

"I take it this is your first visit?" said Edna.

"Yes" said Ruth however hopefully it won't be our last. "Well, firstly congratulations on your wedding and secondly, welcome to Plockton."

"Aw thank you so much," said Ruth as she smiled out the window looking at her husband.

"Okay, let me see if I can direct you to your cottage, however, I'm pretty certain I already know where it will be as Plockton isn't the biggest place in Scotland." Ruth laughed as she moved closer to Edna to show her the address she had written down.

Edna had in fact been correct, she knew exactly what cottage it was that Ruth and Keith had rented for the week. She happily pointed out the directions to Ruth and said she hoped to see her around during their stay. "Just remember," said Edna as Ruth was about to leave the store, "if you need anything at all my dear I am here every day and there is not much I don't know about Plockton and the surrounding areas."

"Thank you so much," Ruth said as she left the general store.

Ruth opened the car with a huge smile on her face "oh, this place is amazing; the people are just so friendly and they know everything. Our stay here is going to be awesome."

Keith looked at his wife with love in his heart "Okay, Mrs V, let's get going so that we can get settled in and go for a walk before darkness falls." Ruth explained to Keith exactly how to get to the cottage, it was roughly a ten minute walk so she knew they could drive there in a couple of minutes.

As they drew up outside the cottage Ruth noticed a woman at the cottage next to theirs looking out the window. As they approached the front door the woman who had been looking out the window came out to the garden. "Welcome to Plockton" she said to Ruth and Keith as they stood in the next-door garden with their bags. "Edna told me you guys were on your way, my name is Alice, I clean the cottage and renew all the bedding when tourists come and go. "Please don't hesitate to give me a shout if I can help with anything." Ruth and Keith both said hello and thanked Alice for her kind words before entering the cottage to begin their holiday.

Keith walked in first, on the table directly in front of him was a welcome pack. In the pack there were chocolates, a bottle of wine and some fruit as well as a lovely card welcoming the happy couple to Plockton and wishing them a fantastic stay for their honeymoon. Ruth jumped up and down with delight; she was just so happy to be there. Everyone so far had been more than welcoming, at least they knew there was no chance of them feeling like they were intruding in this small village as apparently everyone in Plockton welcomed visitors with open arms.

The cottage was very homely, they had everything they could possibly need from clean towels to pots and pans and enough fire wood to last the whole week. They quickly looked around, popped their case in the bedroom then headed out for a walk to familiarise themselves with their surroundings.

Plockton was in deed one of the most beautiful places either of them had ever seen. It didn't take them much time at all to find their way back to the main street where the general store was. Keith noticed a small inn just up from the general store, "let's go see if they serve food," he said to Ruth.

They walked towards the inn when suddenly Edna popped her head around the door of the general store, "Well hello again!"

"Hi!" said Ruth.

Edna walked over to them and held her hand out to Keith, "Edna," she said as she shook his hand.

"I'm Keith, I believe you already met Ruth?"

"Yes, we met when Ruth popped in for directions to the cottage. "I assume you found the cottage okay, and Alice introduced herself?"

"Yes, thank you" said Ruth "your directions were perfect, thanks again."

"Only too happy to help," replied Edna.

"Alice was extremely nice and offered to help if we needed any direction just as you did. What a lovely welcome we have had," Ruth said as she smiled up at Keith who nodded in agreement.

"I'm sure you will enjoy your stay here and don't forget everyone here is happy to help so don't be shy."

Keith asked Edna if the inn sold food, to which she replied, "not only do they serve food, it's all homemade and delicious and reasonably priced."

"Thank you, Edna, we will no doubt see you tomorrow when we pop in to buy some bits and pieces from the store."

"I'll look forward to that," said Edna as she walked back to the store waving at them both as she disappeared.

Food at the inn was indeed delicious, Ruth had the homemade steak pie with all the trimmings and Keith had a traditional Scottish meal of haggis neeps and tatties. After dinner they sat by the log fire and had a couple of drinks before heading back to the cottage. They had both really enjoyed the food and the service and vowed to definitely go back a few times before the end of their holiday.

It was really cold by the time they walked home so Keith decided to put some logs on the fire to make the cottage all warm and comfortable for their first night. Ruth poured some drinks while Keith prepared the fire. Within twenty minutes the room was lovely and warm. Keith and Ruth lay on the floor in front of the fire drinking the wine that had been left for them from the owner of the cottage in the welcome package. Keith looked at Ruth, the reflection of the fire made her eyes sparkle. He just couldn't believe how lucky he was to be here with her, and to have her as his wife. "I'm the luckiest man alive" he said as he pulled Ruth into his arms. Ruth just melted into Keith's arms, she knew that the love he felt for her was real and everything she had ever wanted. They lay there in silence for a while before Keith gently removed Ruth's clothes followed by his own. They made love that night for the first time as a married couple as they had both been too tired on their wedding night. Had there been an earthquake, or any other disaster that night I doubt either of them would have noticed.

The next morning Keith woke early and decided to drive along to the store to pick up some food so that he could make his wife some breakfast in bed. On his return, he was pleased to see that Ruth was still in bed asleep. He cooked a lovely breakfast of bacon, sausage, egg and of course Ruth's favourite, black pudding. He made a pot of coffee and then headed through to the bedroom to see Ruth getting out of bed. "Get back into bed Mrs V, I've made you breakfast so you can't get up yet!" Ruth did as she was told and got back into bed. Keith lay the tray on the bedside table, handed Ruth her breakfast and poured a coffee for them both before clambering in beside his wife with his own breakfast.

"What a perfect way to start a day," said Ruth as she polished off the last of her breakfast. "I could get used to this you know." Keith smiled as he took the empty plate from her and headed to the kitchen to clean up his mess and do the dishes before Ruth got up. "I'm just going to jump in the shower" she shouted. Keith cleared up then headed through to the bathroom, his thought was to join Ruth in the shower, however, to his disappointment she was already done. Ruth stood in the bathroom with a towel around her head and one around her wet body. Keith walked over to her and pulled the towel off her exposing her beautiful wet body. Ruth just giggled as Keith grabbed her and pulled her onto the bathroom floor where he entered her with such a thrust that it took her breath away. Her wet naked body felt wonderful against his, he just couldn't get enough of her. He was so excited that it was all over before it had really started. He looked at Ruth and apologised. "Don't worry my love," she said laughing, "You can make up for it later!"

Keith laughed as he got up off the bathroom floor and jumped into the shower, "Roll on later" he said as he turned the shower on.

That day they decided to go and visit Eilean Donan Castle. It is one of the most recognised castles in Scotland dating back to the thirteenth Century. The drive was beautiful however nothing could have prepared Ruth and Keith for the beauty they saw in front of them as they arrived at the castle. It was easy to understand why so many people flock to its doors year after year. It is without a doubt a Scottish icon and certainly worth the visit. The castle sits on its own little island overlooking the isle of Skye. The castle is owned by the MacRae family who recently started the Conchra Charitable Trust. Their aim is to preserve the building and its artefacts for the nation and future generations. Ruth soaked up the history behind this magnificent building, she just couldn't get enough. She loved to learn, especially when it came to her country, her heritage. Ruth wanted to know as much as she could about Scotland so that she could pass on the history to her children. Her parents had taught her nothing, she didn't even know that in Roman times Scotland did not exist and that the area we now know as Scotland was called Caledonia and the people were known as Caledonians. It was Tony, her father-in-law, who had told her this and he was Italian born. Ruth wanted to make sure that any future children of hers would be able to ask any question about Scotland and she would have the answers. She was also interested in learning about Italy, however, she was confident that her in-laws would be on it when it came to answering questions about their homeland to the grandchildren. Together as a family they would make sure that Keith and Ruth's future children would know everything about their ancestors from both sides.

The Note is Discovered

Graham woke first the next morning. Truth be told he really hadn't slept well and at five thirty a.m. decided to get up. He slipped out of bed as quietly as possible so as not to disturb Angela who he was aware had also been awake a lot during the night. He went next door to the toilet, however on his return Angela was awake, "Good Morning my darling," he said.

Angela looked at her husband with disgust, "Good morning? Really, Graham, good morning?" Graham didn't know quite how to respond to his wife, he could see that his wife was not in a good frame of mind and didn't want to risk making things worse.

Angela jumped out of bed and quickly dressed without saying a word. She then stormed out of the bedroom slamming the door behind her. Graham followed sheepishly behind, down to the kitchen where she was making coffee. Pulling his jumper over his head he said "Let me make the coffee for you Angela."

Angela looked at him with such a glare he couldn't keep eye contact. "No, Graham, I am more than capable of making my own coffee."

Angela made three cups of coffee, one for her, Graham and another for Emily. Graham thanked her for his coffee and suggested that he take Emily her cup. "No, I will take it up as I want to try and speak to her again now that she has had time to take in all that happened with Peter yesterday. "I hope she has managed to get some sleep and will at least get out of bed for a few hours," Angela said as she walked out of the kitchen headed for Emily's room. Graham took a deep breath trying hard not to say anything else before thinking it through for fear of upsetting his wife even more than he seemed to have already. He understood why she was so tetchy however felt rather hurt at the fact she was taking it out on him. He was the one after all that had found Peter hanging in the garden. Surely, he deserved a little compassion? But no, as always, he had to be the one to take the backlash when anything terrible happened to this family. It didn't matter that he was suffering too. It was the same a year ago, Angela had bitten his head off for months after Amelia's funeral.

As Graham turned to put his coffee cup on the table, he noticed a piece of note paper addressed to 'Mum and Dad'. He picked it up and unfolded it, however, just as he started to read it Angela came running in to the kitchen "Emily has locked herself in the bedroom and won't answer when I knock." Angela looked at Graham and immediately knew something was terribly wrong. "What? What's wrong? Why are you looking at me like that Graham?" she said.

"Sit down, Angela, please."

Angela shook her head, "No, no I won't, what's going on? Just tell me for god's sake." Graham handed Angela the note, he watched as the colour drained from his wife's face. Angela dropped to the floor clutching the note to her breast as she screamed "No, no, no, I can't take any more. Haven't we been through enough?"

Graham got down on the floor pulling his wife into his chest, "I don't know what to say, or do, Angela, I just don't know." Angela clung to Graham as they both sat there in the middle of Emily's kitchen, sobbing.

After a week of waiting to see if Emily would return Graham finally said that it was time to go home. "I can't just walk away, Graham, Emily is my child. I need to be here when she gets back."

Graham looked sadly at his wife "She's not coming back love. We lost our daughter a year ago when we lost Amelia, you know that. If she wanted our help, she would have accepted it by now. She had made her wishes extremely clear in the note." Angela nodded, she knew what Graham said was true. As parents they had tried everything to help their daughter to accept the death, grieve for her daughter and move forwards with her life but nothing they did seemed to help. It was time to accept that Emily was the only person who could make choices regarding her future. It was time to go home and try their best to live what was left of their own life. Graham knew that Angela didn't want to hear it but it had to be said "Angela, she's my daughter too, but what else can we do? We have no option other than to respect Emily by doing what she has asked." To stay at Woodland house indefinitely would help no one, it was time to look at the reality of what had happened and accept that Emily was gone. If she returned, as her parents they would always be there for her, however, she had to do what she had to do to survive. "It makes no difference if we agree with her choices or not, Angela." Graham said as he embraced his wife.

Angela looked at Graham with tears streaming down her face, "I know what you are saying makes sense, and I want to go home, however, I feel I will be abandoning my child if I do."

Graham looked at Angela, "Darling you have been the best mother any child could wish for. You have one hundred per cent been there for Emily every step of her life. Now it's time for Emily to do what Emily needs to do."

Angela looked at Graham defeated, "Let's go home Graham, you're right, we need to try and rebuild our own life." They went upstairs, packed up their belongings and left Woodland House hoping that one day soon their daughter would return and need their help. No one could have known that life for them as a family would never be the same again.

On returning to their home Angela couldn't settle, she couldn't get Emily out of her mind. She had already lost two of her children to war, Tom and Dan, both killed in action. Her daughter Molly had married a French man named Sabastian and move to Paris to live. Emily, Peter and Amelia had become the centre of Angela's world. Losing Amelia had been hard on them all as a family however Angela held on to the fact that she had managed to recover and move on from Tom and Dan's death. She had to believe that Emily would also one day be able to move forward and accept her daughter's death. That day however had never come, things had actually gone from bad to worse. Peter had committed suicide and Emily had gone, there was nothing left for Angela. She walked back and forth from kitchen to living-room, again and again. "Is there anything I can get you, my darling?" asked Graham who was extremely worried about his wife's mental health. She had been through so much heartache. Angela had taken a long time to come to terms with the death of their twins, then Amelia dying had broken her heart, but she had Emily to focus on. Now with Peter dead and Emily gone would she be able to cope?

"I just don't know what to do with myself, Graham, I feel so lost."

"I understand darling, I really do however nothing we do or say will change the path that our life has taken so far. All we can do is try to focus on what we can change, our future. We need to accept where we are and somehow learn to move forwards from this nightmare."

Angela looked at Graham and just nodded. "I know."

The next morning Dr Henderson called in to see how Angela and Graham were coping with all that had happened over the last week. He needed to ask them about arranging a funeral for Peter, he couldn't stay in the morgue indefinitely. Angela was mortified that they hadn't been in contact with the doctor or the funeral parlour. They had been so wrapped up in Emily and her note that Peter's funeral had embarrassingly gone to the back of their minds. It suddenly occurred to Angela that they hadn't been back in contact with Cathy about her son's funeral. Angela promised Dr Henderson that they would deal with everything that day. As soon as Dr Henderson left, Angela and Graham headed straight down to the funeral directors and organised a funeral for their son-in-law. They managed to organise the funeral for the 1st December, two days from now. They hoped that would be enough time for Cathy to make arrangements to get to Plockton. Graham called Cathy as soon as he could, she wasn't happy as she had been constantly calling to find out what was going on. She was extremely anxious as she hadn't heard from them regarding her son's funeral. She informed Graham that she had already arranged tickets to Plockton for her and Catherine the next day as they hadn't heard from anyone. Graham apologised once again and arranged to pick them both up at Plockton station. He insisted they stay with himself and Angela until after the funeral. Reluctantly Cathy agreed, she didn't really have much choice as it had taken all her spare cash to purchase the train tickets. She had assumed they would stay with Emily. Graham explained everything, bringing Cathy up to speed with the happenings of the last week. Cathy was really shocked to hear about Emily as she had no idea what had been going on since the death of Amelia. She had spoken to Peter several times and at no point had he made Cathy aware of the issues he had been going through with Emily. Not once had he suggested that he himself wasn't coping.

The next day Graham arrived at Plockton station with five minutes to spare before Cathy's train was due to arrive. The last thing he wanted was for Cathy to be standing waiting when he got there. He felt he had let her down enough and didn't want to let her down any more by being late. Soon the train pulled in and Cathy and Catherine got off. Graham approached them both and immediately hugged Cathy and said, "Dearest Cathy, I'm so deeply sorry for your loss and for my part in causing you more pain and anguish by not keeping you up to date regarding Peter's funeral arrangements. I hope you can forgive me."

Cathy looked at Graham with tears in her eyes. "I know you had no intention of hurting me in any way, going by what you've told me it seems like you have had a lot to deal with, therefore there is nothing to forgive." Graham hugged her tightly and without a second thought thanked Cathy for being so understanding and kissed her on the forehead. Cathy pulled away, she felt extremely uncomfortable being hugged and kissed by Graham and couldn't hide her embarrassment. Graham quickly picked up their luggage and moved towards the exit to avoid further embarrassment for either of them.

On arrival at the house Angela had tea and homemade scone's ready for everyone. Cathy excused herself saying she had a terrible journey and needed to lie down as she felt rather sick. Angela understood and showed Cathy to her room. Catherine sat at the table with Graham and had tea and a scone, she knew that Angela had gone to a lot of effort and didn't want to be rude. She did however feel a little uncomfortable as she didn't really know Angela or Graham and wasn't sure what to talk about, especially given the devastation they had all faced over the last twelve months or so. Talking about Peter, Emily or Amelia felt wrong and really uncomfortable so like most people when they have no idea what to say, Catherine started to talk about the weather. Angela came back into the kitchen and could sense Catherine's discomfort. She offered to take her to her room to allow her to settle in. Catherine stood up immediately, thankful of the excuse to leave the kitchen table without coming across as being rude or ungrateful.

The Honeymoon Ends

The rest of the week was spent exploring Plockton and the surrounding areas. Keith and Ruth couldn't believe how many beautiful places there were to visit, who knew Scotland was so beautiful. This week had been amazing. Both Ruth and Keith were really sad that their holiday had come to an end. It was their last day, the car was packed and all they had to do was put the key under the mat and they were good to go. "Let's go have some brunch before setting off," Keith said to Ruth.

"Okay, however I would like to go for one last walk before we head off, but yes brunch would be good first," was her reply.

They put the key under the mat with Alice watching closely as they did so. Ruth waved as they were about to set off, but before she could even close the car door Alice was by her side. "Goodbye, it was lovely to meet you both. I hope you enjoyed your stay here in Plockton, and hopefully we will see you back here soon." Keith and Ruth both smiled and said that they had a lovely time and would definitely be back. Alice waved them off as they pulled away heading into the main street to have some brunch at the Plockton Inn. Their final meal before heading home.

They entered the inn and sat in the same seat they had sat in on the first day they had arrived, right next to the fire. The bar tender came over to take their order as the waitress didn't start until twelve. They both ordered soup and a sandwich as they didn't want to eat anything too heavy. There was a man who Keith had spoken to a few days prior sitting at the bar. Keith looked over and waved, at that the man headed over to their table. "Hello again, Keith, isn't it?"

"Yes, that's correct, John," said Keith who never forgot a name or a face. He had sat with John a few nights ago at the bar while Ruth chatted to Edna from the general store. "I don't think I've had the pleasure of being introduced to your lady friend, as she was deep in conversation with our Edna the other night."

"Apologies, John, this is Ruth, my wife — Ruth, this is John." Ruth smiled at John and held out her hand as he reached forward.

"Please to meet you, Ruth."

"Likewise," said Ruth, as they shook hands.

"We are just about to have some soup and a sandwich before heading off if you would like to join us," said Keith.

"That would be lovely, assuming you're all right with that Ruth?"

"Absolutely, pull up a seat."

John shouted over to the barman, "Wullie, can you make that another soup and a sandwich, anything will do."

"Nae problem, John," said Wullie as he scurried back into the kitchen to add to the order.

It wasn't long before Wullie appeared with three soups and three sandwiches. As always, the food was excellent, they ate as they chatted. John was a very interesting guy, he was an artist and loved to draw landmarks. He had hand-painted many of the beautiful views around Plockton as well as doing charcoal drawings of most of the castles across Scotland. He was well travelled and knew everything there was to know about every castle across Scotland. Keith found his stories fascinating and had enjoyed talking to him. While they seemed happy to discuss John's drawing and paintings Ruth was more interested in taking a walk before heading home. Ruth could see that Keith was really enjoying John's company and therefore suggested she go for a walk alone while they chatted more about John's artwork.

"Are you sure, darling?" said Keith.

"Yes, I just want to have one last walk in the woodlands, but I know it's more my thing than yours so stay here and chat with John, I'm happy to go alone."

"Okay, if you're sure," Ruth kissed Keith, said goodbye to John and left the inn. Plockton wasn't that big, you walked one way to the harbour and the other towards the woodlands. Ruth set off towards the woodlands enjoying the sun despite the temperature being really low. She loved the outdoors, always had since as far back as she could remember. Perhaps because she was at her happiest when not in the house with her parents. Ruth would be sad to leave this beautiful place and was thankful for the opportunity to have one last walk. She headed into the woodlands feeling really content and happy. She almost felt like skipping she was that excited, however thought better of it at her age. As she entered deeper into the woodlands, she was overcome with the beauty in front of her, the trees were so tall and green and wild flowers grew everywhere. She was aware that she had headed off the path however was so excited at the wild flowers and the beautiful trees that she wanted to see more. She followed a red squirrel as he ran up and down the trees, she was mesmerised by its beauty and at how confident it seemed, and she couldn't take her eyes of it.

Back at the inn Keith and John were deep in conversation about the history of art. Keith had always loved art despite not being able to draw a stick man never mind an actually landmark. He wanted to know all about the different landmarks that John had either drawn or painted. Keith was eager to listen and John was only too happy to talk. Before they knew it two hours had passed and Ruth still wasn't back from her walk. It was starting to get late and they really should be on the road by now thought Keith. He was getting a little concerned that Ruth hadn't returned, however both John and Wullie the barman said she had probably bumped into one of the locals who would be telling her all the history of the woodlands. Keith waited another half hour then decided he should go and look for Ruth. He said his goodbyes to John and Wullie and headed of in the direction of the woodlands to see if he could see Ruth on her way back.

Part of Ruth had been relieved that Keith had stayed behind talking to John as his love for the outdoors was not as great as hers. This way she could take her time and go off track if she wanted without Keith moaning at her. As Ruth was approaching the woodlands, she saw a man taking pictures, he seemed to be taking rather a lot, mostly of the birds flying from tree to tree. Ruth had always loved wildlife and had once tried taking pictures herself however never quite managed to catch her subject at the right moment, either that or the photo when developed was out of focus.

Ruth walked on quietly humming to herself, she was so happy and content and couldn't wait to get back home to tell her nana all about this amazing place. Ruth decided there and then that someday she would move here. She had been saying to Keith all week that she would love to live in a small place like Plockton. Keith wasn't quite so keen however Ruth knew that she would eventually talk him round, as all he ever wanted was for Ruth to be happy.

As Ruth walked deeper into the woodlands, she decided to go off track as some of the trees and the bushes growing around had caught her eye. Ruth loved everything about nature, especially how the trees and plants changed colour with the seasons. Suddenly Ruth felt a terrible pain in her head, it just came from nowhere. She hadn't suffered with headaches before so it hit her by surprise. As she walked on the intensity of the pain grew to the point that Ruth had to sit down. She looked around and saw a large oak tree, she walked over and sat down leaning against it. She would sit there until the pain subsided. Her head really hurt and the pain was causing her to feel sick. One minute Ruth was sitting wondering why she had such a terrible pain in her head, feeling sick and the next, nothing.

Emily was walking happily through the woodlands, nothing new for her, nothing different until she noticed what she thought was a dead body. Emily immediately went to see if this person was in fact dead or hurt and in need of help. She quickly realised that the young girl was still breathing and knew that for some reason she needed to help her. Emily returned to the house for Peter's old fishing trolley then headed back to the spot where she had seen the girl. It took Emily a long time to get the girl off the ground and onto the trolley. She was fully aware that when this girl came around, she would no doubt be in a lot of pain as it wasn't an easy task getting her onto the trolley and she had suffered a fair few bumps while doing so. Emily was sure the girl wouldn't mind as she was taking her to safety out of the woodlands before the storm took hold. Little did Emily know that in taking Ruth back to Woodland House she was actually stopping her from being found by her husband. Going straight into Plockton and reporting that she had found a girl unresponsive would have been the right thing for Emily to do. Despite knowing this Emily had not spoken to anyone in years and finding this girl was not going to change that. Given Emily's situation she had two options, leave the girl in the woodlands with a storm en route or take her to the safety of Woodland House.

Eventually after a lot of pulling and pushing Emily finally arrived home with this strange girl on her trolley. Once Emily had managed to get the girl into the house, she decided she would go into Plockton to the general store as she had nothing in the house to feed this girl. If she wanted to help her, she would need to have food and at this moment in time there really wasn't much of anything in the house.

Farewell Peter

It was ten a.m. on the morning of 1st December, the day they would finally put Peter to rest, there was still no sign of Emily. Angela had cooked breakfast for Cathy and Catherine, however, no one was hungry. Coffee was all they could stomach on this sad day. Cathy just couldn't get her head around the fact that Emily wasn't there to say a final farewell to Peter, her husband, the man who had fathered her child. Why? Where was she?

Angela could sense that Cathy was feeling anxious knowing that Peter would be put to rest without Emily being present. She wondered if speaking about Emily and how she had been unable to cope after Amelia's death would help. However, Angela decided that to mention Emily would probably only make Cathy feel worse so decided just to keep quiet.

Graham walked into the kitchen to let everyone know that Rob from Plockton Inn had agreed to put on a small buffet after Peter's burial as all the fishermen from the village wanted to pay their respects. Cathy just stared ahead, looking out of the window, Graham wondered as he spoke what she was thinking. "Cathy, Peter had a lot of friends in the village, he was extremely popular and everyone just wants to pay their respects and remember Peter for the amazing young man that he was. That said if you would prefer not to have a wake I will understand and will let Rob know that we won't be going back to the inn after the burial."

"No, said Cathy let people come and pay their respects to my boy." At that she walked out of the kitchen saying that she had to go and get ready.

It was eleven a.m. and finally time to go, the hearse pulled up outside along with the funeral car ready to take us to the church. Catherine was sitting in the kitchen waiting on her mother to come downstairs. She waited five more minutes before heading up the stairs to see what was keeping Cathy. Just as she was about to open the bedroom door Cathy appeared all dressed in black with tears streaming down her face. "I can't do this," she said to her daughter. "I just can't watch as my baby boy is lowered into the ground, knowing I will never see him again."

Catherine pulled her mother into her arms and said, "I know this is going to be the hardest day of your life, mum, however you have to go say goodbye. If you don't, you will never be able to accept that Peter is actually gone." Cathy looked at her daughter with tears streaming down her face and nodded, Catherine led her mother down the stairs and out to the car where Angela and Graham were waiting.

On arrival at the church, it was obvious that Peter had been popular, the church was full of well-wishers. The service went as well as any funeral service could go. As soon as the burial was over and the priest had said a few words people started to head towards Plockton Inn to raise a glass to their friend Peter. At first Cathy didn't want to go to the inn but Catherine persuaded her to go. She said it was important for her to listen to people describe the life that her son had in Plockton and how much he had been a part of the community. It would help her and her mother to know how happy Peter had been since arriving in Plockton all those years before. Catherine was right, Cathy did get some comfort from hearing all about her son's life here in Plockton. She actually found herself laughing at some of the stories that his fisherman colleagues told her. Peter had obviously had a wonderful life and despite the fact that it had been cut short he had lived life fully in the years that he had been here in Plockton. That, along with the fact that Cathy knew Peter had a lovely childhood allowed her to feel at peace. There was no bringing her son back so to focus on the fact that he had a good life would enable Cathy to move forward without feeling bitter. She knew that Peter wouldn't want her to feel bitter and angry. She had to let go of these feelings and cherish her son's memory knowing that he is where he wants to be, with his precious little girl, Amelia, and his father.

Cathy and Catherine left Plockton the next day knowing that they would never return. They took with them the knowledge that Peter was at peace. They had no idea what had become of Emily nor did they really care. Truth be told Cathy blamed Emily for her son's suicide. She would however bury those feelings and move forward with her life remembering her boy for the amazing young man he was.

Graham and Angela had hoped that Emily would turn up at the church to say her goodbyes to the man she had loved and who had fathered her beautiful daughter, however she had not. Well not that they knew... unknown to them Emily had been there watching from a distance, not wanting to be seen, she had made sure to stay as far back as possible until everyone had gone. Emily waited for about thirty minutes after everyone had left the graveside to make sure she would not be seen. As soon as she was comfortable that everyone had gone Emily made her way over to Peter's grave to say her final goodbye to the only man she had ever loved. Emily also visited Amelia's grave that day then left the church yard knowing she would never return.

Missing

It was nearly two p.m. and there was no sign of Ruth. She had been gone for almost three hours. Keith was now beginning to get really worried. He had walked for quite a long way into the woodlands however there had been no sign of Ruth. He decided he would head back to the main street just in case, somehow, he had missed her. The last thing he wanted was to go further into the woodlands only to discover Ruth was back at the inn waiting for him.

Keith arrived back at the inn to find John standing at the bar with a pint while talking to Wullie the barman. "Has Ruth been back in since I left?" he asked the guys.

"Nope, no sign of her," answered John. "Have you asked Edna at the general store if she's seen her?"

"No, I'll pop in there now, thanks guys. Oh, and if she happens to come in here and I've missed her, please ask her to stay here as I will come back for her."

"No problem, Keith," they both replied as he moved to walk out of the door.

"Oh, Keith, before you head back off, Alice popped in as she saw your car outside. She does the cleaning at the cottage you had rented and found Ruth's rings in the bathroom. She must have removed them to shower and forgot to put them back on." Keith moved towards John with his hand out and John handed him both of Ruth's rings; engagement and wedding.

"One of these days she's going to lose these forever as she always forgets to put them back on. Thank Alice for me when you see her next."

"Will do and good luck finding the Mrs."

Keith walked along to the general store hoping to find Ruth in there chatting to Edna before heading back to the inn. Unfortunately, when he entered the store Edna was all alone packing shelves at the front of the store with some new produce she had just had delivered. "Hi Edna, you don't happen to have seen Ruth today, have you?"

"Only when I saw you both earlier," she said.

"I'm worried, we went to the inn for some food before heading home. After our food she wanted to go for a walk into the woodlands. I was talking to John, the artist, and Ruth said she was happy to go for a walk alone while we chatted. I had expected her back by now but there is no sign of her."

"That is very strange," said Edna. "I'm sure she will be fine, there are lots of different walks in the woodlands, it may just be that she has lost track of time. It is so beautiful in there, I've lost track of time many times over the years and I know the woodlands well."

"You're probably right, Edna. I'll head back to the inn and give her another hour, however if she isn't back by then I will know for sure that something isn't right as she knew we didn't have much time to spare, we wanted to be home before dark."

Keith headed back to the inn, with still no sign of Ruth, he ordered a fruit juice and sat by the fire waiting for her return. After an hour Keith was really starting to become concerned. He knew Ruth well enough to know that she would be back by now if she could as she hated driving in the dark. She must be lost in the woodlands, there is no other explanation. John offered to go with Keith to help look for Ruth, he could see how concerned Keith was. They headed off together in the hope that between them they would find her trying to work her way back. As they reached the start of the woodlands, they agreed that they would split up and go in different directions. Keith headed straight ahead while John veered off to the left. They agreed to walk for thirty minutes then head back to where they started and take it from there.

As Keith walked further into the woodlands the rain started to come down heavily and the wind was picking up. He was really concerned that Ruth had fallen and was lying somewhere unable to move. He shouted her name as he walked further in hoping to hear her voice calling back. After thirty minutes, he knew he needed to head back just in case John had found Ruth. As he got back to the beginning of the path he had walked along, he saw John approaching without Ruth. "No sign?" said John as he got closer to Keith.

"No nothing," said Keith. "I'm really worried as I know Ruth and she would have come back by now unless she was lost or injured. "The weather is getting worse, we need to find her quickly."

"I agree," said John, "however we need help."

"I'm not leaving here until I find my wife," said Keith.

"I get that, however, we really do need help, Keith. It's getting dark and the weather isn't going to get any better. I'll head back into Plockton and get some torches and see if I can get anyone that will help us with the search."

"Okay, but I think we need to alert the police," said Keith.

"Don't go too far in Keith, stay to the outer edge as you don't have a torch," suggested John "I will be back as soon as I can with help."

John headed back to Plockton in search of help as Keith wandered back into the woodlands continually shouting out

Ruth's name. By now the wind was howling around the trees and the rain was coming down in sheets. Keith's voice was being carried away with the wind and he feared that it may stop Ruth from hearing him. Keith could hardly see in front of him as the rain was so bad. He really didn't know what to do. He had walked and walked and found himself back at the beginning where he started but still no sign of Ruth. He heard voices and as he looked around, he saw John coming towards him with Wullie from the inn and two police officers. "I take it you've had no luck?" John said as he approached Keith.

"No nothing, I just don't know what to do."

The police spoke to Keith and re-assured him that they would work together to try and find Ruth, however, to keep in mind that the weather was going to be an issue and that they may have to call off the search until daylight if they didn't find Ruth soon. Keith thanked the police for their help and told them that he would search all night if he had too. He had no intention of leaving here without his wife. John and Wullie had brought their own torches and one for Keith. It was now six p.m. and getting dark, the police agreed to cover as much ground as possible as a team, however informed Keith that they would call off the search until morning if Ruth hadn't been found within the hour as the weather was too bad for them all to continue searching when it was completely dark. It was far too dangerous and as much as they wanted to find Ruth it was their duty to ensure their own safety and that of Keith, John and Wullie. Keith nodded in agreement however had no intention of stopping looking for Ruth, no matter how dark or stormy it became.

Finally, at seven fifteen p.m. the police decided it was time to stop the search. The wind was really strong, the rain heavy and it was extremely dark. Far too dangerous for anyone to be out in the woodlands. The police called to Keith, John and Wullie to call it a day. Keith was not happy to stop searching and told the police he intended to carry on until he found his wife. The police informed him that it was stupid to continue the search at this point and that he was better to get a night's sleep and start fresh in the morning as soon as the sun came up. To continue in the dark was a complete and utter waste of energy and certainly wouldn't help Ruth in the long run. Nothing the police could say would stop Keith from looking for Ruth. Eventually they had to leave him to do as he pleased despite warning him of the dangers. They agreed to recommence the search at sunrise leaving Keith in the woodlands. John and Wullie agreed to come back, however, agreed with the police that it was too dangerous for them to continue in the dark. Keith said he understood, thanked them for their help and continued the search for his wife alone with the torch given to him by John.

Jane

Jane lay on the bed in Emily's room looking around her and wondering why she felt so calm in this house. Emily had clearly owned this house and had lived here for many years. There was no connection to this house for her so why did she feel so at ease. She picked up the photograph from the bedside table. Emily was the most beautiful woman with long red hair and the little girl in the picture was so like her. Who was the child? Was she Emily's daughter and if so where was she now? Jane once again had that strong feeling of recognition when looking at the photo. She sat up and studied the photo, she really could see a resemblance to herself. How was this possible as Emily clearly had no idea who she was?

Jane lay for over an hour however no matter how hard she tried she just couldn't sleep. She decided to go down to the kitchen to get some water and secretly hoped that Emily would still be awake. She was in luck as Emily was already in the kitchen getting some water. She too could not fall asleep; seeing her old bedroom had stirred up too many emotions. Her brain had gone into overdrive and she just couldn't switch off. "Can't you sleep either?" Jane said to Emily. "I hope my intrusion of the upstairs room isn't the reason for your inability to sleep?"

"Yes, and no," said Emily. "Seeing inside that room for the first time in approximately fifty years has shaken me, I'm not going to lie. However, that's not all that's bothering me, a lot of things from the past have crept back into my mind tonight."

Jane asked if Emily would mind if she sat in the kitchen with her for a while. "Not at all," said Emily, "I'm just going to sit here anyway so we may as well sit together." This was very strange for Emily to say given that she had not wanted human company for over fifty years, nor had she actually spoken to anyone. Maybe Emily finding Jane was meant to be, right place right time. Emily definitely felt comfortable around Jane and for once actually wanted company and wanted to talk. And despite Jane having no idea who she was, she felt comfortable around Emily and in this house so wasn't unduly anxious or upset. There was plenty of time to figure out who she was and what had happened to her, however for now she just felt comfortable and happy chatting to Emily.

Emily made some camomile tea for them both as she thought it would help them to relax. "Can I ask you something?" said Jane.

"Yes of course."

"Who is the little girl with you in the photograph next to your bed?" Emily looked at Jane with tears in her eyes, it had been so very long since Emily had spoken her daughter's name, she started to shake, and tears stung her eyes.

Jane looked at Emily and immediately regretted asking "I didn't mean to upset you, Emily, I'm so sorry I should never have asked, it's none of my business who she is."

"No, it's fine," said Emily as she took a deep breath in. "The child in the picture is Amelia, my daughter." Emily stopped as she had to hold back a scream that was deep in her chest. Jane could tell how uncomfortable this conversation was making Emily and didn't quite know how to respond.

"She's beautiful," she said looking at Emily as she composed herself.

"Yes, she certainly was the most beautiful child. She never complained about anything and just loved life so much. All she did was laugh and play all the time. Her life was so full of love and laughter. She adored the outside, especially in winter, we struggled to keep her indoors, Peter and I." Jane was about to respond however Emily had found her voice and just kept talking about Amelia and her life as a small child. She also spoke of her husband, Peter, and how they met and how her parents loved him even before she did. The story of a young Emily, then Emily and Peter then extended to Emily, Peter and Amelia. The more Emily spoke the happier she seemed and the memories that she had supressed for so many years were just flooding out of her.

Jane was so engrossed in Emily describing her life that she had completely forgotten all about her own life. She loved the passion with which Emily described her life and loved hearing all about the amazing stories of Emily as a young girl falling in love, then a young mother. She did, however, have a few burning questions going through her mind but was way too scared to ask. "Why, if Emily had been so happy, was she living like this now? Why was she so un-kept and alone? What had happened? Where were Peter and Amelia?" Jane was so curious, however, given that Emily had been so upset when she saw the upstairs bedroom door open, and that she had been so reluctant to start talking Jane was aware that to ask anything could be really upsetting for Emily. For this reason, Jane decided just to sit back and listen. If Emily wanted to tell Jane anything then it would have to come from her heart and not because she had been bombarded with questions from a complete stranger. Jane sat back and just let Emily talk. Emily didn't even realise how much talking she was doing; she was so relaxed for the first time in forever and the stories of her life were just flowing out of her mouth. The more Emily spoke the more she felt the need to, the stories just kept coming. It's as if fifty years of silence had never happened, Emily had broken through all her barriers and for the first time in forever spoke freely about Peter and Amelia. Jane sat wondering what had happened to Peter and Amelia as Emily spoke of them so highly and it sounded as if they had the perfect life, so what happened?

Emily finally stopped talking and asked Jane if she would like more tea. "I would love some," she replied. At that Emily headed to the kitchen to get more tea for them both. Jane sat going over everything Emily had spoken about, with more and more questions coming to mind. As Emily entered the room with the two cups of tea, she looked over at Jane and immediately dropped both cups. Jane jumped at the loud crash as both cups landed on the floor and smashed. "What happened?" she said.

Emily stood there frozen with a very strange expression on her face. Jane sat there silent, afraid to speak. Emily moved over to the sofa with both hands up at her face. "I'm so sorry" she said as she sat down beside Jane. "I didn't mean to startle you."

"It's fine," said Jane as she sat up and looked directly at Emily.

"What spooked you?"

For a few moments Emily just sat in silence staring at Jane tears running freely down her face. "I saw you on the sofa relaxed with your eyes shut and you were sucking your pinkie," said Emily finally. Jane couldn't understand why that would spook her.

Jane hadn't even been aware that she had nodded off however as soon as Emily mentioned sucking her pinkie something clicked in her head "I've always done that, as far back as I can remember." Almost immediately she stopped and said, "Oh my god, I knew that was normal for me, how come, when I don't even know who I am?" Emily smiled and assured Jane that her memory would come back and obviously this was proof it had already started.

After a few moments silence Jane stood up and started to pick up the broken cups, Emily immediately helped. They moved into the kitchen where Emily automatically started to make more tea. Jane looked across at her and asked why she had been so shocked at her sucking her pinkie. "Truth be told I've only ever seen one other person suck their pinkie and not their thumb. It's not something you see very often, and it has been many, many years since I last saw it."

Jane was about to speak when suddenly Emily took a deep breath and said "Amelia; Amelia my baby girl, she is the only person I had ever seen suck their pinkie until now."

"How bizarre," said Jane. "Does she still do it?"

As soon as the words were out of Jane's mouth, she regretted them. Emily looked at Jane as the tears ran freely down her face when suddenly she began to sob uncontrollably. Jane was mortified that once again she had managed to upset Emily. She didn't know what to say or do and wanted the ground to open up and swallow her. After what seemed like forever Emily began to settle, her sobbing stopped. She looked at Jane and said "Amelia died when she was three." Jane was horrified that she had managed to bring back so many painful memories without even being aware that she was doing so. Things had become even more complicated and confusing. Not only did she have no idea who or where she was, she was in a strange house that she somehow recognised and felt comfortable in with a woman she knew nothing about until tonight. Now she had almost forced this poor woman to go from telling her all about how happy life was and how amazing her little family had been to now disclose that her daughter had died. Jane felt terrible however there was no way of redirecting the conversation as she had no idea what she could talk about given the only small memory she had was sucking her pinkie and this had been the one thing that had triggered Emily to disclose Amelia's death, which was obviously extremely painful for her.

"I'm so deeply sorry for your loss," was all she could say.

Emily and Jane sat in silence for what seemed like hours. Emily broke the silence, "Peter is also dead." Once the words were out, she told the whole story from Amelia's headache to Peter's suicide to rejecting her parents and any other human contact right up to her leaving until her parents went home then her silent return to Woodland House. Jane sat there saying nothing as she processed everything that Emily said. Things started to fall into place. Jane could now understand the locked doors, the pain on discovering one open. The state Emily had allowed herself to become, black missing teeth and matted hair. The house being so cold and dirty with almost empty cupboards. Poor Emily, she had been through so much. She had kept everything locked away until my intrusion into her life which has opened a lot of wounds. Jane felt so terribly guilty and said as much to Emily. "No, no that's not true," Emily said very quietly. "Yes, finding you and bringing you here has opened a wound — however, it has also helped me. I haven't spoken to another person in fifty years. Now I've let down my barrier and have decided to talk once more. You haven't caused me any pain, I've done that by locking everything away. In doing so I have not allowed myself to accept my loss and try to heal from it all. So you see, finding you has helped me to find myself again, something I never imagined would ever happen. Finally, I am free to accept life as it now is and move forward, that's down to you Jane so please do not feel bad about anything."

Keith

The rain was getting heavier and heavier and the wind was so strong Keith could barely stay standing. He knew that to continue in this weather with a tiny torch and no sense of where he was in dense woodland would be suicide. He was extremely frustrated knowing that he had no real option other than to turn back. He guessed he had searched for a good couple of hours after the others left and had achieved nothing. He arrived back at the inn at nine thirty p.m. drenched. John was still at the bar with Wullie whose shift had ended.

"No luck then mate?" John said as Keith walked into the inn alone.

"No sign of her, I just don't understand how she could just disappear." Wullie had gone to fetch a towel for Keith and asked if he would like a hot coffee or a pint. Keith opted for the coffee as he needed to get some heat inside him and also wanted to stay alert. He asked if there were any vacancies in the inn to which Wullie replied there were. He paid for a room, had his coffee and headed upstairs with Wullie showing him the way.

Keith decided not to tell his parents or Lyn what had happened as he didn't want to worry them. He decided just to say they had agreed to stay another couple of days. Anna who knew her son like no other had a really bad feeling despite Keith reassuring her that everything was okay. She knew only too well how responsible both Keith and Ruth were when it came to work, so for them to both decide to extend their honeymoon and give no regard to their jobs was extremely unlike either of them. Anna asked her son why it had taken him until ten thirty p.m. to call. All he said in reply was "does it matter?" Anne knew at that moment not to push her son as she could hear frustration in his voice. In her mind, she knew something was wrong however knew her son well enough to let it go until such times as he wanted to talk. Without another word Keith hung up the phone and turned his mind back to his next move regarding the search for Ruth.

It was eleven p.m. and last orders at the bar. Keith had gone back downstairs for another coffee as he couldn't relax, he walked back and forth constantly looking out the window for the weather to break. John who was still standing at the bar informed Keith that he had arranged with the police and Wullie as well as some other locals to resume the search at six a.m. John finished his pint, he bid Keith goodnight and left saying he would see him soon. Keith had to go back upstairs as the bar area was being locked for the night.

Back in his room Keith kept imagining Ruth in all sorts of situations, none of which had a good outcome. Despite being a positive person, he couldn't think of one situation in which Ruth would be fine. He knew her only too well, she would never not come back unless she couldn't. He was driving himself crazy imagining all sorts.

At six a.m. sharp Wullie opened the bar area so that the police could discuss their strategy in the search for Ruth with the volunteers. There were four police officers and six locals including Wullie and John. The woodlands and surrounding areas could easily be covered with them if they split into groups of two. Keith was really grateful to the local volunteers and the police. The police had a map of the woodlands and surrounding areas which included Woodland House and the old, abandoned cabin that Emily had used years before. They stressed that everyone should be vigilant at all times as the weather had been treacherous overnight and the ground would be dangerous in parts, especially around the area near the stream. "The key objective here" said the police officer, "is to find Ruth Vasillio as quickly as possible especially since we have already lost so much time due to the weather conditions and night fall."

At six fifteen a.m. sharp they all set off together towards the woodlands. The police had said that they would go straight to Woodland House to see if Emily had come across anyone during her walk back and forth from the general store given that she had been twice the day before which was totally out of character. They didn't hold out much hope of Emily answering the door never mind talking to them, however, they had to give it a try. Two volunteers agreed to head to the abandoned cabin and the rest spread out over the remaining areas including the stream.

Keith paired up with John given that they knew each other and John had local knowledge of woodlands and surrounding areas. As they approached the woodlands, they all split into their groups and agreed to meet back at this point every couple of hours for a re-group. The police, of course, had walkie talkies and could communicate with each other if they came across anything. And so, the search for Ruth Vasillio commenced.

Back at Woodland House

Finding Jane and bringing her back to Woodland House had opened up a part of Emily she forgot even existed. They had both fallen asleep in the living room after Emily had chatted about her past and told Jane all about Amelia and how she died, the autopsy, the result, her inability to accept her daughter's death, her guilt. Everything down to Peter's suicide, her parents trying everything they could to get through to her, Dr Henderson, her leaving, writing the note, the abandoned cabin, her return to Woodland House and everything from that dark period of Emily's past. The period she had locked away and not allowed herself to think about for the last fifty years. No wonder Emily had fallen asleep, she must have been exhausted talking for the first time in so many years and bringing all the good memories up followed by so many bad. All of it must have drained her, Jane thought as she herself drifted off.

Emily woke as she heard a tapping at the front door. She glanced over at Jane who was sleeping soundly, sucking her pinkie. She got up and headed upstairs to look out and see who was at the door. She looked out the window from her bedroom and saw two police officers. Emily immediately knew they would be looking for Jane however she didn't want to let her go, not yet. Emily was aware that having Jane here had somehow enabled her to speak again and to remember her past. Having Jane around made Emily feel comfortable, in a way that she really couldn't remember feeling for such a long time. She knew she was ready to start living again and that this was somehow down to Jane. If she gave her up what would happen, would she automatically retreat back into herself and go back to living as she had for the past fifty years? No, she couldn't, she didn't want to, she needed Jane here, she wanted Jane here, so, for this reason she would not answer the door, not yet, not until she felt strong enough.

Emily was aware however that the police knew she lived there so would definitely come back at which point Jane could be awake and that would be a disaster. For this reason and this reason only, she decided to open the door. Emily went down stairs and opened the door a tiny crack, rubbing her eyes as if she had just been woken out of a sleep. "Good morning Emily, we are so sorry to bother you at such an early hour however we are searching for a tourist who has gone missing. Emily looked from one to the other with a blank look on her face. "As I said we are searching for a woman who was in Plockton on honeymoon with her husband. She went for a walk in the woodlands yesterday and hasn't returned since. The weather was extremely bad last night and we wondered if perhaps she had taken shelter here. The police went on to describe Ruth but Emily just shook her head and closed the door. The police knocked again and asked Emily why she had gone back into Plockton the day before, in the afternoon. Emily looked at them both for a few seconds, screwed up her face and once again shut the door. Emily had no idea the pain she would cause by lying to the police that morning. The police had no option other than to leave Emily in peace.

Emily returned to the living room where Jane was still fast asleep. Emily sat and stared at Jane sleeping with her pinkie still in her mouth. She wondered if Amelia would still have sucked her pinkie at Jane's age. A part of Emily felt guilty for not letting the police know that the girl they referred to as Ruth was actually asleep on her sofa. However, Emily needed to know why this girl had fallen into her path. Why, out of all the people who had tried to get Emily to speak, why Jane, why now? She wanted to try and understand why, after fifty years this strange girl who seemed to come from nowhere made her want to speak again, made her want to live once more.

Jane woke to see Emily sitting staring at her but instead of feeling shy or embarrassed she actually felt safe and comforted. Who is Emily? Why does she make me feel so at ease? It's not as if she is a beautiful wee old lady that would automatically draw you to her and make you feel safe. She was old and shrivelled with hardly any teeth and those she did have were black and broken and her hair was so badly matted I doubt she would ever be able to sort it without shaving her head. Her clothes were hanging off her and really dirty. I'm not sure she has changed clothes or had a wash in a very long time. She looked like a witch out of a kid's story book and yet I feel so at ease around her. Why?

Emily smiled at Jane as she sat up. "Can I get you something to eat, or a cup of coffee?" she said.

"I would love a coffee please," said Jane. Emily walked out of the living room and entered the kitchen and for the first time in as far back as she could remember she actually felt hungry. She filled the kettle and sorted the coffee cups; then popped some bread under the old grill that she hoped would work as it hadn't been used in years. To her surprise the grill lit up perfectly. She made four pieces of toast as she was certain Jane would want some as soon as she smelt it. Toast had that effect on most people for some reason.

Jane could hear the kettle boil and smell bread toasting. Her stomach rumbled as she moved closer to the kitchen. Emily had

153

been right, the smell had got to Jane. "I'm making toast for us both," she said as Jane walked through the door.

"Thanks," said Jane. "I didn't realise I was hungry until I could smell the bread toasting."

"Just what I thought," said Emily.

They ate their toast and drank their coffee in silence. There didn't seem to be a need to fill the silence, they both seemed to be very comfortable around each other. It was Jane that spoke first, "Would you mind if I have a shower as I feel really dirty."

Emily looked surprised as she hadn't even given it a thought that Jane would perhaps want to freshen up. "I will put the immersion on, however, if I'm honest I don't know if it will work, as I haven't used it in a very long time."

Jane looked at Emily and smiled, "Emily why did you stop looking after yourself? You've told me all about Amelia's death and what happened to Peter and then you wanting your parents to leave you alone and I kind of get it, but why stop looking after your own health?"

Emily sat for a few moments just looking at Jane, "truth" she said. "I hoped that I would die, I wanted so badly to be with my Amelia and Peter. To be once again reunited with them both. I wasn't as brave as Peter, I couldn't kill myself despite thinking about it many times. So, instead, I punished myself for being alive by not eating much or washing or sleeping in a bed or caring for myself in any way. I hoped every day that it would be my last, however it never was, for some reason I was supposed to live."

Emily tested the water after an hour and sure enough it was hot. She was really surprised as it hadn't been used in such a long time. "The water is hot little one if you want to go shower. I will go get you some towels but I can't guarantee what state they will be in I'm afraid."

"I'm sure they will do just fine," Jane replied. Emily returned with two towels and handed them to Jane who thanked her and headed up to the bathroom to shower. While Jane was in the shower Emily decided she wanted to go into her room that she had shared with Peter. She had a strange urge to be near him and that was the closest she could get. She went upstairs quietly and opened the door with shaking hands. As soon as she walked through the door, she could feel him, his love was all over this room. They had gone together when choosing the furniture and all the added extras to make the room theirs. Every way she turned there was something to remind her of Peter. She slowly walked over to her dressing table where she sat every night brushing her hair while Peter sat on the bed and watched. She sat on the chair and picked up the brush. There was still hair from when she last used it, how was that possible when it was so long ago. She touched the hair and immediately had a vision of herself back then brushing her long beautiful hair. She looked in the mirror and she could see Peter smiling at her. She could hear Amelia in the room next door playing, fifty years melted away, and in that moment, she was back there at her happiest with her perfect life, the perfect family.

The search continues

It was eight fifteen a.m., and as discussed, the volunteers and the police all met back at the agreed spot, however there was no sign of John and Keith. To be honest, the police were not surprised that Keith had not returned as agreed, however were surprised with John as he should have known better than to continue the search without an update.

Not one single shred of Ruth having been anywhere in the woodlands had been found. The Police had covered Woodland House, the abandoned cabin which was barely standing these days and the stream. The volunteers had pretty much covered every other route that Ruth could possibly have taken. The only other area of woodlands to search was so dense they would have to use a helicopter as no one could get there easily on foot. If Ruth was in there, she must be badly hurt. They also now had to consider that perhaps someone had taken her. The only other option to consider is she may have fallen into the stream, been knocked out and drowned.

Keith and John had searched long and hard looking in every inch of woodland surrounding them even off the walking tracks and into the dense woodland but there was no sign of Ruth. "We need to turn back," said John.

"I can't go back without my wife," was Keith's reply.

"I understand what you are feeling, Keith, however we need to head back as one of the others may have information or better still may have found Ruth."

"I guess it's possible," said Keith as he nodded to John to lead the way. They headed back to find no one there, by this time it was nine thirty a.m. The police and volunteers had re grouped and decided to go back to town as there was nothing more they could do on foot. Keith looked at John "What now?" I guess we head back to the inn to find out if there is any news.

They headed back to the inn. On their arrival Wullie was there and told them there had been no luck, however the police had decided it was time to get the helicopter out and the divers to make sure there was no one in the water. Just as Keith was about to speak one of the police sergeants, walked through the door. He had come to see if John and Keith had returned. Wullie spoke first, he said that he had brought John and Keith up to speed with the next step of the search. Sergeant Cornwall thanked Wullie and said he would take it from there. He explained that the helicopter would circle the woodlands in search of Ruth, while they waited on a specialised diving team to arrive to check the water.

"The diving team should be here within the hour as time is of the essence. We need to move as quickly as possible as the weather is about to turn for the worst late afternoon and darkness will follow. There really is nothing more you can do other than stay here and await news of our findings."

Keith looked at Sergeant Cornwall and said "If you think I can just sit here and wait, you must be crazy! My wife is out there somewhere and I need to keep looking for her, I can't just give up and sit here drinking coffee waiting for your guys to get back to me, surely you can understand that."

"I can one hundred per cent understand your need to keep looking, Mr Vasillio, however we have covered every inch of woodland that is possible to do so by foot. There is no other option other than to let the helicopter team search in areas we can't get to. I would have police out there on foot still searching, if I thought there was the tiniest chance we could cover more land, but we've covered it all, I can assure you." Keith looked at the Police Sergeant and nodded in agreement. John asked Wullie to get coffee for him and Keith while he moved over to the fire to sit down. Keith followed and sat next to John as he had no other option than to just wait for news. The not knowing what had happened to Ruth and the thought that she was hurt somewhere and had been out in the bad weather all night was killing him, but what else could he do? He couldn't sit still for more than a few seconds; he passed back and forth just praying that Ruth would be found.

Three hours passed when finally, Sergeant Cornwall returned to tell Keith that they still hadn't found Ruth. The helicopter had gone over every inch of woodland and found nothing. The diving team had checked the water and once again nothing. Keith looked as if he was about to pass out. "So what happens now?" he said.

"We have exhausted every avenue there is regarding her being somewhere in the woodlands. We need to now start thinking that someone has taken her."

Keith looked shocked at the thought of someone having taken Ruth. "The best thing you can do Mr Vasillio is to return home and let us get on with our investigation on the disappearance of your wife. We will of course contact you daily with updates."

"How am I supposed to just go home without Ruth and act as if nothing has happened, how is that possible?" Keith said angrily as he looked back and forth from Sergeant Cornwall and John.

"Obviously it's not going to be easy, Mr Vasillio, however staying here is only going to cause you more anguish. Going home you will have your family for comfort and you will be in your own environment. Staying here would just be silly as there is nothing you can do here to help any further than you already have. You've done all that you can here so please Mr Vasillio go home to your family."

Keith didn't know what to do for the best, he was torn between staying in Plockton but not being able to help, or going home and not being able to settle. He decided it was time to call his parents. He asked Wullie if he could use the phone to call his mother. "No problem," said Wullie as he showed Keith where the inn phone was.

Keith dialled his parents' number and waited with bated breath for Anna to answer. On the third ring the phone was picked up "Ciao residenza Vasillio posso aiutarti?" said nonna.

Keith was surprised as nonna rarely answered the phone given that her English was so poor. "Nonna e Keith e mia madre li per favour?" Keith was aware that his voice was shaky and just hopped that nonna hadn't noticed.

Keith was relieved when nonna replied "Si amore mio la prendero per te." Keith could hear nonna calling on Anna, she really didn't realise how loud she screamed when she wanted someone, poor nonna screamed so loudly that everyone in the house always jumped out of their skin. Anna came to the phone a few seconds later, "Hello my darling, how are you and Ruth?" At the mention of Ruth's name and the sound of his mother's' loving voice he just couldn't hold back, Keith started to sob, and Anna couldn't understand a word he was saying. John who was standing beside Keith motioned to him that he would take the phone and explain everything to Keith's mother. Keith handed him the phone and dropped to his knees.

"Hello Mrs Vasillio, my name is John. I am a friend of your son, well, we met a few days ago however we have become friends." Anna was about to start a chat with John as she normally would, however quickly remembered that her son had been so upset that she couldn't understand him.

"What's going on John? Why is Keith so upset, why are you speaking to me and not Ruth?" John took a deep breath and told Anna everything, from the early lunch to Ruth going for a walk to Alice coming into the Inn with Ruth's rings to the initial search on foot to the police helicopter and divers coming up with nothing. He explained that they were now considering Ruth as a missing person and would be starting an investigation into her disappearance. John continued to tell Anna that Sergeant Cornwall who was in charge of the case had advised Keith to go home and be with his family, and how he was too upset to leave Plockton.

"Please put my son back on the phone, John, and thank you for explaining everything to me."

John handed the phone back to Keith "Keith, listen to me, come home, the police will do everything they can to find Ruth. You need to be surrounded by your family, not staying in a strange town with people you barely know. Please darling just come home." Keith knew in his heart his mother was right and with a croaky voice agreed. He hung up the phone and told everyone that he would head back home but asked if John would take his number and call if he heard anything. John agreed that he would, however, knew that there would be no need as the police in Plockton would make sure that Keith was the first person to know any little detail if and when they came across anything. Keith finished his coffee, said his goodbyes, and headed home with an extremely heavy heart. He should have been heading home with his wife to start married life, not alone, having no idea what had become of Ruth.

Guilt

Emily decided she wanted to go into Amelia's room, however she wanted to wait until Jane came out of the shower to ask if she would mind going into the room with her. She felt like she needed support as she didn't feel strong enough to enter Amelia's room for the first time in fifty years, alone. She sat on the double bed in her old room picturing life as it had been when Peter and Amelia were still both alive and well.

Jane came out of the bathroom wrapped in a towel with another one on her head. She saw Emily sitting on the bed, so looked over and asked, "You wouldn't happen to have something I could wear would you as my clothes are dirty." Emily smiled as she walked over to the wardrobe, she opened the door and said that Jane was welcome to try on anything, however apologised that is was nothing of fashion. "As long as it's clean it doesn't matter if it's fashionable or not, it's not as if I'm going anywhere, is it?" she said to a smiling Emily. Emily walked out of the room to give Jane privacy to try on one of the dresses. Jane picked out the plainest dress from the wardrobe and pulled it over her head. To her surprise It was a perfect fit, however it still left her with the small problem of knickers. Hers needed to be washed and even if Emily had some, which she doubted, she wouldn't really want to put on someone else's under garments. Jane decided it wasn't a big deal as the dress was quite long and would be fine until her clothes had been washed and dried.

Jane walked out of the room with a towel still wrapped

around her head. She nearly jumped out of her skin as Emily was standing there silently waiting on Jane to get dressed. "Oh, my goodness, I nearly had a heart attack, I thought you had gone downstairs Emily."

"No," said Emily, "I wanted to ask you a favour, but first you must sort your hair. I don't have a hairdryer but I do have a brush. It's in my room on the dressing table, however, it still has some of my old hair in it, so I will clean it first."

Emily walked into the room and began to pull the old hair from the brush, Jane couldn't help herself "No, please don't. Please leave the hair, it's all we have left of you when we were happy."

Emily stopped and looked directly at Jane as she said "All we have left, from when we were happy?"

"I'm sorry, I'm not sure why I said that, but it's true it's all you have left of your former self, the happy you when you brushed your hair every night while Peter sat on the bed smiling at you."

Emily looked at Jane with a shocked look on her face "Did I tell you that Jane?" she said.

"Erm, I'm erm, not sure, I guess so. I don't know I just had a vision of you sitting brushing your hair while Peter sat on the bed and admired your beauty."

"That' is very strange as I don't recall telling you that however you are, in fact, correct. I would brush my hair every night before bed and Peter would always watch with a loving smile on his face. That is one of the reasons I have not brushed my hair in many years. I just couldn't face it without Peter."

"I'm so deeply sorry for everything you have gone through Emily. I'm just glad that you found me and we have managed to help each other. Without you I could be dead by now and you would still be locked away in the house never speaking to a soul."

Emily looked at Jane and said, "Everything happens for a

reason, I know that now."

Jane brushed her hair using Emily's brush as Emily sat on the bed and watched. Emily couldn't help but wonder what Amelia would have looked like. She thought how nice it would have been to be sitting there watching her baby girl as a grown woman brushing her hair.

Emily looked at Jane and asked her if she would help her to try and wash her hair and perhaps cut out the matted lumps. Jane said she would do it if Emily was sure that she didn't mind having short hair as Jane was pretty certain that most of the hair would need to be chopped off. Emily replied that she wasn't fussy as she couldn't look any worse than she already did and they both laughed. Emily undressed and got into the shower, once she was finished washing her body Jane came into the bathroom and Emily sat down in the bath while Jane tried hard to tease out as much of the matting as possible. Eventually, she just had to cut most of Emily's hair off using a blunt pair of scissors from the kitchen drawer that were partly rusted. Emily's hair was at last matt free albeit there wasn't much hair left. What was left Jane washed several times to get it clean. Once she was happy that all the dirt was gone, she suggested that Emily try washing her body again as she still looked really dirty. "Fifty years without washing will do that to a person!" Emily replied as they both laughed again. Jane left Emily in the bathroom while she went down stairs to dispose of the matted hair. For the first time in fifty years Emily was clean, well as clean as anyone can be after so long without washing.

Jane came back upstairs just as Emily came out of the bathroom wearing one of the dresses from her wardrobe. It was way too big for her however at least she was clean. Jane said to Emily that it was amazing to see her look so well, so completely different. Emily seemed pleased at what Jane had said. Jane remembered that Emily had said something about asking her a favour, she turned and asked Emily if cutting her hair had been the favour she intended to ask. Emily looked at her and said "no" I have something more important to ask you." Jane looked at her in anticipation of what she was about to say.

Back to Plockton

Keith sat at the kitchen table with his head in his hands. He had barely said a word since he had returned from Plockton. Anna looked at her son with a feeling of helplessness, there was nothing she could do or say that would make her son feel any better. As a mother she felt like she had failed him. A mother is supposed to protect her son but there was no way of protecting Keith from the pain he was going through. She cried silently inside for herself as well as her son, she had fallen in love with Ruth and was so pleased to have a daughter in law who loved her son the way a mother wanted her son to be loved. Anna was convinced that Ruth was dead but she couldn't bring herself to say as much to anyone let alone Keith. She put her hand on her son's shoulder and gave a little squeeze just to let him know that she was there if he needed her. Keith put his hand on top of hers and said "I can't live without her mum, I just can't."

Tony walked into the kitchen and on seeing his wife and son so upset decided he wanted to do something, anything, to help, but what could he do. He looked over at Keith and said, "if there is no news by morning, I think we should drive back up to Plockton as a family so that we are all together when Ruth is found."

Keith looked up at his father with tears in his eyes, "Thank you Dad, I needed someone to say that as I had already decided I was going back. To have you all with me, all of us together as a family waiting, would be great." Anna looked at Tony, and smiled. She had wanted to suggest the same thing but was worried it would be the wrong thing to say so had remained quiet. They knew that nonna would just tag along as she was happy no matter where she was as long as she was with her family.

The next morning, they still had no news from the Plockton police. Keith phoned them to ask for an update however Sergeant Cornwall was out of the office and the desk sergeant, despite knowing about the case, didn't have the latest update. He assured Keith that he would get back to him as soon as he managed to speak to Sergeant Cornwall. Keith said there was no need as he and his family were heading back to Plockton so would speak to Sergeant Cornwall on arrival. On hanging up the phone it suddenly dawned on Keith to call ahead to make sure there were rooms available in the Plockton Inn for them all. He called and Wullie answered the phone after a couple of rings. Keith recognised Wullies voice straight away and asked if he had three rooms available for him and his family. Wullie was pleased to hear from Keith despite knowing there was still no news regarding Ruth. He assured Keith that he would make sure that three rooms were ready for them arriving later that day. "How long will you need the rooms for?" said Wullie. Keith hadn't thought that far ahead and in reality, had no idea how long they would need the rooms. That would depend on the investigation into Ruth's disappearance. Wullie said not to worry and that they would sort alternative accommodation if needed at a later date. On that note Keith hung up the phone and continued to pack his stuff up. As soon as everyone was ready Tony packed the car while Anna pulled together some sandwiches and drinks for the journey. Before long the Vasillios were on their way to Plockton.

As soon as Edna saw Keith's car pulling up, she ran across to him and flung her arms around him. "I'm so deeply sorry

Keith, I want you to know that we are all praying for Ruth's safe return." Keith hugged her and thanked her for her kind words. He was so wrapped up in finding out from Sergeant Cornwall what the latest update was that it completely slipped his mind that Edna had not been introduced to his parents or his nonna. Anna stepped forward as Keith moved away from Edna. She put out her hand and introduced the family. Edna said if they needed anything during their stay in Plockton that she would be happy to assist. Anna thanked her and followed Keith into the inn. Keith was standing at the bar waiting on Wullie to get the keys for the rooms.

Just as Wullie came back into the bar with the keys John walked through the door. "Keith how are you?"

Keith looked over at John and instantly John felt stupid for asking. "I'm back as I just can't rest without knowing what has happened to Ruth. My family have come with me so that we will all be together when she is found." John looked at Keith and tried hard to look positive, however he had already assumed Ruth was dead but obviously didn't want Keith to see what he was thinking. Just at that moment Sergeant Cornwall came into the bar, his colleague had informed him that Keith had called and had said that he and his family were heading back up to Plockton.

"Mr Vasillio," he said as he walked towards Keith. "I believe you called earlier today looking for an update on your wife's case."

"That's correct," said Keith. Sergeant Cornwall looked at Keith and said that he was happy to discuss the case in detail with Keith however would prefer to do so in private. Keith asked Wullie if it would be all right for him to take the sergeant through to the office to talk in private.

Wullie looked across the bar and said, "No problem, please

come through." Keith and Sergeant Cornwall followed Wullie into the back office where he left them alone to discuss Ruth's case.

Sargent Cornwall spoke for about fifteen minutes. Keith was quickly becoming frustrated as he really didn't say anything different from what Keith already knew. Keith was just about to lose his patience with Sergeant Cornwall when suddenly the conversation changed. "We do however have a witness who saw Ruth that day," said the Sergeant.

"Okay," said Keith. "So what has he said?"

"We haven't managed to speak with him yet, it was a man passing through Plockton who had decided to have a walk in the woodland before carrying on with his journey. We only discovered he had been in Plockton this morning. He called to ask if a small Dictaphone had been found in the woodland area. He went on to describe how he had been passing through and got out for a walk. He is apparently doing research on the history of Scotland. It wasn't until he returned back to Glasgow that he noticed his Dictaphone was missing and has been calling all the places he had visited to see if it had been handed in."

Keith looked at the Sergeant with frustration clearly written all over his face, "So, what has all this got to do with Ruth?" he said angrily.

"Mr Vasillio, I understand how upset you are and how frustrating the whole situation is for you however please let me finish talking. I'm on your side, we want your wife found as soon as possible just like you do."

Keith apologised, "I'm really sorry I'm just cracking up, the not knowing is killing me."

"I fully understand. Anyway, this gentleman called to discuss his missing Dictaphone, as soon as the PC who took the call heard the date and approximate time this gentleman had been in the area of Plockton woodlands he asked the man to hold the line while he came and discussed the situation with myself. I took over the call as I wanted to ask if he had seen anyone. Apparently, this Mr Gulam had been walking in the woodlands when he saw a woman who matches the description of your wife. He really didn't think anything of it at the time as a lot of people like to walk in woodland areas alone. I told him how important every detail was, and asked if there was any possible way he could return to Plockton so that we could have a chat. He has agreed to come back the day after tomorrow. He also mentioned that he had taken a lot of photographs and offered to look through them to see if Ruth happened to be in any."

"The day after tomorrow?" said Keith, "Why not tomorrow?"

"Mr Vasillio, we are grateful that Mr Gulam is prepared to come back to Plockton to discuss the situation with us however we cannot then force him to come at a time that suits us. He needs to agree to come on his own terms, he's not a suspect, at the moment, he's a witness."

"So, you think he may have had something to do with Ruth's disappearance, you think he could be a suspect?"

"That's not what I said Mr Vasillio, in fact quite the opposite. We have no reason to think Mr Gulam had anything to do with your wife's disappearance. It would be very unlikely that someone would contact the police asking about a lost Dictaphone if he was responsible for the disappearance of a woman from the exact place he is asking about. It would make no sense," said the Sergeant. "As soon as I've managed to have a chat with him, I will come and tell you everything we discussed. My job is to keep you informed and do everything possible to find your wife. Not to keep you in the dark, so I promise you I will come and update you as soon as possible after my meeting with Mr Gulam."

Keith knew in his heart that what Sergeant Cornwall was saying was correct, he was just really frustrated that someone out there could have some valuable information and yet they had to wait until he had the time to come forward. Keith wanted the police to force him to come to Plockton sooner, however he knew he was being unrealistic. If this guy did have some valuable information, it would be worth waiting for. He was just so impatient as he missed Ruth so much and just wanted to know where she was. The not knowing was killing him and he knew he wouldn't be able to hold it together much longer.

He thanked Sergeant Cornwall for his time and the update and agreed to meet him back at the station at four p.m. the day after tomorrow. By then Sergeant Cornwall will have managed to speak to the witness and will have looked through all the photographs he had taken on the day that he saw Ruth, the day she disappeared.

Emily's Return to the General Store

Emily woke early the next morning. She crept upstairs and could see Jane was still asleep so decided now would be a good time to go into Plockton to pick up more supplies. Emily pulled out the old fishing trolley from the garden shed then headed back to the front door to make sure it was locked. She had already locked the back door, she needed to be sure that Jane couldn't come looking for her just in case she was recognised.

Emily set off pulling her old trolley, she hadn't stopped to think about her appearance, she was just so happy for the first time in years. Before she knew it, she had reached the general store, which she hadn't been in for a couple of days. Emily wandered into the store with a completely new vibe about her. As soon as Edna set eyes on her she did a double take. She was so shocked at the difference in Emily's appearance, she was almost unrecognisable. Edna was embarrassed as she gasped so loudly that Emily looked directly at her. Edna's face immediately turned red, she wasn't sure what to do next, however without thinking she said "Emily, you look erm, so different. I mean you look great. It's so nice to see you." What happened next almost caused Edna to pass out.

"Well thank you, Edna," Emily replied. Edna looked so shocked it actually caused Emily to giggle.

"Emily, oh my goodness you spoke, oh my I can't believe it, it's been what fifty plus years!"

Emily smiled and said "Well it has taken a long time but

finally I'm ready to live again. I want to move forward with my life and stop living in the past."

"That is amazing news, Emily, I'm so pleased, it's just a shame it's a few years too late for your mother and father." Although Emily had been talking to Jane about her whole family, she hadn't thought about whether or not her parents would still be alive.

"Can I assume from that they are both dead?" she said to Edna. "I'm sorry Emily, they moved away from Plockton twenty-five years ago. I heard from John the artist who travels back and forth to Edinburgh and Glasgow that your mother died ten years ago followed by your father the year after. Apparently, your mother had a brain aneurysm that burst and your father never got over it and died of a broken heart." Emily stood looking at Edna with a shocked look on her face.

"I'm so sorry, Emily, I did try to talk to you some years ago to let you know however you always seemed to be in some form of trance and didn't respond to anyone. It must be such a shock to hear that they are both gone, I'm so deeply sorry."

Emily could feel her legs wobble, she quickly sat on the fishing trolley, she needed a moment to catch her breath. Her parent's death had come as a shock but it was the fact that her mother had a brain aneurysm that had shocked Emily the most. For the first time since Amelia had died, Emily realised there was nothing she could have done to prevent what happened. Amelia was obviously born with the aneurysm as was her mother, unfortunately, Amelia's had burst at a very early age. Her mother had at least lived her life before hers had finally burst.

"Can I get you a glass of water, Emily?" said Edna.

"No thank you, I just need a moment, I'll be fine." Emily could feel herself shaking and for a second, thought she was about to pass out. Just at that moment Alice walked into the general store, she didn't notice Emily for the shelving unit. "Edna," she said, "Have you heard any more regarding the disappearance of Ruth Vasillio?"

"No nothing," said Edna as she was trying to nod sideways to alert Alice that Emily was in the store. Alice however hadn't noticed and just kept wittering on and on about Ruth leaving her wedding ring in the bathroom and how maybe she had left him, maybe she realised during the honeymoon that he wasn't the one. Emily could hear everything Alice was saying, now she knew that Jane was in fact Ruth Vasillio and that she was married and had been on her honeymoon, her guilt intensified right there and then, however not enough to speak up, well not about Ruth anyway.

She stood up, "Alice," she said, "I see gossiping is still your favourite thing to do, some things never change." Alice spun round to see who was talking to her and couldn't believe her eyes when she realised it was Emily. Not only had she not heard Emily speak in forever she didn't expect to see her with an almost shaved head wearing clean clothes.

"Emily, oh my god Edna, it's Emily Wilson" said Alice with a shocked look on her face. "She spoke, did you hear that, Edna, she spoke,"

"Yes, Alice I heard. Emily and I were talking before you came in babbling. I had just informed her that her parents had both died." said Edna with a stern look directed at Alice.

"Oh, I see," said Alice, "Sorry." Alice looked from Emily to Edna and back again, she still couldn't get her head around the fact that Emily was not only standing right there in the store but she was clean and she actually spoke.

Emily walked around the store picking up different bits and

pieces and popping them on her trolley. Alice looked at Edna and gave her a strange look as if to say, what's going on. Edna ignored Alice as she was too busy watching Emily roam around the store humming to herself. Edna was pleased that Emily had finally opened up and began to talk again, even if she was left wondering why? why now? What's changed?

Emily moved past Alice without a sideways glance and headed straight to the till to pay for the goods on her trolley.

"Can I get you anything else Emily or is that everything?" said Edna. "That's all for today but I'm sure I will be back in a couple of days."

"I did notice that you had been in a couple of times before today, your routine has changed."

"Yes, I erm just decided I should come into town more often," said Emily nervously laughing as she paid for her shopping, worried that Edna would suspect she knew more about the missing person.

Edna gave Emily her change and said, "Once again, Emily, it's great to see you looking so well and talking, I always knew the day would come that you would come back to us."

"Thank you, see you soon," said Emily as she walked out of the store pulling her trolley. She gave Alice the most awful look as she passed by and omitted to say goodbye to her despite Alice waving and saying "Bye, Emily."

Emily set off home with all her shopping on her trolley feeling pretty happy, however, also a little worried that Edna suspected something. As she reached the house, she could see Jane at the window, she didn't look happy at all. At that moment Emily forgot all about Edna and the general store as she opened the front door. Jane rushed towards her angrily asking "Why, why did you lock me in the house, Emily?"

"I'm sorry, I didn't mean to upset you in any way however I needed to go to the shop and buy some more supplies. You were still asleep and I didn't want to disturb you. I didn't think about locking you in, I was more thinking about locking others out as people walk past here sometimes and I didn't want a stranger walking in." Emily looked really upset as she spoke that Jane automatically apologised for being annoyed.

"I understand you needing to lock the door, I just thought you could have waited until I was awake, and we could have gone to the shop together. It would be good for me to go into Plockton as someone may recognise me." Emily was worried, she tried hard not to show her emotions and said they could both go into town together the next time they needed supplies. Emily just wanted another couple of days with Jane. She had no idea why Jane was so important to her, but she was and she wasn't ready to lose her, not yet. Luckily Jane didn't pick up on Emily's nervousness and moved towards Emily to help her in with the shopping. Emily felt so bad, however, she just needed a little more time.

Amelia's room

Jane had now been with Emily for three days and had managed to get Emily to talk, to shower, to change her clothes, to cut, wash and brush her hair. More importantly, to talk about her past, about Peter and Amelia and her parents. Jane had no idea of the tragedy Emily had endured over the years. She had lost both her brothers in the war, her sister had moved away never to return and the worst of it all, Amelia dying and then Peter's suicide. No wonder Emily had shut herself away for so many years, that said it was lovely that finally she was able to move forward.

Emily decided it was time to approach Jane regarding the favour she wanted to ask her. She opened the living room door and looked at Jane, "Can I ask you that favour now I feel that I'm ready"

"Of course," said Jane. "I will help in any way I can."

"I feel the need—" Emily took a deep breath and started again "I feel the need—" for some reason the words just wouldn't come out. "I'm sorry Jane I—" once again Emily paused." Jane looked at Emily and could see that she was physically shaking, "Do you want me to leave? Is that what you are trying to say?"

Emily looked shocked "No, no, no I just want to, I feel the need to unlock Amelia's bedroom, it has been locked ever since Peter committed suicide. I just, I just couldn't cope with either of the rooms being touched. As I said before I just needed to know they were locked and safe from anyone trying to remove any of Amelia or Peter's things. Having now been into the room I shared with Peter, I feel the need to unlock Amelia's room. I need you to do this with me as I really feel the need to do this tonight, however, I know I am not strong enough to do it alone. Will you help me, Jane?"

Jane looked lovingly at Emily and said "oh, Emily, of course I will help. I will do anything to make life easier for you, after all, you saved my life." At that moment Emily felt a pang of guilt knowing that she knew Jane was actually Ruth, a missing wife who had been honeymooning in Plockton. If I can just have another few days to become stronger, I will tell Jane that the police are looking for her. I just need a few days that's all. Surely it can't hurt anyone me keeping quiet for a few days. If only Emily knew the impact of Ruth (Jane) being missing was having on the Vasillio family especially Keith, I'm sure she would have reconsidered.

Jane approached Emily and gave her a warm hug and said "Whenever you are ready, I'll be there by your side."

Emily smiled and said "all right, let's do this." Emily walked towards Amelia's bedroom with Jane close by her side. Her hands were shaking as she put the key in the lock. She tried several times to unlock the door however the lock seemed to be stuck. Jane said that she would go down to the kitchen and bring up some butter, for some reason this seemed to be a reasonable thing to suggest.

Emily looked at Jane and said, "If you think it will work then yes go ahead and bring the butter upstairs and we will try it." Jane quickly ran downstairs and returned a few seconds later with the butter. Emily pulled the key out of the lock and Jane covered the key with the butter. At first it didn't seem to make any difference however on their second attempt the lock actually opened. Emily stared at Jane afraid to believe the door was actually unlocked.

"It's unlocked," she said with a surprised look on her face.

"Shall I go in first Emily or would you like to?"

"Can you please go in first?" she replied. Jane gently pushed the door open and what happened next was a complete shock to Jane and Emily.

As soon as the door was open and Jane entered the room, she had vivid flashbacks, flashbacks of her as a child lying on the bed in front of her with her father standing over her. The strange thing is that it wasn't Martin who was standing over her it was Peter. Jane walked over to the bed and sat down, she seemed to be in a trance. Emily just stood and watched as Jane lay down on the bed. Emily was fixated with Jane, she couldn't take her eyes off her. Jane curled up in a ball and started to suck her pinkie. Emily ran over to Jane grabbing at her and telling her to get off Amelia's bed. "What are you trying to do to me?" she screamed at Jane. "Why are you lying on my baby's bed sucking your pinkie?" Jane didn't respond she just lay there looking straight ahead of her. "Get up Jane, now, get off Amelia's bed, this was a mistake. I should never have let you come into this room, get up."

Suddenly Emily backed off as Jane started to talk; she was speaking like a little girl and asking her daddy for one more story, "Please Daddy just one more story." Emily stumbled backward holding her hands up to her face. What was going on? Why was Jane speaking like a tiny child? This is exactly what Amelia would say to Peter every night when he tried to tell her it was time to sleep. Emily backed away from Jane, she couldn't understand what was going on, she was shaking from head to toe, and she wanted Jane to stop talking, to get up and get out of Amelia's room.

Jane continued to plead with her Daddy, despite no one being in the room, to please read her one more story. It was as if she was convinced her daddy was in the room, she kept looking up saying, "Please, Daddy, please." Exactly what Emily would hear every night when Peter put Amelia to bed. Why was this happening? Why was Jane acting this way? Emily ran from the room downstairs into the living room, she threw herself on the sofa and cried into the pillow. This was all too much for her, a few hours ago she had felt the happiest she had felt in many years and now all the hurt she felt all those years ago was once again filling her heart.

Emily must have cried herself to sleep as when she woke Jane was sitting on the chair opposite her. Emily sat up and stared at Jane, "What the hell was all that about in Amelia's room earlier?" she screamed.

Jane sat there silent for what seemed like an eternity, "Well" said Emily, "Speak to me, Jane, and tell me what that was all about."

Jane looked at Emily, tears started to stream down her face, "I can't," she said. "What do you mean you can't? You were on my child's bed sucking your pinkie and asking your daddy to read you another story, in a child's voice... why? Why would you do that to me Jane, why? I told you everything about my past as I trusted you, I just don't understand what's going on." She stared at Jane who just kept looking down with tears streaming down her face. "Jane," she shouted, "speak to me."

How could Jane explain to Emily what happened, it had all taken her by surprise and she was still trying to digest it all so how could she possibly begin to try and explain to Emily. Even if she knew how, what would Emily think? She is likely to think that Jane is some lunatic. However, the truth has to be told, but when would be the right time, and would Emily believe her?

The Witness

Mr Gulam arrived at Plockton police station at exactly 2pm, as agreed. He walked up to the police woman at the desk and asked for Sergeant Cornwall. "Who may I say is asking?" replied the policewoman.

"Please tell him it's Mr Gulam, the witness regarding the missing woman. As soon as Sergeant Cornwall heard that Mr Gulam had arrived, he asked his colleague to show him into his office and offer him tea or coffee while he finished a few things he was doing.

When Sergeant Cornwall entered his office, Mr Gulam was seated and had a cup of tea. "Hello, Mr Gulam, thank you for taking the time out of what I'm sure is a busy schedule to come all this way to help us with our enquiries regarding the disappearance of Ruth Vasillio."

"No problem at all," said Mr Gulam. "I'm only too happy to help in any way I can as I know how I would feel if my wife was missing."

Sergeant Cornwall and Mr Gulam chatted for about an hour. Mr Gullam was telling the sergeant all about his project and why he had been in Plockton that day. He had also printed off all photographs taken in and around the Plockton woodlands just in case he had caught anything on camera without knowing it.

When asked when he had first spotted Ruth, he said it was pretty soon after entering the woodlands. He said he noticed her as she seemed engrossed with the beauty of the trees and bushes in the woodlands and was singing to herself. However, she quickly headed off track and out of sight. "It's not often you see someone head off track in woodland unless they are from the area, I presumed she was local given the direction in which she was heading."

"Did you keep to the walking tracks yourself, Mr Gulam?"

"Yes, at first, however as I got deeper in, I did veer off track a little as I wanted to take photos of some of the birds as I'm also a keen bird watcher. That said I only veered off track a little and as soon as I got the photos I wanted I headed straight back to the path as I didn't fancy being lost in the middle of the woodlands with no knowledge of how to navigate back to town."

"Sensible," said sergeant Cornwall. They continued to discuss timings of when he had noticed Ruth to give the police a better timeline of when she was last seen. They also looked through the photos, however there was nothing caught on camera that could been seen by either of them. Mr Gulam did say that he was happy to leave the photos with the sergeant to allow him to have a more thorough look. The sergeant thanked him for his time and said he would be in touch if they needed to speak to him again. With that Mr Gulam shook the sergeant's hand and bid him farewell.

Just as Mr Gulam was about to walk out the door, he turned to Sergeant Cornwall and said, "Oh I just remembered I did see someone else in the woodlands that day," Sergeant Cornwall looked at Mr Gulam, interested to hear more about who else he had seen. Maybe this would be a vital clue in finding Ruth.

"Can you describe the person you saw?"

"Yes, it was an old woman, she was really small with really dirty clothes on, and it looked like her hair was badly matted, or it could have been those dreadlock things that some people do to their hair. Then again she looked a wee bit old for that kind of thing."

"Ah, that would be Emily," said sergeant Cornwall disappointed. "She lives in the woodland, has done for many years. She doesn't communicate with anyone, however, comes in to Plockton for food supplies." Mr Gulam nodded at the sergeant's acknowledgement of the old lady and once again said if he was needed at any time just to call as he exited the office.

Sergeant Cornwall took all the photographs and handed them to a colleague "get someone to look at every inch of these photos, tell them to use a magnifier, if necessary, we need to see if there is anything in any of the photos that will help us trace Ruth Vasillio."

"Oh, and send someone back up to Woodland House to ask Emily if she noticed anyone on her walk that day as Mr Gulam said he saw her not long after he saw Ruth."

"Okay, Sarge, I'll get someone on it right now."

Sergeant Cornwall was in his office when his colleague Pete came rushing in, "Sarge, we've found something."

Sergeant Cornwall jumped up, "Okay, let's have it." Pete walked around the Sergeants desk with a photograph in his hand. It was a beautiful photo of a bird landing on the ground, the angle it was taken from caught it beautifully as the bird was about to land with full span wings. "Nice picture of a bird Pete, but how does that help us in our investigation?"

"That's what I thought at first sarge, but when looking closely with the magnifying glass we are able to see a partial foot."

Sergeant Cornwall took the picture and the magnifying glass to look for himself. As Pete said, there it was in the bottom right-hand corner of the picture, a partial foot. They couldn't be sure if it was an old shoe or if there was a foot inside the shoe. Sergeant Cornwall decided it was time to call Keith Vasillio and get him to look at the picture to see if he recognised the shoe. "Pete, get Keith Vasillio on the phone now, ask him to come in as soon as possible."

"On it Sarge," said Pete as he walked out of the office. "Pete, before you go, did someone go back up to Woodland House?"

"Not yet Sarge, we've got a couple of officers off sick so we are short staffed. I'll head there as soon as I call Mr Vasillio."

"No hang fire, I'll go myself once I've spoken with the husband and know for sure if this foot/shoe belongs to Ruth Vasillio."

"Okay, Sarge, I'll make the call now."

Keith arrived at the station within ten minutes of the call from Pete. His hands shook terribly as he entered the police station, he was so worried about what he was about to discover. He was taken immediately into Sergeant Cornwall's office. "Please take a seat Keith. Can I get you a drink?"

"No thanks, I just need to know what you've found out. Sergeant Cornwall pulled out the photograph and explained to Keith what they had seen with the magnifying glass. Keith looked closely at the picture and immediately recognised the shoe as being Ruth's. He had bought them for her last Christmas. "So, what now?" he asked the Sergeant.

"I think it's time I went to speak to Emily Wilson."

"Who is Emily Wilson? And what does she have to do with Ruth disappearing?" asked Keith. "She is a local who lives in Woodland House which is in the middle of the woodlands. Our witness who saw Ruth that day, said he saw Emily not long after seeing Ruth, so I think it's worth going to see her."

"Why haven't you been there before now?" asked Keith.

"We have, however it's not as simple as ringing the doorbell and talking to Emily. It's a long story, however Emily hasn't spoken to a single soul in over fifty years since losing her daughter and husband. Some of my colleagues went to Woodland House to ask if she had seen anything during the search for Ruth. Emily however had been uncooperative and basically shut the door in their face. Without good cause there really was nothing else we could do. However, now that we have a witness who says he saw Ruth and Emily within a close proximity and time line as well as a photo clearly showing a shoe that belongs to Ruth, I feel that I should go and see Emily to see if I can perhaps get her to at least listen to me and perhaps acknowledge whether or not she remembers seeing anyone that day.

"Okay, so let's go," said Keith almost running out the door. "Hold on Mr Vasillio, it's important we deal with this situation in the correct manner. For this reason, I really believe that it would be better for me to go alone. Emily hasn't spoken in many, many years and as I already said, when my men tried to speak to her the other day, she was unresponsive and just shut the door, I want to try and avoid this happening again. Keith looked really upset however knew there was no point trying to argue his case as Sergeant Cornwall obviously had detailed knowledge regarding this woman so clearly had thought this through.

"Promise me you will come straight to the Plockton Inn as soon as you have spoken to this Emily?"

"I can assure you, Mr Vasillio, I will come straight there. Please however remember that this isn't going to be an easy task and may take a while and still turn up nothing."

Keith looked at the Sergeant, "I understand," he said before shaking his hand and leaving the sergeant to do his job.

Keith arrived back at the Inn to find his parents and nonna

sitting by the fire drinking coffee. He sat down and explained everything that the sergeant had just told him about the photo and the woman Emily, everything. "We just need to hope that despite everything the sergeant has told me about this Emily, she finds it in her heart to open up and speak to Sergeant Cornwall. Hopefully given that she was in the woodlands around the same time she saw something."

"Let's hope so," said Tony to his son looking at Anna with a concerned look as he spoke.

Anna turned to look at her son, "Everything will be okay, darling, we just need to remain positive." Tears stung Keith's eyes once more, he was losing hope.

Jane Speaks Out

"Emily," said Jane, "Please sit down, I need to talk to you and I'm not sure how you are going to respond. I'm not even sure how to say what it is that I need to say." Emily sat down worried that Jane had remembered who she was and had somehow figured out that Emily knew.

"Jane let me explain," began Emily.

"No, please Emily, I need to say what I have to say and I need you to please just remain quiet until I've finished. That said it's not going to be easy so please give me time to try and explain things the best I can." Jane took a deep breath and looked straight at Emily, finally she began to talk. "When I first woke up here, I had no idea where I was, however, I didn't feel lost or upset, just a little frustrated at the lack of clarity in my head. I recognised but didn't recognise the house. I know that doesn't make sense and this is why I need you to be patient with me. I remember looking around and knowing this wasn't my home but knowing that it felt safe and extremely familiar. I looked around and as you know I entered the upstairs room, you know the one that was locked." Emily nodded however said nothing she wanted to let Jane continue as she could see how difficult this was for her. "I had been in your room first and I saw the picture that I now know is of you and Amelia, however at the time it felt so familiar to me as if the photo could have been of me and my daughter. This frustrated me more as I had no idea if I was a mother or not." Jane stopped and looked at Emily, "Bear with me Emily, I need to get some water, would you like some?"

"Yes, that would be nice," said Emily as she followed Jane into the kitchen. Jane's mouth was really dry and she was finding it harder and harder to breath. She needed to take a moment and drink some water. Emily kindly kept quiet allowing Jane to recommence where she left off once she had had a drink. "I then looked in the wardrobe in your room and saw only woman's clothes, old fashioned woman's clothes," Jane giggled with nerves. "Sorry, I now know these clothes are your clothes and I'm not trying to be mean." Emily just smiled and waited for Jane to carry on. I can't really remember what room I tried next but the room I now know to be Amelia's remained locked, the other one as you know opened." Jane took another deep breath before she carried on, "As soon as I went into that room I could feel happiness, it felt like I had been there in happier times. When I looked in the wardrobe there were some really pretty woman's and men's clothes which drew me to them. I couldn't help myself, I took a shirt, it was a blue checked shirt and I held it to my face and inhaled. I can't explain any of this as it wasn't something I would usually do in a stranger's house but it was as if I had no choice. I felt as if I had hugged the person wearing this shirt many times, it was just so familiar and comforting. I know you will be thinking I'm crazy by now, I know that I do when I hear myself but I must tell you everything, crazy as it sounds."

Emily looked really confused and could see the need in Jane to continue. However, she looked at Jane and said, "Stop, please, this is just weird, why would you want to hold Peter's shirt next to your face? Why would you feel as if you had hugged my husband while he wore that shirt? This is too much, I'm not sure I understand any of this, nor do I want to. I think maybe it's time you left."

"Please, Emily, I need to finish."

"No, I need some space. I can't listen to this any more."

"I understand this is all very confusing for you, Emily, however please understand that as confusing as it is for you, I'm just as confused, if not more so. I have no idea what is really going on but I have to tell you everything. I promise as soon as I've told you everything I will leave."

Emily walked away holding her hands to her ears, "I need space, leave me alone, please." Jane wanted so badly to continue however had no option other than to respect Emily and give her the space she asked for. "I will go into the living room and give you some space, however, I'm begging you to allow me to stay until I've told you everything." At that, Jane walked out of the kitchen leaving Emily alone with her thoughts. Emily's head was spinning, so many things said, she was so confused. She wanted to scream at Jane to get out of her house and to never return, however something inside of Emily told her not to. She needed to know the rest of what Jane had to say, she needed Jane to stay at least until she had told her everything. Emily had to listen to all of what Jane had to say even if she did sound crazy. Despite feeling upset at the thought of Jane being in the room she had shared with Peter and her touching Peter's clothes she needed Jane to finish what she had to say, Emily knew now for sure that she needed to know.

Emily walked into the living room where Jane was sitting looking out of the window with the strangest look on her face. Emily just stood and watched Jane until finally she turned to see Emily standing in the doorway. "I'm so sorry about all of this Emily. I have no idea why I ended up here, or who I am but I do know that for some reason I am meant to be here, here with you and telling you all of this."

Emily sat down, looking directly at Jane she said, "Okay, so you entered my private room, a room I had locked year's previous, you touched my husband's clothes, clothes I had locked away as I wanted no one to touch them. Emily's voice was full of emotion as she clearly visualised in her head that day, the day she locked that door walking out of that room for the very last time. "How can you even begin to make me understand this? To see this as being normal behaviour?"

Jane looked at Emily, "I have no idea how I can help you make sense of this, I'm trying so hard to process everything myself. What I do know however is that it wasn't just Peter's clothes that drew me to them. I sat at your dressing table and the smell of your perfume, albeit extremely faint made me feel something. The hair in your brush was so familiar to me I had to touch it, to smell it. When I did, I could see the woman from the photo in the other room sitting brushing her long, beautiful hair. I felt like I was actually there watching her, watching you and it made me feel like I belonged. I didn't feel as if I was a stranger looking through someone else's things. I felt like I belonged there with her, you. This is so difficult for me Emily, please try to understand that I didn't want any of this. I don't want to upset you in any way, but I must continue, I must tell you everything."

Emily sat there in silence, something inside of her told her that Jane had to continue not only for her sake but also for Emily herself, she needed to hear this. Jane was now crying, the tears were streaming down her face, she had no control over them. Emily felt a strong pull on her heart, she wanted so much to comfort Jane. Emily sat frozen to the spot, torn between wanting to comfort Jane and wanting to run out the door and not come back. A few minutes passed, which seemed more like an hour as both Emily and Jane sat looking at each other in silence.

Finally, Emily spoke, "Okay, Jane, for some reason my heart is telling me to listen, to let you tell me everything you need to despite my head telling me to run and never come back. These last few days have seen me speak, wash, cut my hair and more than anything feel alive again, however, today I feel like it has all slipped away from me again. I really feel like I have stepped back and the pain I feel is almost unbearable. However, my heart is telling me that I must let you continue, so be it Jane, continue, try to help me understand all of this."

Jane sat silent for a moment thinking carefully about her next words as she knew she could risk sending Emily over the edge depending on how she put across the next few things she had to say. "Okay, well when I went into the bathroom, I had a similar experience, I could visualise myself in the bath, in the shower with a man standing above me, a man I called Daddy however he wasn't my father. When I went into the shower the other day, I felt happiness like I hadn't felt in such a long time. It was as if I had finally returned home. This is so difficult for me Emily as I really am not trying to upset you, however, I know that everything I'm saying sounds crazy and I know this whole thing is so confusing but I promise you I'm not making any of this up. I need to try and understand all of this and to try and help you to understand."

Emily was holding her head in her hands; she was struggling to keep it all together. Jane looked out the window "When you came back to the house and I hid, I had no idea who you were or why we had both ended up in this house. I was so terrified I just couldn't make sense of anything. I hurt all over however there was no sign of any injury, I had no idea who I was and how I got to this house, however, I recognised myself in the photo upstairs, that I now know to be you. I felt so comfortable and at the same

190

time so uncomfortable. I had all the weird feelings that I have just described to you and had no idea what it all meant. When you spoke and I came out from behind the sofa, I immediately felt safe. You explained that it was your house and that you had found me in the woodlands. You explained everything about your life to me over the next few days and I really felt as if I was part of it all. I had no idea why and was afraid to say anything about my feelings, thoughts and visions. Despite your silent past, and me having no idea where I had appeared from, we seemed to make each other feel secure, you began freely talking about your past. I was more interested in finding out more about you and this house than I was in trying to discover who I am."

Jane stopped for a moment watching Emily with her hands up at her face and her head bowed down. She was truly afraid of how Emily would react to the next thing she was about to say. "Emily, you asked me to help you and I wanted to, not because you had helped me, but because I felt drawn to you and wanted so much to make you happy. When you said you were ready to unlock Amelia's room, I knew how difficult that choice must have been for you and was only too pleased that you wanted me to do it with you." Emily looked up and she was silently crying as she listened to Jane. "When the door opened and we went in to Amelia's room I can't even begin to imagine how you must have felt. Then to see me on your child's bed and experience me acting in a strange manner sent you over the edge. I know that but I truly couldn't stop. Emily, I know this is going to sound weird, I have to say it, I think I'm Amelia. I feel it in my heart." At that moment Jane was ready for Emily to explode and ask her to leave, however Emily just sat there and stared at Jane for what seemed like forever. "Emily, did you hear me?" said Jane.

Emily looked at Jane, she got up and walked over to where

Jane was standing. Emily put her hands on either side of Jane's face and pulled her head down until she was looking directly into her eyes. As she did so she was crying freely. She just stood there, staring at Jane speechless. Jane didn't feel uncomfortable, in fact she was struggling not to pull Emily towards her and hug her. Jane felt she had come home to her mother and wanted so much to comfort her and be comforted by her. Jane looked down at Emily, "I've been having visions, visions of us all over this house, not just you and me but Peter." There were no photos of Peter on show in the house however Jane went on to describe Peter to Emily. She described him exactly as he was before he took his own life, before Amelia died. She even told Emily little things that it would have been impossible for her to know unless what she was saying was true.

Emily remained silent, so Jane continued to talk about her visions. Every one she described was so vivid in her mind. Emily could see from Jane's expression the love she felt as she described every detail of her memories. "It's very strange for me as I have no idea who I am and how I got to be in Plockton woodlands, however I do know I was meant to come here and be with you, Emily, of that I have no doubt. I look at you and I feel so much love for you it's killing me as I just want to hold you and never let you go." Emily's head was spinning, so much information, so many details, private moments being described by Jane in detail. How was this possible? Could Jane actually be a reincarnation of Amelia? As if reading Emily's mind Jane said "My grandparents are Angela and Graham Laird, your mother and father. I also have a grandmother Cathy who visited a couple of times with my aunt Catherine, my father's, Peter's mother and sister."

"Oh my god how is this possible?" said Emily as she pulled

Jane into her arms, "Amelia, my Amelia, how can this be?"

She pulled back and looked at Jane "your pinkie, you suck your pinkie," Emily was sobbing as she pulled Jane back into her arms. "Amelia, it's really you, my baby girl, my beautiful baby girl. I don't know how and I don't care I just know that you have come home to me, oh, Amelia, I've missed you so much, I love you my darling, I love you." Emily just kept pulling back and staring at Jane then pulling her in to her arms again.

Emily confesses

Emily and Jane had spent the whole night discussing the past. Emily was amazed at everything that Jane could tell her about her life as Amelia. It was a very bizarre night for both Emily and Jane as neither of them had ever experienced anything like this. Jane wasn't even sure she had ever believed in reincarnation and said so much to Emily. Emily had always believed but had never experienced anything that could prove it until now. There was never a moment since Amelia died that Emily ever thought that this day would ever come.

The time had come for the truth all round. It was up to Emily to explain to Jane that she had something she needed to discuss that would upset her. It was time to tell Jane her name isn't Jane, its Ruth Vasillio and her husband and family were looking for her. Emily had to work out not only how to tell Jane the truth but to help her to understand why she hadn't told her immediately once the police had come asking questions. Emily knew there was no option other than to tell Jane everything, she was however terrified that Jane would be so angry that she would leave and never return. Emily couldn't bear the thought of losing Amelia, not again, not when she had her back in her life, albeit she was Ruth not Amelia. Her vivid memories had brought back all the love and joy Emily had felt all those years ago as the mother of this amazing child.

"Jane," said Emily almost silently, "Did you just say my name, Emily?"

"Erm yes, I did, however it's not your name." Jane assumed that Emily was referring to Amelia.

"Emily, I don't want to lose you from my life, however I wouldn't feel right if you continue to call me Amelia. I know that sounds weird given the lengths I've gone to convincing you that I am Amelia. That was my life, long ago. I'm me now, an adult, not your beautiful little girl any more."

"I know, I know, that's not," Emily stuttered as she was extremely nervous. "I, I have something I need to tell you about your life before I found you."

Jane stared at Emily with wide eyes, "My life before you found me? But you said you had no idea who I was or where I came from. You said you found me in the woodlands and had no idea how I got there."

"That's all true," said Emily. "Well, what do you mean you need to tell me something about my life, how can you possibly know anything about me all of a sudden?" Emily decided there was no point delaying things any longer, it was time to pull the plaster off no matter what it revealed. "Your name is Ruth Vasillio."

"Ruth Vasillio?"

"Yes, you are married although I have no idea what your husband's name is."

"Husband? So, I have a husband? But I have no wedding ring on my finger!"

"I can't explain that, all I can do is tell you what I know. A few days ago, there was a knock at the door very early morning. It was two of the local police looking for a missing person. They described you, I'm so sorry Ruth but I shut the door on them shaking my head, allowing them to believe I was still not talking and that I had no idea what they were on about."

Ruth felt sick, her head was all over the place, she was trying so hard to remember, something, anything. "A husband, Ruth Vasillio, what else do you know?"

"That morning, after you had cut my hair, the morning I left you sleeping and locked the door."

"Oh my god, you did lock me in," Emily looked ashamed, "Erm yes, well no, well kind of. I obviously didn't want anyone to come into my house so locking the door would prevent that, but, yes, I also thought if I locked the doors, you couldn't get out. I'm so sorry Ruth, I really am."

"Why, why would you not tell the police I was here, why did you keep me here pretending you had no idea who I was when in fact you knew? The police could have taken me to my husband, I could be with him now."

"Be with him? Who Ruth, be with who? You don't even remember him. You had no idea you were married. What you did know is that you ended up here for a reason, you were meant to come home."

"Home?" said Ruth, this is your home not mine. This is a different life and I have a right to know who I am Emily, surely you understand that?"

"Yes, of course I do. I know that, I just knew there was something about you and I needed a few days to work it all out. I had no idea what was in front of us both, I just knew I needed to know why you ended up in the woodlands, why I needed to bring you to my home, why you had such a profound impact on me. Why I chose to talk again, wash, dress, cut my hair. Why after all these years, what was it about you that made me want to live." Ruth looked emotional as she listened to Emily. "I understand all of that, Emily, I needed to understand too but surely we could have done both." Emily looked at Ruth with a sad expression on her face, "I don't believe that Ruth. I think if I had told you about the police visit, told you who you were, we would never have got to this point. We would always have wondered why the universe brought us together, why we both had such strong unexplainable feelings."

"Perhaps," said Ruth. "Anyway, that day that I went into Plockton for supplies, I heard some of the locals talking about the search for you. I knew I should have said something right then but I just couldn't. I just knew in my heart that we needed more time."

Ruth didn't know how to respond to Emily, she was extremely confused. In her heart she knew that Emily would never do anything to hurt her but her head was telling her that Emily should have been honest. Ruth genuinely felt that she would still have wanted to get to know Emily as she knew something was connecting them and needed to know what it was. Yes, Emily keeping quiet had enabled Ruth to discover what that connection was and maybe just maybe that would never have happened if Emily had told Ruth straight away who she was and that the police were looking for her, but surely that should have been her decision to make and not Emily's. Ruth looked up at Emily who by now was shaking from head to toe, worried that Ruth would run from the house never to return. Emily couldn't bear the thought of losing Ruth, not now that she knew about her past. She just couldn't bear the thought of losing Amelia all over again. Ruth could see that Emily was really upset and was clearly shaking, she looked at her and said "I don't condone what you did, I don't fully understand why you did it however I do kind of understand as I also needed and wanted more time with you to discover more about my connection to this house and you. I wish however you had trusted me and told me the truth as I would then have been the one to decide how to move forward."

Emily smiled at Ruth, "I wish I had little one, but I can't take back what I've done, I can't change things. What I can do though is help you now. Help you to remember your life with your husband and your family. If you can remember a previous life then I'm certain you will remember this one. I can be by your side every step of the way if you want me to."

"Given that I don't know another soul, I would appreciate you helping me Emily, oh and just so we are clear I forgive you for not telling me about the missing person search for me just as you forgave me my intrusion into your life."

"All things happen for a reason," they both said at once. Just at that moment Emily looked at Ruth, "it begins now little one, I can hear a car approach."

The knock on the door

Emily was mid-sentence when there was a loud knock at the door. Ruth looked across at Emily unsure about what she should do. Was she ready to face this? Was she strong enough to accept that she had a life outside of these four walls? She knew Emily wouldn't allow her to come to any harm, with that thought she smiled at Emily and said "Let's do this."

Emily walked towards the front door, opening it to see Sergeant Cornwall and a young PC. "Come in," said Emily as she walked back into the living room. Sergeant Cornwall followed Emily into the house and on into the living room. Once there, Emily sat down and didn't say another word. She looked at Sergeant Cornwall as he entered the room and could see the shock on his face when he saw Ruth sitting on the chair by the window.

"Mrs Vasillio" he said as he approached Ruth. "Are you all right? Where have you been?" Ruth looked at the sergeant with a confused look on her face. Despite Emily telling her what her name was and that the police were looking for her she felt a strange feeling in the pit of her stomach being referred to as Mrs Vasillio given that she had no memory of that being her name. She had become so comfortable being called Jane and had resigned herself to staying there with Emily. Ruth knew however that she needed to know the truth, discover who she was, what her life was like. She needed to know who her husband was, to see him to see if that would spur her memory.

Ruth stood up and walked towards the sergeant with an outstretched arm ready to shake his hand, "I believe so" she said to the sergeant. "I think you need to know that I have no memory of who I am or why I'm in this area or how I ended up in the woodlands. It's also important for you to know that Emily here, she saved my life. Had she not brought me back here I'm sure by now I would be dead."

The sergeant looked from Ruth to Emily and back again, "Perhaps," he said, "or perhaps we would have found you and saved a lot of anguish for your family and police resources." Sergeant Cornwall then looked directly at Emily and asked why she hadn't told the police that she had found Ruth when they came searching.

Emily was about to speak when Ruth interrupted. "I asked her not to," said Ruth. "You did? Why would you do that? Why wouldn't you want to know who you are, who you left behind?" Ruth looked flushed, "I'm sorry sergeant my intention was not to cause any trouble. I just needed a couple of days to get my head together, to try to figure a few things out. I was sure my memory would come back so I asked Emily not to inform anyone that she had found me." Sergeant Cornwall didn't look convinced however he had no way to disprove what Ruth had just told him. Emily looked at Ruth, thankful for her explanation to Sergeant Cornwall. Emily had just got her life back and didn't want to end up on the wrong side of the law. Despite feeling that the truth had somehow been twisted to protect Emily, Sergeant Cornwall had no option other than to accept what had been said. He went on to explain to Ruth who she was and what had happened on the run up to her being found by Emily in the woodlands. What they didn't know was what actually happened to Ruth that day, why she was found unresponsive and why she had no memory.

Sergeant Cornwall explained to Ruth that Keith, her husband, and her in laws were in Plockton. I need to call Plockton Inn and tell your family you have been found safe, then we can head back to town where they will be waiting for you.

The look of fear on Ruth's face couldn't be mistaken. "Are you all right Mrs Vasillio?" asked the sergeant as he looked at her questioningly.

"No, not really," replied Ruth. "I don't know these people and I feel safe here, I want to stay here with Emily, assuming that's all right with you?" she said as she looked across at Emily.

"No problem with me," said Emily in return. Sergeant Cornwall looked a little surprised to learn that Ruth wanted to stay where she was. "Don't you want to find out all about your life, who you are and where you live? Your husband has been going out of his mind with worry as have the rest of your family."

Ruth looked at the sergeant and said "Yes of course I want to know everything about my life, but I need to do things my way. I can't just go with complete strangers to a completely strange house. If it's all right with you Emily they can come and speak to me here." Emily looked at Sergeant Cornwall "It's fine with me" she said looking for his approval. Sergeant Cornwall wasn't sure this was a good idea as he could sense that there was more to this story, the house, Ruth's relationship with Emily, something wasn't right about all of this. However, his hands were tied, if Ruth wouldn't budge and Emily had no issue with that then he had no other option other than to get Keith Vasillio out here to Woodland House.

"Fine," he said. "I will call Plockton Inn to inform your husband that you are safe and well, then explain to him that your preference would be to meet with him here. I will then send my PC back to pick him up. "I don't want them all to come here," said Ruth "It's going to be hard enough for me facing one stranger."

"No worries, I'll make sure that's made clear to your husband." Ruth looked at the sergeant, "would you mind referring to him by his name as it's freaking me out every time you say, your husband."

"No problem," said the sergeant apologising for upsetting her.

Emily was in the kitchen making tea and coffee when the PC arrived back with Keith. Ruth saw the car pull up, she looked at Sergeant Cornwall and asked, "Can I go get Emily as I want her with me when this man comes in."

"If that's what you want, then yes of course," he replied. Ruth ran into the kitchen to tell Emily that they had arrived and that she needed her to be by her side when they came in. Emily nodded, she took Ruth's hand and walked back through to the living room where Keith stood waiting. Sergeant Cornwall had let them in and quickly explained that Ruth had no memory and was feeling extremely vulnerable.

As Ruth and Emily entered the room you could feel the tension. Keith wanted to run up to Ruth and embrace her in his arms, he was so relieved to see her alive and well, however after listening to what the sergeant said he thought better of it. "Ruth, darling, I'm so relieved to see you, I've been worried sick. We have been searching and searching for you for days now. I can't believe you have been here all this time, we've had helicopters and divers searching for you." Keith could see the distress in Ruth's face and it was killing him. "None of it matters now, you're safe and well my darling." Ruth couldn't find the words, she had no idea what to say to Keith as she had no recollection of him whatsoever. She just stood and stared at him trying to find something, just a little thing, anything to make him familiar to her, but there was nothing.

Emily could sense Ruth's discomfort and decided to speak for her. "I'm sorry Keith, Ruth has no memory of anything from her life and it's not easy for her. I'm afraid you will have to be patient with her. "Can't you see she's scared? This whole situation has been so traumatic for her."

Keith looked at Emily clearly irritated that she was doing the talking for Ruth, however he loved Ruth and knew that Emily was making sense, she was looking out for Ruth and for that he should be grateful. "I understand," he said. "All I want is to help my wife regain her memory. I'm sure you can understand that in order to do that we need to talk about her life, our life together." At that moment Ruth ran from the room, she was so overwhelmed by everything that had happened over the last few days and now all this on top of it all was just too much. She headed up the stairs and without thinking about it headed straight for Amelia's room and through herself on the bed.

Downstairs, Sergeant Cornwall, Keith and Emily discussed the best way forward. They had to take into consideration that Ruth was extremely confused and vulnerable. They needed to find a way of helping Ruth first and foremost, otherwise nothing would be achieved. Sergeant Cornwall suggested that they take a trip to the hospital with Ruth despite her having no visible physically injuries there was clearly a problem with her memory and the best move would be for her to be assessed at the hospital. They could then work out the best plan of action for everyone involved. Keith and Emily were both in agreement, everyone was on the same page in so much as they all wanted what was best for Ruth.

An Anxious Ruth

Emily suggested that she go and speak to Ruth alone. Sergeant Cornwall agreed despite seeing the irritated look on Keith's face.

"I guess Emily is the only person that Ruth trusts right now. She doesn't know me at all and doesn't remember you so I think Emily should be the one to go and speak with her," he said looking directly at Keith.

"I guess so," Keith said reluctantly.

Emily found Ruth lying on Amelia's bed, only this time it didn't upset her, in fact it actually made her smile as she could see how comfortable Ruth was. "Hey little one, how are you feeling?" she said as she sat on the bed next to Ruth.

"I'm exhausted and confused and my head hurts. I just don't know anything any more. I want to remember my life of course I do but it's just all too much for me at the moment, especially after just realising I had a previous life. My head is all over the place and I'm not sure I can handle all of this right now."

Emily understood exactly what Ruth was saying, "If you want me to ask Sergeant Cornwall and more importantly Keith to give you a few days then that's exactly what I will do. That said, I do agree with the sergeant that perhaps a visit to the hospital would be a good idea. After all we have no idea why you ended up in the woodlands the way you did when I found you." Emily could see Ruth trying hard to process everything, it was no wonder her head hurt, so much information over a few days, poor Ruth. Emily wanted to tell everyone to go and to leave Ruth alone, however, she knew in her heart that wasn't going to help

Ruth in the long run.

Ruth sat up, "Okay let's get this over with, let's go to the hospital however I don't want Keith to come with us I feel anxious enough without a stranger being by my side listening to what the doctor has to say. I want to have time to process what they tell me before I have to share it with a man I don't know, or can't remember. I want you to come with me and if Sergeant Cornwall wants to come that's fine but he can wait outside I don't want anyone in the room with me except you."

"Deal," said Emily as she hugged Ruth, "Come on then little one."

Emily and Ruth went downstairs into the living room where Keith and Sergeant Cornwall were waiting. Emily explained to them both exactly what Ruth had said to her in the bedroom. It was clear that Keith was not happy at being told he could not go to the hospital with his wife. Now that he knew she was alive and safe he wanted to keep her close, however he had to respect Ruth's wishes therefore agreed to go back to Plockton Inn and wait for news.

Sergeant Cornwall instructed his colleague PC Edwards to take Keith back to the Plockton Inn then to return to escort Ruth and Emily to the hospital. Keith looked at Ruth, "please let me know how you get on as soon as possible. I understand you don't remember me however I'm your husband and I can't help being worried sick about you. I need to know that you are all right even if you don't want me to be around you at the moment." Ruth smiled apologetically as she understood that this situation was also extremely difficult for Keith.

"We will be in contact soon," said Emily as PC Edwards led Keith out to the car.

Emily made tea for Sergeant Cornwall and Ruth while they waited on PC Edwards to return. Ruth sat in silence while Sergeant Cornwall talked to her about who she was and what had happened on the lead up to her going missing. Ruth listened intently however nothing he said seemed to trigger anything. They drank their tea in silence and before long PC Edwards was back to escort them to the hospital.

Hospital Assessment

On arrival at the hospital Sergeant Cornwall spoke with the on-duty doctor and explained everything that had happened to Ruth over the last few days. He obviously didn't mention anything about previous lives, reincarnation or anything like that as Ruth and Emily had omitted to discuss that with him. The doctor assured Sergeant Cornwall that they would do all necessary assessments to try to get to the bottom of what had happened to Ruth and why she had no memory.

The doctor asked Ruth to come into the examination room. Ruth looked at Emily and nodded towards the door, Emily looked directly at the doctor for approval to go in with Ruth. The doctor said "If you want Emily to come and sit in while I examine you that's not a problem." Ruth smiled and both women entered the examination room followed by the doctor. The doctor closed the door and signalled to both women to take a seat. "I'm Dr Robertson," he said while taking a seat "So Ruth, why don't you tell me in your words what you remember." Ruth looked a little nervous, so Emily took her hand. Ruth immediately felt comforted and began to recount what she knew about the day that Emily found her, which wasn't anything really other than she woke in a strange house.

Emily spoke to the doctor "I saw Ruth slumped against a big oak tree in the woodlands. I obviously checked that she was still breathing which of course she was. I knew the weather was going to turn nasty as all the warning signs were there, you know what it's like, doctor, I'm sure." The doctor nodded. "I went back to my home and pulled out my husband's old fishing trolley, I often use it when going into Plockton for supplies. I tried to wake Ruth however she was unresponsive. I then tried for quite some time to get her on to the trolley. I can only assume that's why she felt so sore all over for a few days following. I eventually managed to get her onto the trolley and back to my house. She still hadn't come round." Emily continued to explain the rest of that day to the doctor. He was not concerned about any of the rest of the story as his aim was to try figure out why Ruth had collapsed that day and why she had no memory. Judging Emily or Ruth as to why they hadn't contacted the police was not on his radar.

Dr Robertson asked Ruth to climb up onto the examination bed where he proceeded to do a physical examination. He could find nothing of concern, however informed Ruth that he would be referring her for a CT scan and would run some bloods. He suggested that Ruth stay in the hospital overnight as she was slightly dehydrated so he wanted to get some IV fluids into her. He also felt it would be beneficial if she was monitored overnight. Another benefit to staying overnight was that as an inpatient he could arrange bloods and the CT scan while she was there. If she was sent home, it could take weeks for an outpatients appointment to come through. Given the doctor's advice Ruth reluctantly agreed to stay in hospital overnight. "Can Emily stay with me while I have blood taken and while I have the CT scan?" Ruth asked the doctor.

"She can wait with you, however, she will be unable to go in the room with you while you have your scan." Ruth looked at Emily, however before she could say anything Emily had agreed that she would stay for as long as Ruth needed her.

Ruth was taken to a ward and assigned a bed within the hour.

Emily sat by her side while she settled in as Dr Robertson had gone to inform Sergeant Cornwall what the plan was. The Sergeant told the doctor that he would go back to Plockton Inn and inform the relatives that Ruth was being kept in overnight. The doctor then proceeded to make arrangements for Ruth to have a CT scan later that day and have her bloods taken.

Within twenty minutes a nurse appeared to take a full blood count from Ruth. Ruth had no idea how she would react to the needle as she didn't know if she was okay with blood being taken or not, luckily it didn't bother her one way or the other so all went well. Emily asked the nurse if she had any idea what time Ruth would be taken for the CT scan. The nurse said she would go and ask and get back to them as soon as she had an answer. The nurse was only away a few minutes when a porter turned up to take Ruth for her scan. Emily went with Ruth down to the scanning department and sat in the waiting room while Ruth was being scanned. Within twenty minutes Ruth was out, and on her way back to the ward with Emily by her side. The nurse who had taken the bloods came back into the ward to tell Ruth that the doctor would be back to see her within the next two to three hours and that Emily could stay with her until then if she wanted to, both Emily and Ruth were pleased.

Ruth and Emily were sitting chatting when Dr Robertson entered the ward. He asked them both to follow him to a small side room as he wished to discuss Ruth's scan in private. Emily looked at Ruth, she could see the look of fear on her face. Emily quickly put her arm around her, "I'm here little one, and everything will be fine," she said as they both followed the doctor into the side room. The doctor motioned to Ruth and Emily to take a seat. He remained standing, he had what looked like x-rays in his hand. Ruth was soon to discover that these were in fact the scan pictures that she had taken of her head earlier that day.

The doctor proceeded to explain his findings "We have discovered that you have a brain aneurysm,"

Emily immediately flung her hands up to her face, "No, no not again please, please don't let this be happening I've only just found you."

Dr Robertson looked at Emily clearly confused at her reaction. Despite this he continued to speak to Ruth who was completely silent. "You have been extremely lucky in that the aneurysm hasn't burst. It is however pressing on part of your brain that would cause memory problems. This would explain why you have had memory loss. It also explains the fact that you passed out in the woodlands the day you were found. My concern is that it may burst, you have been given a warning and the next time you may not be so lucky. For this reason, we feel it is necessary to remove the aneurysm as soon as possible. We have booked you in for surgery tomorrow. Ruth was speechless, she just stared at the doctor. She didn't know how to feel about the news, she was just so confused by everything going on in her life right now her brain was in overdrive.

Emily was standing by her side with tears running down her face, "Is the operation risky?" she asked Dr Robertson.

"No operation is without risk, however we have successfully removed aneurysms bigger than this one in the past. I am confident that this aneurysm can be removed successfully and would expect a full recovery within approximately six to eight weeks. That said I would expect Ruth to experience some headaches for the first few weeks as this is pretty standard after any brain surgery." Dr Robertson looked at Ruth "Do you have any questions, Ruth?" he asked.

Ruth looked at Emily who was still crying then back at the

doctor, "Will my memory come back?"

"I can see no reason why not as the pressure caused by the aneurysm will be gone. What I can't tell you is how much of your memory will come back and when, as all patients are different." Ruth smiled at Dr Robertson and thanked him for his time. Dr Robertson said he would see Ruth first thing next morning. He informed Emily that she was welcome to stay for another hour however would have to leave after that. He turned, wished both ladies good day and left the room.

"Emily," said Ruth, "Can I ask you something?"

"Of course, you can," said Emily, "anything."

"I know that Dr Robertson will have updated Sergeant Cornwall and he will have informed Keith, however I was wondering if you could go and speak to Keith for me?" she said looking at Emily with a strange look on her face.

"No problem," said Emily, "however, why are you looking at me like that, is there something else you want me to tell him?"

Ruth took a deep breath and said "I want you to tell him everything. I know it's not going to be easy however I need him to know everything. Dr Robertson is pretty sure my memory will come back but I'm worried that my past life will fade away. I must love Keith as we are newly married, so that means I trust him. I may not remember you or anything about Amelia and I can't bear to not know. If Keith knows and he can tell me everything then I will know that it's true and that part of me, Amelia, really did exist. I don't want to lose you Emily and I'm worried, look how I've reacted to Keith because I can't remember. I don't want to feel like that about you, I want to know it's all true and for you to remain part of my life. It's really important to me Emily, will you do it? Please say you will." How could Emily refuse when all she wanted was to remain part of

Ruth's life and this would make that possible.

"I will go to Plockton Inn when I leave here, and I promise you little one I will tell Keith everything." Ruth grabbed Emilys' hand and pulled her close to her, she hugged her so tightly poor Emily couldn't breathe. Emily kissed Ruth on the cheek and said she would return the next day to wait on Ruth returning from surgery. Ruth smiled, kissed Emily goodbye and went back into the ward to rest.

The Operation

As promised Emily went straight to the Plockton Inn. Keith was sitting with Sergeant Cornwall when Emily walked over to them. The Sergeant had just told Keith all about the results of Ruth's CT scan and informed him of the pending operation to remove the aneurysm. Keith was devastated that Ruth was having to go through a brain operation however relieved that the aneurysm was found in time and hadn't burst. He was happy to hear that there was no reason that Ruth shouldn't recover 100% from the operation and regain all or most of her memory. He wanted to go to the hospital however was advised against it by Sergeant Cornwall as Ruth had given strict instructions that she only wanted Emily at the hospital. Emily interrupted the sergeant as she had an update regarding Ruth and needed to speak to Keith alone. The Sergeant excused himself as his job was done and left Emily with Keith to discuss Ruth and her wishes going forward.

Emily began by telling Keith that Ruth had agreed for him to go to the hospital next day and wait with Emily for her to have her operation and return to the ward. She did however make him aware that just because the operation would be over not to expect too much from Ruth regarding recognition, just to play it by ear. Keith was just so pleased that Ruth had agreed for him to be there, he didn't care about anything else. Emily then told Keith that a lot had happened over the few days that she and Ruth had spent together at Woodland House and that Ruth had asked her to explain everything to him. Keith listened intently to the whole story before saying anything. He was completely shocked at everything Emily told him however had no reason to disbelieve her as she would have no reason to want to make something like this up. He wasn't a great believer in the afterlife or reincarnation however he couldn't prove or disprove therefore all he could do was listen to Emily and try to understand everything that both she and Ruth had gone through together. It certainly helped him to understand the bond that was clearly visible between the two women. Once Emily had told Keith everything she asked if he wanted her to help him explain things to his family. Keith said he would tell them everything but not at the moment. The important thing right now was to get Ruth through the operation and on the road to recovery. Once things had settled down, he said that Ruth and he would explain everything to the family. He knew in his heart that this is what Ruth would want as they had always tackled difficult conversations together. Emily understood and said she would see Keith the next day at eight thirty a.m. outside the hospital.

As soon as Emily left, Anna, Tony and nonna joined Keith. They had been waiting patiently to learn all about Ruth's results, they had been so worried about her. Keith explained everything to them, the aneurysm causing the loss of memory and finally the operation Ruth needed to have. The Vasillio's where worried sick, nonna started to cry "La mia povera Ruth ha gia passato cosi tante cose e ora questo."

Tony looked at his mother angrily, "Ma stop it. Ruth will be fine." He was worried about Keith as he had been through so much over the past few days, this was just another pressure for him to cope with. Tony didn't want his mother to put any more pressure on his son. He knew Keith would be upset seeing nonna cry and would try to comfort her when he needed all his strength to get through the night and what would be one of the hardest days of his life tomorrow.

Nonna looked at Keith, "ragazzo mio, mi dispiace che tuo padre abbie ragione Ruth è forte, lei starà bene." Keith pulled nonna into his arms and kissed her on the forehead, "Ti amo Nonna, ti amo."

Keith didn't sleep much that night as he was so worried about Ruth and what must be going through her mind. He wished with all his heart that he could be going through this instead of her. Ruth had endured so much in her life, why did she have to suffer more and something so serious, life threatening even. He walked across the room at least a hundred times willing the time to pass so he could go to the hospital. Finally, it was light outside and he could at least go for a walk to try and clear his head before heading off to the hospital. On his way downstairs he bumped into his mother who hadn't slept much either. She asked where he was going as it was too early to go to the hospital. Keith explained to his mother that he needed to go for a walk and try to clear his head.

Anna looked at her son, all she could see was worry in his eyes "Ruth will be fine darling, I'm sure of it."

"I hope so mum, I really do as my life is nothing without her." Anna felt helpless, as there was nothing she could do to help her son feel better. As a mother it was killing her knowing she could do nothing to alleviate the pain and anguish her child was going through.

"Let me walk with you, Keith" she said as she put her hand on her son's' chest.

"I want to be alone, Mum, I just can't bear to talk to anyone right now. I just need to be alone to try get my head straight," he replied.

"I understand my Darling, however if I promise not to speak, just to walk by your side, would you allow me to come with you?"

Keith looked at Anna and just nodded as he slipped his jacket on. "Let me get my jacket, give me a moment." At that Anna went back into her room to pick up her jacket, however by the time she returned Keith was gone. Keith needed to be alone to try and process everything that Emily had told him about Ruth and Amelia.

Keith had agreed to meet Emily at the front of the hospital at eight thirty a.m. as Ruth was due in theatre at nine a.m. Keith just wandered around until finally arriving at the hospital at eight fifteen a.m. To his surprise Emily was already waiting. "Good morning, Emily" said Keith as he approached.

"Good morning, Keith. You look as if you've not slept in weeks," she replied.

"The truth is, I haven't, well not much anyway. Last night was a right off, I just couldn't close my eyes as every time I did, I was scared of what my dreams would bring."

Emily knew exactly what Keith meant as she felt exactly the same. "Let's go and see if everything is still on schedule," said Emily as she walked through the hospital doors. Keith hesitated for a moment, terrified that they would discover Ruth's aneurysm had burst and she had died during the night. Emily could sense what he was thinking and put her hand on his arm "I'm certain all is well Keith, let's go and see if we can see Ruth before surgery." Keith smiled at Emily as he followed her up to the ward. The nurse on the reception said that Ruth had already gone down to be prepped for surgery. Keith and Emily both felt disappointed despite being told the day before that they would be unable to see Ruth prior to her operation. They had hoped that they would at least see her being taken to theatre and would have the opportunity to wish her luck. The nurse told them that they could wait in the family room and someone would come and tell them once Ruth was back from theatre. She did advise them not to expect to see anyone for quite some time as the operation would likely take three to five hours. Keith and Emily both thanked the nurse and entered the family room where they would both wait for the operation to be over.

After five hours Keith was beside himself with worry, he was convinced something had gone wrong. Emily remained calm and kept reassuring him that all was well and that Ruth would be back up to the ward soon despite being worried herself. She refused to think the worst and needed to stay positive for Keith. After another forty-five minutes Keith was about to go and ask the nurse if there was any news. However just as he stood up, the door opened and the nurse they had spoken with earlier walked in the room. "You will be glad to know that the operation is over and Ruth is now in recovery. We will keep her there for an hour or so then all being well bring her back up to the ward. I can tell you however that the operation went extremely well, a little more complicated than expected but it's all over and the doctor expects Ruth to recover her memory in full. The recovery period will take approximately eight weeks, however all patients differ. Ruth will stay with us here for five to ten days depending on how she herself responds. Keith thanked the nurse for the update then turned and grabbed hold of Emily nearly knocking her off her feet. He was so relieved that Ruth had come through the surgery and was alive that he needed to hug someone. Emily responded by hugging him back and laughing out loud. The relief for both of them brought laughter and tears. Emily encouraged Keith to go and call the Plockton inn to let his parents and nonna know that Ruth had made it through the surgery and was going to be fine.

At that moment it suddenly hit Keith that no one had contacted Lyn. He looked at Emily with a look of horror on his face, "Oh my god, Lyn, no one has told Lyn what's going on!"

"Emily looked confused, "Who is Lyn?" she asked.

"Lyn is Ruth's nana. The last she knew was that we had

extended our honeymoon. I've been so worried about Ruth going missing, then being found and now the operation, it completely slipped my mind to call her."

"Perhaps that's not a bad thing Keith. At least now when you tell her you can be confident that Ruth has come through the other side. I understand you are upset at leaving her in the dark but I truly believe it has worked out for the best."

"Perhaps," said Keith as he headed to the pay phone to call and let his parents know the good news. Keith called the Plockton Inn and as luck would have it Anna was sitting reading in the bar when Wullie answered the phone. On speaking to her son and learning that all had gone well she gave out a deep sigh and burst into tears, tears of relief as she had been certain that Ruth would not come through all of this, not that she would ever have let Keith know that.

Keith asked his mother if they could all head home and if she personally could go and tell Lyn everything. Anna gasped as she too realized that no one had been in contact with Lyn. "Of course, I will go and see Lyn, we will leave first thing in the morning as it's already started to get dark."

"Thanks Mum," said Keith as he hung up the phone. Anna knew not to expect to see Keith that evening or the next morning as she knew he would be home late and away back to the hospital first thing. None of that matters. Ruth was going to be fine. The Vasillio's would all be together again soon.

Ruth's Recovery

Ruth stayed in hospital for six days following her surgery where slowly but surely, she started to remember who she was. She remembered parts of her life she would have preferred not to however she much preferred knowing everything as opposed to knowing nothing of her life. Keith stayed at the Plockton Inn despite Emily inviting him to stay at Woodland House. He visited Ruth every day and stayed until he was thrown out by the nurses. Emily visited for one hour each day as she respected that Ruth and Keith had a lot to talk about. The Vasillio's had gone home and Anna had told Lyn everything. Lyn was obviously upset at the whole situation however was only too pleased to hear that her granddaughter was well and truly on the mend. Keith kept them all updated daily, each day telling them that more and more memories were returning to Ruth. On day three Tony asked Keith to book a room at the Plockton Inn for Lyn as he was driving her up there the next morning now that Ruth was getting stronger.

Emily worried that Ruth would forget about the things they had discovered while being together in Woodland House but didn't want to bring it up as she couldn't risk upsetting Ruth, she needed her in her life. Three days after the operation Emily and Ruth were alone when Ruth decided to bring up the subject of Amelia. Emily was so excited that Ruth could remember everything and still wanted Emily to be part of her life. She wanted to grab hold of Ruth and hug her but didn't want to risk hurting her so jumped up and down with excitement instead.

Ruth laughed at the sight of Emily jumping up and down like a child, secretly wishing she could join her.

When Keith told Emily that Lyn was arriving the next morning Emily suggested that she stay at Woodland House. Keith didn't want to upset Emily however Lyn knew nothing about Emily or Ruth's experience regarding Emily and Woodland House. He decided to speak to Ruth and ask her opinion. "I will ask Ruth what she thinks and let you know." he said. Ruth thought it was a great idea, she fully intended telling her Nana everything and thought that if she stayed with Emily, it would give them a chance to get to know one another as Ruth had every intention of bringing Emily into her family no matter what anyone else thought. When Emily visited that afternoon, Ruth told her that she was going to tell her nana everything and said she would like her to be there with her. Emily agreed however suggested that Lyn have a couple of hours alone with Ruth first. Ruth was happy with that and agreed on a time for Emily to come in the next day. Before leaving Emily suggested that once Ruth was strong enough to leave hospital, she go and stay at Woodland House until she felt she had enough energy to face the journey home.

Ruth reached across and took Emily by the hand "I would love to, Emily, thank you." Emily felt like she was walking on air, she was just so happy. As Emily turned to leave Ruth pulled her back, "Emily, I want you to know that I consider you as family and never want to lose you from my life." Emily couldn't believe her ears, she had longed for Ruth to say something like this and finally she had. Emily knew there and then that she would never be alone again, she had a second chance to live the rest of her life happy.

Ruth's nana arrived the next day and was so happy to see

Ruth sitting up smiling as she walked into the ward. She hugged Ruth gently for fear of hurting her. Ruth squeezed her grandmother as hard as she could without causing herself pain. They both cried with relief that everything was going to be all right. They talked nonstop about everything that had happened to Ruth including Emily, the house, the feelings Ruth had experienced and finally Amelia. To Ruth's surprise Lyn looked at her and said "I'm not surprised in the slightest, I've always said that you were an old soul from the day you started to walk and talk." Ruth was delighted that her nana had taken everything so well and couldn't wait for her to meet Emily.

A few moments later Emily walked into the ward. Lyn immediately recognised her from the description Ruth had given her. Lyn put her hand out towards Emily "I just can't thank you enough for finding my Ruth. She has told me all about your past and I know it couldn't have been easy for you stopping to help Ruth let alone take her into your home." Emily blushed.

"Ruth has helped me so much, she helped me more than I helped her. I'm not sure how much she has told you, however prior to finding Ruth I hadn't spoken in fifty years. Now not only am I speaking, I'm living life again and that's all down to Ruth."

"It sounds like you both helped each other. I'm a great believer in fate and fate brought you both to the same path in order for you to meet. I honestly believe that especially given everything Ruth has explained about her visions in your home." Emily felt so relieved that Lyn believed in the afterlife and in reincarnation. She had been worried Lyn would think Ruth had been hypnotised or something. Life going forward would be so much easier given they all believed.

Lyn immediately took to Emily and agreed to go and stay at Woodland House with her until Ruth was strong enough to go home. Keith had also agreed that when Ruth was released from hospital it would be a good idea for them both to stay with Emily until Ruth felt strong enough to leave Plockton. Later that day Lyn went with Emily back to Woodland House where Keith met them for dinner. This gave them the opportunity to discuss Ruth and everything she had gone through before and after meeting Emily. The night turned into morning as they all chatted so comfortably.

The next few days passed quickly and before she knew it Ruth was packing up her things to leave the hospital. Keith was by her side helping her pull everything together. Emily and Lyn had remained at Woodland House preparing a welcome home dinner for Ruth. In the last few days Emily and Lyn had become pretty close. The one thing they had in common was their love for Ruth and their need for her to be happy.

Ruth and Keith arrived at Woodland House met by both ladies who had come running outside as soon as they heard the car pulling up. Lyn instantly pulled Ruth into her arms as soon as she stepped out of the car. Emily took a step back for fear of looking too eager to see Ruth. She didn't want Lyn to feel like she was treading on her toes, not now especially given the relationship they had built. Ruth walked up to Emily and hugged her tightly, Emily's heart felt as if it was about to burst out of her chest. It was at that moment she realised Ruth actually wanted her in her life and didn't feel pressured into staying at Woodland house.

As Ruth walked into Woodland House, she had a strange feeling knowing that both her lives were crossing over. Here she was with Emily, her mother from a past life and Lyn her grandmother from this life. It was a lot for her to take in but she knew that she needed to do this, she needed to spend time with both of these woman as she recovered from her surgery. Keith was just so happy to have Ruth out of the hospital and on the road to recovery that he would have agreed to almost anything.

Lyn had helped Emily get the house ready for Ruth returning from the hospital. They cleaned everything top to bottom to make sure there was no possible way that Ruth could pick up any infection. As for sleeping arrangements, Emily remained in the room she had been staying in. They changed the bedding and cleaned what had been Peter and Emily's room ready for Ruth and Keith, and Lyn was happy to sleep in Amelia's single bed in the small room. This meant that each of them had their own space to escape to if they felt the need given the complexity of the relationships.

Ruth was astonished at how clean the house was. She felt even more at home than she had the last time she was there. It just felt right that she should recover in Woodland House. Ruth's memory was coming back more and more, not only memories of her existing life but also memories of her past life as Amelia. It was comforting for Ruth to have Keith there to discuss her personal life, Lyn to discuss memories from her childhood and Emily to discuss and remember good times as her daughter. It was certainly a lot for Ruth's brain to handle however she seemed to be soaking it up and had never felt more content than she did at this moment in her life. As she remembered more and more about her present-day life, she began to wish that Anna, Tony and nonna would come up to Woodland House. She discussed the possibility with Keith who was really pleased that Ruth remembered how close they all were and had the need to have them around her as she recovered. Keith spoke to his parents later that day who were only too happy to learn that Ruth wanted to see them, they couldn't wait to see their son and daughter-in-law.

Keith agreed for them to come to Woodland House the next day. Emily was excited to be part of what seemed such a loving family and couldn't wait to welcome the others for dinner the following evening.

Keith met his parents and nonna the next afternoon at the Plockton Inn. Anna ran over to her son as soon as she set eyes on him, he grabbed her in a bear hug and swung her round while nonna and Tony watched laughing. He had a quick chat with Wullie bringing him up to date with Ruth's recovery then the Vasillio's all headed to Woodland House together.

Emily was nervous and excited at the same time, what if Keith's family didn't understand the connection between her and Ruth? What if they thought it was all nonsense, she would once again be alone, a stranger to those around her. Emily couldn't bear the thought of going back to having a life of silence. A life of nothingness, she couldn't lose Ruth, not now, not ever. However, she needn't have been worried as everyone took to her instantly. When they sat as a family having dinner it was Ruth who brought up the subject of Amelia. Up until that point the Vasillios had merely thought of Emily as a good Samaritan who had found and nursed Ruth in what was a terrible time for her. Tony sat in silence as he really didn't believe in anything that he couldn't 100% prove so just let everyone get on with it. Anna and nonna had been fascinated by the whole story and needed all the details which of course Emily and Ruth were only too happy to give them.

After dinner Tony and Keith went outside for a walk and a father son catch up as Tony was concerned for his son. "What do you make of all this Amelia, Ruth stuff?" Tony said to his son as they walked around the garden.

"To be honest Dad, I never really considered anything

remotely like this before. However, Ruth knows way too much about Amelia, Emily and Peter for it not to be true." Keith said to his father looking at him as he spoke. "I know it all sounds very weird however how could Ruth know so much about a family here in Plockton back in the 1930s when not only had she not yet been born, she had never been to Plockton? I have no option other than to believe my wife, Dad, unless you have another explanation?" said Keith.

Tony looked at his son with a concerned look on his face, "I just can't get my head around it, Keith, but just because I can't understand it, doesn't mean I won't respect Ruth and Emily. If they believe it and it makes them happy then so be it." Keith hugged his father, relieved that Tony was just going to go along with things despite his lack of belief.

The women chatted more about Ruth and the cross over between her prior life and her present life. Nonna and Anna were fascinated at the details Ruth was able to give of a life that once was her life. They loved the passion in Emily's voice as she spoke of Ruth/Amelia as her mother. It was certainly a much more loving upbringing than the one Ruth had endured in this life time. It was just so tragic that it ended when Amelia was so young. Emily had certainly gone through a lot losing her daughter then her husband and finally losing herself. It was fascinating that she had come across Ruth in the Woodlands and that she had actually saved her from the same death as Amelia and her mother. "Fate, definitely fate," said nonna in her attempt to speak English, as she got up, she walked over to Emily and hugged her. Emily was so pleased that this family had embraced her into their family fold. Emily felt she had been given a second chance to live the rest of her life with meaning. She refused to let herself think about Ruth and Keith leaving Woodland House as the thought was too upsetting. She would cross that bridge when the time came, until then she wanted to soak up the love that was present once again in the four walls of her home.

After a lovely few days, spending lots of time at Woodland House the Vasillio's headed home. They had agreed to spend Christmas together and promised to return on the 24th December. Keith, Ruth and Lyn would remain at Woodland House until the New Year.

.

Christmas

Ruth got stronger day by day and became much happier knowing that her both lives had crossed over and she had the ability to speak about both with love. She would sit with Emily and talk about Peter for hours on end then sit with Keith and talk about how they met and how their life had progressed. They would talk and talk but never once did Ruth discuss going home, it just wasn't on her agenda for now and Keith didn't want to risk upsetting her so had decided to allow Ruth to take the lead with regards to when they would discuss leaving Woodland House. In the meantime, he was happy doing odd jobs around the house and garden. Emily and Lyn had gone into Plockton to pick up paint as they had decided to freshen the house up for Christmas. Ruth was confined to the house and garden as she recovered from her surgery. The doctor had insisted she do nothing that would physically exert her until at least the end of January.

Soon it was Christmas Eve and the house looked the best it had in decades. It was all freshly painted and Emily and Lyn had even made Christmas decorations. Keith had gone into the woodlands and cut down a tree for Ruth to decorate as she had asked specifically if she could at least do that job, promising to take her time and not over exert herself. Everything looked perfect when finally, the car drew up outside and the Vasillio's descended upon Woodland House for a family Christmas. Everyone was on top form and excited to spend time together over the festive period.

Anna and nonna had gone shopping to make sure that everyone including Emily had a small gift to open on Christmas morning. Before leaving that evening to head back to Plockton Inn Anna popped all the presents under the tree with the clear instruction that no one should open their gift until after Christmas dinner. Ruth laughed at the look on Anna's face as she looked at Keith and said "Keith, I'm warning you, no peeking, no shaking, no nothing until after dinner when we are all together."

Keith smiled and hugged his mother "I promise," he said as Anna got in the car. Nonna winked at Keith as she too got into the car.

The next day the Vasillio's arrived at noon. Nonna and Anna had agreed to do most of the cooking given that Lyn needed to sit most of the time, Ruth wasn't to get overly excited and Emily hadn't cooked a Christmas dinner in forever. Emily was on table duty while Lyn kept Ruth company. Lyn was glad to have some time alone with her granddaughter as she hadn't spent time alone with her in such a long time. Lyn was concerned at the lack of conversation regarding Ruth's childhood as Ruth. She seemed to want to discuss her childhood as Amelia but didn't feel inclined to discuss her present life childhood memories. Lyn needed to ask the question, "Ruth, darling, do you remember your parents?"

Ruth looked at her Nana, "Yes, of course I do" she replied.

"It's just that you never seem to want to talk about them."

Ruth looked sad as she responded to her beloved Nana, "You know why nana, my life growing up was not the best. The only good memories I have are those spent with you. I don't like talking about my early days as it doesn't make me feel good. I only feel sad when I talk about my parents and my life growing up with them."

Lyn looked at her granddaughter "I'm trying to understand

Ruth as I know your childhood was far from perfect but to hear you talk about your life as a child with Emily as your mother breaks my heart. I see love all over your face when you talk. I would do anything for my son to have given you such loving memories. I know I can't change the past but surely there must be at least one thing from your childhood that brings a smile when you think about it?" Ruth sat silent for a few moments

"Nana," she said "I'm not going to lie to you as I love you too much for that. My childhood was terrible, I have NO good memories with my parents, NONE. I have lovely memories visiting you and I talk of those times often with love in my heart but I won't make up a memory of my parents to make you feel better. I'm not going to patronise you Nana."

Lyn had tears in her eyes as she turned to Ruth, "I'm so sorry my darling, I should have done more. I know your life was terrible, I should have taken you to live with me when you were a baby."

"Nana, you know they would never have allowed that. You did everything you could when you could and I will always be thankful that you are my Nana. I couldn't ask for a better nana. You have always done your best by me and have never made me feel anything other than loved. I adore you Nana always remember that."

Lyn looked across at Ruth with tears in her eyes "and I adore you, Ruth. All I want is for you to be happy and I guess seeing you here with all the love around you confirms that. I just wish things had been different."

"I know," Ruth replied. "Let's just live for the future, Nana, as I'm certain we are going to make lots of happy memories."

Soon they were all sitting at the table eating a delicious Christmas dinner. For the first time in a while Woodland House was once again silent, only this time it was a happy silence as everyone enjoyed their meal. Once dinner was over Anna said everyone could open their gifts. There was a loving chatter amongst them as they opened and discussed their individual gifts. The room was full of laughter and good cheer, just how it should be in a house like this on Christmas Day. Emily looked around the table, she was happier than she had been in forever, if only Peter was here.

Time for normality

A few days into the New Year Keith decided it was time to talk to Ruth about going home. He wasn't expecting her to leave that day or even the next, however felt it was time to agree on a date. He felt it was time to get back to work and some form of normality. Not just for his sake but also for Ruth. Thankfully Ruth was not surprised when he brought up the subject. He had been worried that perhaps it was too soon however to his surprise Ruth agreed that it was time to get back to normal. They couldn't just stay with Emily at Woodland House indefinitely, they both had jobs to get back to. Ruth said that she would talk to Emily later that evening, however would prefer to do it alone. Lyn was still living with them so Ruth informed Lyn that she was going to speak to Emily so could she please go to her room after dinner to allow Ruth time to talk with Emily alone. Lyn agreed as she also felt it was time she was heading home.

After dinner Ruth asked Emily to come sit with her in the lounge after the dishes were all cleared away. Lyn excused herself saying she wanted an early night, Keith said he had a bit of a headache so was also having an early night. Once Ruth and Emily were alone, Ruth began to talk, "You know how much I care for you Emily and how grateful I am that you found me and for all that you have done for me since that first day."

Emily looked at Ruth with sadness in her eyes as she guessed what Ruth was about to say. She always knew this day would come however had hoped it wouldn't be for another while.

"You're leaving, aren't you?"

"Sadly yes, it's time for me to get back to my life. I have a job and a house and people who care for me. I can't just stay here forever and forget about that life."

"I know," said Emily, "and I understand. I'm going to miss you that's all."

Ruth stood up and walked over to Emily. She knelt down on the floor by her side, "Listen to me Emily, I'm not leaving you. I'm going home but I will be back and you are welcome to come to stay with me anytime you want. My home is your home as you have made yours mine. We are family." Emily looked away from Ruth as she felt her eyes fill with tears. She didn't want to upset Ruth and tried so hard not to cry in front of her.

The harder she tried the more the tears came, Ruth pulled her close "I love you Mum," she whispered into Emily's ear.

Emily couldn't hold back any longer she hugged Ruth tightly as she sobbed, "and I love you little one, forever."

The next day would be Ruth's last spent together with Emily, Keith and Lyn at Woodland House for a while. She wanted to build as many memories of them together so planned the day starting with a family breakfast. Ruth made pancakes with Emily's help as Lyn prepared a large pot of tea. Keith just sat and watched as the women prepared everything around him. He was happy just to chill while everyone else sorted out his breakfast. The day started and ended with a lot of laughter. By the time everyone was ready for bed they all had sore ribs from laughing so much.

The next morning Ruth woke early. Keith had packed the car the night before to allow them to have a relaxing start to their day. Ruth showered and dressed then headed downstairs. As she walked through the kitchen door, she noticed that Emily was already sitting at the kitchen table. "Good morning," said Emily as Ruth pulled out a chair at the table.

"Good morning," Ruth replied. As always, the conversation between the two just flowed, there was never an awkward moment's silence. After a while Keith joined them followed closely by Lyn who had already been up and out before anyone woke. Lyn had gone for a walk around the garden taking in all it's beauty. Keith and Tony had really cleaned the garden up and had planted some beautiful flowers and bushes. Lyn was also sad to leave as she and Emily had grown very close and she loved Plockton, almost as much as Ruth. Not one of them had an appetite so no one had breakfast. Emily was adamant however that they needed to take some sandwiches for the journey and had prepared them earlier. She walked over to the fridge, reached in for the sandwiches and put them into a plastic bag ready for the journey. Saying goodbye was difficult for them all especially Ruth and Emily despite knowing it wasn't for long. Ruth cried so hard as she clung to Emily, "stay safe and remember I'm only a drive away. I love you." Emily didn't want to let go of Ruth, she wished she could have just another few days, however, in her heart she knew it would always be another few then another as it would never be enough. Emily pulled back and looked directly into Ruth's eyes, no words were needed, they both felt the connection and the pain of being parted. Keith walked around the car opening the door for Ruth. Once Ruth was in the car Keith hugged Emily and said he would bring Ruth back soon. Lyn had been first to say goodbye and was already in the car waiting to leave. The car pulled away as everyone waved goodbye leaving Emily all alone in the garden. Despite having lived a life of silence alone for decades she felt lost and alone. She had no idea what to do with herself as she walked back into the house.

Once inside she sat down and allowed herself to finally grieve for Peter and Amelia. Emily must have cried herself to sleep as when she woke it was dark outside. For the first time since Peter had taken his own life Emily felt peace. She had finally accepted that her life had changed and there was nothing she could do about it. Living alone in silence was no longer an option, Emily had felt her heart beat once again on finding Ruth, she had made the choice to live again and had no intention of turning back. Onwards and upwards, there was no other way. It was time for bed, and in the morning, she would start planning her trip to go see Ruth and Keith.

Emily's Visit

It had been six weeks since Ruth left Woodland House and Emily had been out and about every day talking with the locals and even having a drink in the Inn. It was so lovely for the older generation of Plockton to finally see Emily living her life again and enjoying herself. Ruth had agreed with Emily to call once a week. As Emily didn't have a phone, they had arranged for Ruth to call the Plockton Inn on a Sunday at three p.m. This was the sixth Sunday since Ruth left and Emily waited patiently in the Plockton Inn for the phone to ring. At exactly three p.m. on the dot the phone rang and as predicted Wullie called over to Emily, "Emily it's for you, it's Ruth."

Emily almost ran to the phone, Sunday was her favourite day as she knew she would be speaking to Ruth. "Hello little one, how are you today?" she said as she took the phone from Wullie. "I'm really good thanks, in fact I have some news for you," said Ruth.

"You do?"

"Yip I do, if you turn around and look at the door there will be a surprise there for you." Emily spun around almost knocking over Wullie as he was heading back behind the bar. To her surprise Keith was standing by the door. Emily squealed with excitement, she didn't know if she should run over and hug Keith or continue talking to Ruth, she was so confused.

Keith walked over and gave Emily a massive hug knocking the phone out of her hand "I'm here to take you for a little holiday. Ruth has arranged for you to stay with us for a couple of weeks so we'd better go and pick up your stuff."

Emily stood there silent; she was so happy. She quickly realised that she had dropped the phone and scrambled to pick it back up "Ruth, Ruth are you there? I'm on my way," she squealed as she hung up without even saying goodbye. Ruth was left hanging on the other end of the phone laughing at Emily's childlike excitement.

Emily skipped out to the car with Keith following close behind laughing at her enthusiasm. They headed to Woodland House where Emily quickly pulled together a few changes of clothes and some other bits and pieces for her stay with Ruth and Keith. Before Keith even had time to have a cup of tea Emily was ready to leave, "No time to waste," she said to Keith as she started walking out the front door. Keith just laughed and followed her back out to the car. Emily smiled for the entire journey, every time Keith looked at her she was staring straight ahead with a huge grin on her face. There was no hiding the fact that she was really excited to be going to see Ruth. It had only been six weeks since Ruth left Plockton however to Emily it may well have been six years as she had missed Ruth so much.

Before long Keith pulled up in front of the house. He parked the car and helped Emily with her bag. Ruth came running out to greet them as soon as she noticed the car pulling up. "Emily, I've missed you so much," said Ruth as she pulled Emily into her arms.

"I've missed you all so much too, especially you little one," she said in reply. "I can't believe it's only been six weeks since you left Plockton, it feels so much longer. How have things been?" she asked as Ruth let her go.

"Things have been marvellous for me since coming home.

Being back in this house has enabled me to remember so much more of my life. Also being back at work around my friends and colleagues, albeit only one day a week has been really good for me. That said I have really missed the tranquillity of Plockton, Woodland House and your company, hence the reason I sent Keith to pick you up. I hope you didn't feel pressured to come here?"

Emily looked at Ruth with a look of disbelief, "Pressured? No way, I prayed every day that you would invite me to come stay."

During the first few days of Emily's stay Ruth took her to visit Lyn and also the Vasillio's. Everyone made Emily feel so welcome, she was overwhelmed with their graciousness towards her. She really did feel part of their family, it was so lovely having that feeling of belonging again.

Ruth introduced Emily to her friends and colleagues as her aunt. They had decided between them that no one needed to know the truth as too many people would more than likely have a negative comment and both Emily and Ruth didn't want any negativity in their life that could potentially damage their relationship. They knew the truth and the people most important to them knew, so as far as they were concerned anyone that needed to know already did, no one else mattered.

For the first time in Emily's life, she found herself doing things she had never done before like going into a shopping centre, visiting the cinema, and going to McDonalds. Emily was amazed at all the things she hadn't known existed. She wished so much that Peter had been there to experience all these new things with her. She felt sad knowing the number of years she had wasted by locking herself away in the four walls of Woodland House. Time could not be turned back so there was no point in

Emily dwelling on what she had no power to change. She did however have the choice to live the rest of her life making sure she was happy and that is exactly what she was going to do.

At the end of her two-week visit, Emily had really enjoyed her visit and didn't want to leave. She knew however that she needed to allow Ruth and Keith to get on with their life as a newlywed couple. No one wanted a third wheel in those early years, as Emily remembers only too well. As she prepared to leave, she spoke to Ruth about future visits, "I would love it if I could come for a few days every couple of months. I would of course get a bus as I wouldn't want Keith driving all that way. I would also love it if you and the rest of the family would come to stay at Woodland House as often as you would like."

Ruth looked at Emily lovingly, "I would love you to visit often, and yes we will definitely be returning to Woodland House, all of us."

The journey back to Plockton was not a sad one as Emily knew she would be seeing Ruth again soon. Her life had changed so much over the last few months, she felt so grateful that she had found Ruth during one of her daily walks in the woodlands. Since that day, not so long ago the journey of her new life had begun and she never looked back.

Emily and Ruth had visited back and forth over the last year, taking turns. It became a regular part of their routines. Before long it was Christmas again and Emily had invited them all to spend Christmas once more in Woodland House. Only this year she had changed the house about a little to accommodate Tony, Anna and nonna as she wanted them all under the one roof. Emily had moved out of her room and made it up ready for Anna and Tony to use during their stay. She had also bought a cot bed from the general store which she had set up in a small room at the back of the house that she never used. It was more like a cupboard than a room but it did have a small window and the cot fitted nicely. It would be perfect for nonna during her stay. Emily herself would sleep on the sofa in the living room, this meant she could have her wish, all the family sleeping under the same roof over the festive period. Emily couldn't wait for their arrival, she had decorated the whole house with Christmas tinsel and had acquired a rather large tree which both John and Wullie had helped put up. She was ready, all she needed now was her family to arrive.

Christmas 1985

A whole year had passed since the family had been all together at Woodland House. Emily was all prepared when at last Ruth and Keith pulled up with Lyn in the back of the car. Tony was close behind with Anna and nonna. All back together for what was going to be the best Christmas ever.

It was Christmas Eve and everyone had settled into their rooms. Tony and Keith sat in the living room drinking beer while the women where in the kitchen getting started on the preparations for the next day. There was a lot of laughing going on in the kitchen. "I'm not sure they are getting much done through there with the amount of laughing going on," Keith said to his father. Tony just laughed as he was sure nonna would be making sure everything was perfect. Nonna always loved being in the kitchen, especially if she was cooking for the family. "Enjoy your beer son" said Tony as he sat back to enjoy his.

Once all the preparation for the Christmas dinner was done and everything cleared away the women joined Tony and Keith in the living room. Just as they sat down to relax, Keith suggested they should walk into Plockton and go to the Inn for a few drinks. It was cold outside but dry, a nice walk into town and a seat by the fire at the inn would be a lovely start to their Christmas celebrations. Everyone quickly agreed and went to get their coats, all except Ruth who had gone upstairs straight from the kitchen. "Ruth darling, grab your coat, we are all going to walk into Plockton for a few Christmas drinks."

Ruth had gone to get a gift that she had made especially for Emily. "Can you all go ahead, except Emily, can you ask her to wait for me," Ruth shouted down the stairs.

"Okay love, but don't be long, we will start a slow walk." Ruth appreciated that Keith had listened to her and asked Emily to wait while the rest of them carried on into Plockton. She had been worried that he would be paranoid letting her walk in the woodlands again without him.

Emily waited patiently downstairs while Ruth rummaged through her bag looking for the gift she had made Emily. Finally, she found it and headed downstairs. Emily was sitting waiting in the living room wondering why Ruth wanted them to be alone as Ruth walked in. "I made this gift for you Emily. I hope you like it and are not annoyed with me."

Emily looked at Ruth and repeated, "Annoyed with you, why would I be annoyed at you making something for me?"

"Just open it and you will see." Ruth said nervously.

Emily pulled the wrapping paper from the gift and immediately started to cry. "I hope those are happy tears?" said Ruth.

Emily looked at her with her mouth wide open, "Oh Ruth, thank you so much it's beautiful." In her hand she held a photo frame and in the frame was a photo of Amelia as a baby that Ruth had taken from one of the albums Emily had shown her earlier in the year. Next to that photo was one of Ruth as a baby. "I hope you're not angry at me for taking the photo of me/Amelia as a baby from one of your albums. I only did it so that I could make you this gift for Christmas."

Emily looked at Ruth with love in her eyes "Little one, I could never be angry with you. I love you, I love this. I will treasure it and take it with me everywhere I go." Ruth was delighted, she definitely got the reaction she had hoped for.

Ruth and Emily soon caught up with the others. They all laughed at Lyn being pushed in a wheelchair by Tony on two wheels. Lyn screamed as Tony kept tipping her back and running ahead with her. The others following behind making all sorts of jokes about poor Lyn and her recently acquired wheels. Ruth loved being wrapped up in the middle of such a loving family. Life couldn't get much better, especially now with the news that Keith and Ruth had up their sleeve. Ruth wasn't sure she could keep quiet much longer.

Plockton Inn was busy with all the locals. They were all pleased to see Emily as she walked in with the others. Small places like Plockton rarely embrace strangers into their fold however this lot had happily accepted Emily's new found family as locals since they had brought Emily back to them. Tony parked Lyn in her wheelchair by the fire, one of the local lads got off his seat and offered it to nonna so that she could sit with Lyn. Tony ordered a round of drinks, beer for him and Keith and wine for the ladies. Keith looked at Ruth who had already prepared for this moment. She nodded at him as if to say, "I've got it covered."

Wullie put the Christmas tunes on and the party at the Plockton Inn began. Everyone was in the party spirit and sang along to the Christmas songs as they belted out the speakers behind the bar. At one point Edna from the general store tried to climb up on the bar, luckily John spotted her and whisked her off her feet for a dance. Given the small amount of space in the bar dancing room was minimal however John and Edna gave it their best shot. Emily had never seen Edna drunk like this and couldn't stop laughing. It was so good being part of the community once again. Too many wasted years...

On Christmas morning everyone was woken up by the sound of Christmas songs playing loudly down in the kitchen. Emily and nonna were already up and were in the kitchen preparing breakfast for everyone. Bacon and eggs all round with freshly made bread and butter. The smell soon made its way up the stairs and before long everyone was gathered in the kitchen waiting for their breakfast.

They all had the most amazing day as a family, the dinner was perfect the weather outside was beautiful albeit cold, everything was just as they had all hoped. With all the dinner dishes cleared away and everyone sat relaxed in the living room it was time to exchange gifts. Keith had always handed the gifts out from under the tree and this year was no different. Soon there was wrapping paper everywhere and people thanking each other for their lovely gifts when Anna suddenly stopped and said "wait a minute, there are still some gifts under the tree."

Keith looked at his mother and said, "Yes there is one for each of you from Ruth and me, however we wanted to wait until everyone had opened all their other gifts first. We want everyone to open their gift from us at the same time." Anna looked from her son to Ruth and back again with a questioning look on her face. Ruth started to giggle as Keith nervously picked out the remaining gifts and handed them to each person one by one. I'm not sure nonna even knew what was happening as she had polished off a good few wines with the Christmas dinner.

Ruth and Keith stood together holding hands as they asked everyone to please open their gifts. Suddenly Anna screamed as her package was ripped open enthusiastically "I knew it! I knew it!" she screamed as Lyn and nonna struggled to open their packages. In each package there was a tiny pair of white booties, Ruth and Keith were going to be parents. This was their

Christmas gift to their family.

After all the kissing, cuddling and congratulations suddenly Tony looked at Ruth and said "wait a minute, you were drinking wine in the bar last night. Is that not bad for the baby?" Ruth smiled as she told everyone how Wullie was in on the surprise and she had been drinking fizzy water.

Anna laughed and said, "I had my suspicions until I saw what I thought was you drinking wine, ha ha I should have known you would have covered your back." She couldn't stop smiling, her face was beginning to hurt as she just couldn't stop herself, she had a permanent smile on her face, she was going to be a grandmother.

Everyone was so excited that no one had noticed Emily had left the room. It wasn't until Ruth looked over to where Emily had been sitting that she noticed she was missing. Ruth looked at Keith "Where is Emily?" suddenly everyone stopped and looked at the empty seat. Ruth immediately left the room in search of Emily. She was so worried that the surprise had been too much for her. Ruth was kicking herself as she started to imagine all sorts of memories being dredged up for poor Emily.

Keith had followed Ruth, "I'm sure she's fine Darling she may have gone to the bathroom," but Ruth wasn't convinced. The song that had been playing in the background finished and before the next one began there was a moment's' silence. It was then that Ruth could hear Emily moving about in the kitchen.

Ruth could see she had been crying as she walked up to her "Oh Emily, I feel so selfish. I should have thought about your feelings and the memories all of this must have dredged up for you."

Emily looked at Ruth with a shocked look on her face "No, no little one, I couldn't be happier. I left the room as I felt it wasn't my place to be there."

Ruth was speechless for a moment, "Wasn't your place? Why? What do you mean?" Emily looked at Ruth and Keith as they both stood looking at her for some sort of explanation to help them understand what she meant.

"Anna and Tony are going to be grandparents, Lyn and nonna are going to be great grandmothers, you are both going to be parents. So, you see it was a moment for all of you to share."

Both Ruth and Keith started to talk at once, Keith stopped and let Ruth continue as it was clear they were both on the same page. "Oh Emily, my darling Emily, you are also going to be a grandmother, yes, maybe not in the conventional way but to Keith and me it makes no difference. We adore you, we all do and no one in this house thinks of you any differently to how we all think and feel about each other. Emily you are one of us, part of this family. I thought you knew that."

Emily looked up to see tears falling from Ruth eyes, "Please don't cry little one," she said.

"Then please accept that you are family and my, our child, needs you in their life, just like he or she is going to need the rest of us. Keith and I, well we can't do this alone." Emily hugged Ruth, Keith hugged them both and they all laughed.

"Okay," said Emily, "let's celebrate." Just at that she turned to walk out of the kitchen as the others were making their way over to join in the group hug. Life couldn't get any better.

January 2nd 1986

It was January 2nd and the festivities were over for another year. Everyone had enjoyed Christmas and New Year together as a family. Unfortunately, the reality of life must take over and the festivities soon become a distant memory.

The plan was for everyone to leave on the 3rd January as Ruth was due back to full time work on Monday, January 6th. Tony and Keith worked together to take down all the decorations and the tree so that Emily would be left with a tidy house. Ruth and Anna packed up their stuff ready to leave the next morning while Lyn and nonna sat drinking tea with Emily chatting in broken English mixed with quite a lot of Italian that neither Lyn nor Emily fully understood. The buzz in the house was electric as everyone chatted together while going about their business.

As this was their last day together as a family for a while Tony wanted to treat everyone to a meal in the Plockton Inn which he had pre-booked with Wullie on Hogmanay. It was his way of saying thank you to Emily for her hospitality and a way of celebrating the news of Ruth and Keith's pregnancy. The meal was booked for six p.m. so they had all day to relax once they had all the decorations down and the packing done.

Ruth wanted to go for a walk in the woodlands with Emily to spend some quality time one on one before leaving the next day. It wasn't going to be so easy for Ruth to visit as often given she was returning to work full time. Emily loved spending time with everyone but the prospect of time alone with Ruth excited her. It had been a while since they had time alone as usually Keith would be with them.

Emily and Ruth set off straight after lunch at twelve thirty. Emily wanted to take Ruth the last walk she had taken Amelia on the day she collapsed. She felt strong enough now and wanted more than anything to walk the path with Ruth. As they approached the big oak tree Ruth suddenly had the strangest feeling in the pit of her stomach. She stopped suddenly, turned to look at Emily, "Mummy, you and daddy gave me the best life. You laughed with me every day, read stories, played in the snow, the rain and kicked leaves in this very spot so many times. My short life was perfect, never forget that Mummy, never." said Ruth, once again in the strange voice she had used on the day she lay on Amelia's bed. Only this time Emily wasn't upset, she didn't scream at Ruth, she hugged her and they cried together.

Ruth had to sit down as suddenly she felt drained. She needed a few minutes to get her breath back. Emily was only too happy to sit for a while as she wasn't as young as she used to be and the walk had taken it out of her. They sat in silence for a few moments, Emily remembering the precious moments spent here with Amelia and Ruth reflecting on everything that had happened since they met. Their relationship was certainly different from most however they both loved each other very much and really enjoyed spending time together especially outside in the Woodlands.

Finally, after twenty minutes or so Ruth and Emily decided it was time to head back to Woodland House to relax for a while before getting ready to go out for their farewell dinner as a family. They walked back to the house holding hands, chatting and laughing together, both feeling happy and content with life. "I'm looking forward to when the baby arrives and we can bring him or her on this very walk," said Ruth. Emily smiled despite knowing it would never happen.

It was a quiet afternoon for all the family, the festivities had certainly taken it out of them. However, at 5five thirty p.m. they all showed up downstairs ready to set off into Plockton for a nice family meal. Everyone was in good spirits and looked forward to a pleasant evening in the Plockton Inn. The Inn was busy as usual however Wullie had set up a lovely table in the back corner for Tony and the family to enjoy their meal. Tony thanked Wullie for the effort he had put into setting the table as it looked amazing, even nonna approved and that was something. Wullie smiled at Tony, "my pleasure Tony, you know me, only too happy to help a fellow out with a wee surprise." Tony laughed as they all took their seats at the table. Wullie handed them menus before taking the drink orders. He left them to look over the menu while he arranged the drinks for them. Before long everyone was eating their meal of choice and the chatter around the table was loud and full of laughter. There was no denying the love around this table.

They all arrived back at Woodland House after a very enjoyable evening. Nonna and Lyn both said goodnight and went straight up to bed. Tony, Anna Keith and Emily had a nightcap while Ruth had a hot chocolate. The evening had finished off what had been an amazing family Christmas and New Year, life was good.

The next morning Keith woke early, it was only six fifteen a.m. so he decided to leave Ruth asleep as she needed her rest, especially now that she was pregnant. He knew that Emily would be in the kitchen making coffee as it was her daily routine to get up at six a.m. and put on fresh coffee before the others got up. Keith crept out of the bedroom quietly as he didn't want to disturb Ruth. He made his way down to the kitchen however was a little confused as there was no smell of freshly brewed coffee and no sound of anyone moving around. Perhaps Emily had decided to sleep late this morning, he thought as he walked into the kitchen. Keith knew that Emily liked to be the one to make the morning coffee however decided it would do no harm for him to do it this morning given that Emily had decided to sleep in. Soon the smell of fresh coffee filled the air, Emily will come through any moment now, I just hope she's not upset at me for making the coffee he thought. Five minutes passed, ten minutes, still no Emily. Keith waited another five minutes then thought he would go and peek in the living room as perhaps Emily had gone for an early morning walk. Keith stuck his head around the door and could see that Emily was still asleep. He didn't want to disturb her as she never slept late so he went back to the kitchen to drink his coffee.

When Ruth finally woke, she could hear muffled voices coming from downstairs. She jumped out of bed assuming she had slept late and was worried that everyone would be waiting on her. However, when she looked at the clock it was only seven thirty a.m., she knew Nana never got up before eight a.m. so knew there was no rush. Ruth was going to jump in the shower before dressing and heading down for breakfast now she knew she had time. As she walked out of her room and started to walk towards the bathroom, she heard a loud scream coming from downstairs. The scream startled her, so much so she dropped her wash bag which clattered off the floor waking Nana who came rushing out of her room. "What happened?" said Nana to Ruth as she saw the back of her disappear down the stairs. Nana realised something was wrong and followed Ruth down the stairs. As Ruth reached the doorway of the living room, she saw Anna standing over Emily with her hands up at her mouth. Tony was doing CPR on Emily while Keith had jumped in the car to go fetch the doctor.

Ruth ran over to Emily "No, no, no please no," she screamed as she dropped to the floor next to the sofa that Emily was lying on. Tony finally stopped trying to bring her back, there was no hope, Emily was gone.

Anna knelt down behind Ruth and put her arms around her to try to comfort her. "She's gone, Darling, I'm so sorry, Tony tried his best, however, she must have already been dead," said Anna as she put her arms around Ruth. Ruth pushed Anna off, she jumped up and started to push down on Emily's chest sobbing as she did so, "Emily please, no, mamma, no please don't leave me, not now, I need you more than ever, please, please, someone help her," screamed Ruth as she looked around at the others.

"She's gone Ruth, there is nothing more we can do, I'm so deeply sorry," said Tony as he walked towards Ruth with open arms. Ruth pushed past him and ran out the front door. She ran and ran crying and screaming as she ran, she had no idea what she was doing or where she was running to she just knew she needed to get away, away from Emily's lifeless body. She couldn't bear to see her lying there with no breath left in her lungs, no voice, no heart beating. Ruth couldn't bear it, she just kept running. Suddenly she found herself at the large oak tree, she flung herself to the ground and just sobbed.

Keith ran into the doctor's surgery shouting "Help, help it's Emily she's not breathing." Dr Henderson heard the commotion and asked his patient to excuse him for a moment.

"Keith, please follow me."

"You need to come now, Doctor, Emily needs you urgently." Dr Henderson looked at Keith with pity in his eyes, "Keith she will be gone by the time we get there, please come into this office so I can explain in private." Keith was confused, he heard the doctor loud and clear however didn't understand how he could be sure that Emily would be gone. Keith followed Doctor Dobbin into the office. "Please take a seat," he said as he motioned to the seat at the opposite side of the room. "Emily came to me a couple of months ago. She had been suffering pain for quite some time so we ran some blood tests. I suspected that she had cancer and it was confirmed when her test results came back. She refused all treatment saying she wanted the last of her life to be spent happily with the people she loved the most. I told her she would be lucky to see in the New Year however she wanted to take her chances. So you see Keith, Emily chose to die her way. If she had taken chemotherapy, it would have made her very ill and potentially only given her another couple of months. There was no saving her Keith, she had a stage four aggressive cancer. She was better to enjoy what time she had left."

Keith looked at the Doctor with sadness in his eyes when suddenly he jumped up, "Ruth, oh my god, Ruth, I need to get back to her.

Dr Henderson asked Keith to wait a few seconds as Emily had left a letter for him to give to Ruth when the time came. Keith followed the doctor out into the waiting room while he pulled out Emily's file which contained the letter addressed to Ruth. He passed the letter to Keith and said, "I will follow you back to Woodland House once I finish with my patient who is mid-consultation. I need to come and pronounce Emily dead then arrange for the undertakers to come and pick her up. Emily didn't leave any lose ends, she made sure everything was taken care of to spare Ruth any additional pain. Keith thanked the doctor as he walked out of the surgery eager to get back to his wife.

When Keith arrived back at the house Tony informed him

about Ruth, her reaction to Emily's death and subsequent running out of the house. Keith knew exactly where to find her, he headed straight for the large oak tree. He could see Ruth perched up against the tree sobbing as he approached. She looked up and as soon as she saw Keith she ran into his arms "Keith, Emily is gone, she's dead." she sobbed.

"I know Darling, I know, I've just been to see the doctor. He will be at the house soon to sign her death certificate and allow the undertakers to take her."

"No, they can't, I haven't said goodbye, Keith don't let anyone take her, I need to see her," she screamed at Keith.

"Ruth, we need to head back now if you want to say goodbye to Emily" Keith said as he embraced his wife. Keith explained everything to Ruth as they walked back to Woodland House, however he wasn't sure how much of what he said had been taken in by Ruth. He decided just to walk the rest of the way in silence, he could explain it all to her later after she had said her goodbyes to Emily.

They reached Woodland House just as Doctor Dobbins' car was pulling up. "I'm so deeply sorry for your loss Ruth" said the Doctor as he followed Keith and her into the house. Emily was still in the same position as no one wanted to move her. Tony had considered taking her into the bedroom however Anna had objected, she was afraid to move her just in case it caused issues later when the doctor arrived. The Doctor walked into the living room assuring Ruth that she could take her time to say goodbye once he had examined Emily and officially pronounced her dead. Ruth waited by the door while Dr Henderson did what he had to do. As soon as he was finished Ruth ran over to Emily throwing herself on the floor next to her. She put her head on Emily's chest and sobbed. Keith didn't know what to do, he had no idea how to comfort his wife. He had never seen Ruth so upset, not even when her parents died, nor when she finally had grieved for them. The way she was with Emily was something Keith had not expected. Dr Henderson signed the death certificate and handed it to Keith "Just be there and allow her to do what it is she needs to do until she is ready. There is no rush to call the undertakers, give Ruth some time." Keith thanked Doctor Dobbin and he showed him out to his car. "Thank you, Doctor, for everything."

Keith and the others left Ruth alone with Emily. It broke Lyn's heart to see her granddaughter so upset however she knew her well enough to give her space. Lyn would be there for her if and when Ruth decided she wanted her. Keith explained everything to his parents, nonna and Lyn that Doctor Dobbin had told him back at the surgery. Everyone was in shock, not one of them had suspected that Emily had been ill, she had hidden it very well.

After what seemed like forever, probably about an hour, Ruth appeared in the kitchen. "It's time," she said as the tears rolled down her face, "It's time to call the undertakers."

Anna walked across to Ruth and put her hand on her arm "I'll deal with it, Darling," she then looked at her son. "Take Ruth upstairs Keith, she will need to rest." Keith nodded and helped Ruth up to her bedroom. She lay on the bed and sobbed until finally she drifted off to sleep. Keith had lay on the bed just holding her while she cried. Now that she was asleep, he thought he had better go down stairs to see what was happening. Anna had called the undertakers and they had been and taken Emily to the morgue. The undertaker informed Anna before leaving that Emily had made plans for her funeral and paid for it. The only detail left to deal with was a date and time. The one thing Emily could not take control of, however she would have if she could have. The last thing Emily wanted was to leave any of her loved ones, especially Ruth, with a funeral to plan.

Keith went into Plockton firstly to inform all the locals, especially Edna, of Emily's death. As he had guessed, word had already spread. He then went to the Inn to use their phone, he contacted Ruth's boss to explain what had happened and to inform him that Ruth would obviously not be returning to work. Her boss was extremely compassionate and told Keith that Ruth could have as much time as she needed. Keith then proceeded to deal with his own boss, who sadly wasn't quite so compassionate. Keith was left feeling so angry when he finally got off the phone to his boss. He couldn't believe how cold his boss had been considering he knew everything that Keith had gone through with Ruth the year before. John was at the bar and had heard the conversation, "Don't let your boss bother you mate, just forget about him and focus on the family. Let me know if there is anything we can do to help."

"Thanks," said Keith as he turned to leave.

Wullie called him back. "Keith, mate, it goes without saying that we are all sorry for your loss as a family and I just want to say that we will put on a wake for Emily as a way of celebrating her life. Just let us know what date and time the funeral is and we will organise the wake." Keith was blown away by the kindness shown by the locals of Plockton.

"Thanks, all of you, thanks for everything," said Keith as he left to head back to Woodland House.

When Keith arrived back at the house Ruth was awake, she was sitting drinking coffee with Lyn while Anna dealt with all the funeral arrangements and nonna made some food for everyone. He walked into the living room and sat next to his wife. Ruth snuggled into his shoulder and just held his arm as if she never wanted to let go. Keith sat silently allowing Ruth to just snuggle with no need to talk. After a while Keith remembered the letter Dr Henderson had given him, it was in the kitchen on the dining table. Keith sat forward, "Ruth, darling, Doctor Dobbin gave me a letter this morning when I went to his surgery. It's a letter that Emily wrote when she realised, she was dying. She gave it to Doctor Dobbin with the strict instruction to give it to you on her death." Ruth took a deep breath and tried to talk however all that came out of her mouth was a sob.

"Shall I go get it for you?" said Lyn. Ruth nodded at her nana who then got up and went to fetch the letter. Ruth remained snuggled up to Keith afraid that she would fall to pieces if she let go.

Lyn came back with the letter in her hand. It was in an A4 brown envelope with Ruth Vasillio written on the front. Lyn tried to hand the envelope to Ruth however she was shaking uncontrollably and just shook her head. Keith looked up and took the envelope from Lyn. "Do you want me to read the letter to you Ruth?" he asked. Ruth nodded at Keith as if to say, yes go ahead. When Keith opened the envelope there were a further two envelopes inside, one addressed to Ruth and the other addressed to MY FAMILY.

Keith looked at Lyn, "Can you please go and ask my parents and nonna to come into the living room?" Without hesitation Lyn went to fetch the others. Once everyone was sitting Keith began to read the letter addressed to them all.

"To my beautiful family,

If you are reading this letter, then I am already gone. It breaks my heart to leave you all, you have become so important to me, each and every one of you. You have given me something I thought I would never have again, a reason to be happy. I spent too long in my own bubble locked away from the world, locked away from life. One by one you came into my life and showed me that there was happiness in the world. I thought I would never feel alive again but I did, albeit for only a while. I need you all to know that no matter how long it was you all made me feel a life time's worth of love. I made peace with myself, I accepted the wrong decisions I made over my lifetime and put them behind me. I can now move on to the afterlife knowing I die happy. The only regrets I have is that I didn't meet you all sooner and I will never have the opportunity to meet our new arrival. All I ask of you is that you look after one another, cherish every day and do not let Ruth forget me.

Love to you all from the bottom of my heart,

Emily.

Keith struggled to read the letter without crying and by the time he was finished there was not a dry eye in the room. It was Anna who managed to speak first "I hope she knew that we all felt the same way about her, she was an amazing person with a huge heart and I for one will never ever forget her."

Keith looked at his wife "Ruth do you want me to read your letter in private?" he asked.

"No, I want us to be all together while you read it." Keith tore open the second envelope to find not only a hand written letter but also an official letter, Emily's will. He looked around him, "Emily's will" he said with a shocked expression on his face. Ruth looked at her husband "Why would Emily's will be in with a letter to me?"

"I guess she wanted you to read it first," replied Keith.

"What do you want me to do Ruth?" he asked, looking questioningly at Ruth.

"Read the will first," said Ruth.

Keith read through the will quickly, there wasn't much to read. Emily had left everything to Ruth, Woodland House, all her possession's and any money Emily had. Ruth looked shocked, she hadn't expected that at all. "I don't know what I expected, but it certainly wasn't this," said Ruth looking around her.

Tony smiled "Who else would she leave her estate to Ruth?"

"I guess I just hadn't thought about it," she replied. Ruth looked at Keith trying to take in the fact that they had just inherited Woodland House. "Keith, this house is ours, all of it."

"Emily clearly loved you very much Ruth and to be honest, Dad's right, who else would she leave it to?"

Ruth just kept saying, "it's all ours, it's all ours. But without her what's the point?"

Anna looked at Ruth, "The point is, Ruth, that Emily was happy that you brought this house alive again. Leaving it to you was her way of making sure it never fell silent again."

Ruth cried hard wishing Emily was still there. Anna asked Ruth if she wanted to take a break to digest the will before Keith carried on and read the letter Emily had written to her. "No, carry on Keith, read the letter please," she replied through her tears. Keith nervously unfolded the handwritten letter addressed to Ruth.

My beautiful little one,

If you are reading this then I am gone. Please do not be sad as I had accepted it was my time. You gave me so much love over the past year, enough to make up for a life time of love lost after losing Amelia and Peter. You came into my life out of nowhere, and brought me back from the dead, I may have been breathing but I wasn't living. I had given up that luxury many years before when it had been taken from Amelia and then Peter. I believe it was fate that brought you to Plockton and into my life. I never expected to feel alive ever again or to love someone but believe me Ruth, I loved you with every breath I had in me. That day that you told us as a family that you and Keith were going to become parents was one of the happiest, yet saddest, days of my life. I left the room and told you it was because it wasn't my place to be part of the celebration, that was a lie. I only said that, as I didn't want to tell you the real reason I left the room. I left because I knew I would not be alive to welcome your little one into the world and that thought devastated me, I needed time alone to digest and accept that. One thing I do know is that your baby will be loved and cherished like no other. Knowing that makes me happy and makes the fact that I won't be there more palatable. Anyway, my little one I just needed to explain that to you.

By now you will know that I have left Woodland House to you and I hope you can someday live there with Keith and the baby. I know you have a home and a job that are important to you and I don't expect you to give that life up, I just want you to have options. Amelia loved Woodland House and the surroundings so much and I know you feel the same. It would be my dream for you to bring up your children there but the choice must be yours. All I ask is that you keep the love in those four walls, part time, full time it doesn't matter. You brought the house back to life when you arrived and the good times shared with the family there over the past year have enabled me to go in peace. I love you, my Darling, be happy and look after your beautiful child. I will watch over you both and try to keep you safe.

Until we meet again

Emily (Mum)

Leaving Woodland House

Ruth, Keith and the family stayed at Woodland House until after the funeral. Emily was given a beautiful send off, the whole of Plockton turned up, old and young. The wake in the Plockton Inn was full of chatter, lots of laughter and memories of Emily as a child, teenager and mother. There was no talk about the silent years as there was nothing to say that would bring happiness. There was however a lot of talk about the last year and how Emily had thrived when Ruth came into her life.

Edna and all the older locals who had known Emily since childhood were so happy to learn that Woodland House had been left to Ruth. They had taken to her and Keith as if they had been born in Plockton and been part of their community since. Alice, the 'gossip of Plockton' wondered what Ruth's intentions were with regards to Woodland House. Most people would just leave well alone and wait and see what happens but not Alice, she went right up to Ruth during the wake, "Ruth are you going to stay on in Plockton and live in Woodland House?" she asked.

That was the last thing Ruth had expected to hear, who thinks about something like that at a wake? Emily had told Ruth about Alice and how much she loved to gossip so Ruth, despite not expecting the question was not surprised by it. "We have no idea what we are going to do, Alice. At the moment our only concern is giving Emily the best send-off possible then allowing time to grieve for her." Alice just smiled and walked away, she had not heard the response she wanted but she had quickly learnt that

Ruth was very much like Emily and didn't like to be put on the spot.

The next day The Vasillio's left Plockton taking Lyn with them. Ruth and Keith had to stay another few days to allow Ruth time to tie up some lose ends regarding the transfer of the Woodland House title from Emily Wilson to Ruth Vasillio. Given that the will was freshly signed and straight forward there was no hold up, everything went smoothly and Ruth soon became the soul owner of Woodland House and all it contained. Ruth had wanted the title to be transferred into joint names, her and Keith, however, given that the will named only Ruth, it was not possible. This was something Ruth could have changed in the future if she wished to.

Now that all paperwork was complete Ruth and Keith could leave Plockton, however before leaving Ruth wanted to take some time to go through all of the personal possession's belonging to Emily, Peter and Amelia. She understood the pressure being put on Keith by his boss so suggested he return home alone and go back to work. She was going to take a week or so to herself and go through the house room by room. Keith was a little anxious at first however knew there was no point trying to change Ruth's mind, once she decided on something there was no budging her. He made her promise not to do any heavy lifting and to get plenty of rest as he packed up the car ready to head off. Ruth promised that she would be sensible and said that she would call him in a few days. They kissed goodbye and Keith drove away waving frantically in the rear-view mirror at his wife. Ruth went indoors closing and locking the door behind her.

Ten days after leaving Keith returned to Plockton to pick up Ruth who had packed up all the possessions that she wanted to keep that had belonged to Emily, Peter and Amelia. Keith helped her store them away in the attic of Woodland House. The rest she had boxed up to either go to charity or the bin. Together they packed up the car and set off to say their goodbyes to the locals, hand in the goods to the local charity shop and dispose of the boxes to be binned.

It was with a heavy heart that Ruth left Plockton that day as she had no idea when she would return, however return she would.

The New Arrival

It was 26th May 1986 when Ruth felt the contractions start. The baby wasn't due for another week however Ruth knew in her heart that today was the day. She called Keith at work to give him a heads up that her contractions had started. She told him not to rush home as first babies usually take forever. Her words however, fell on deaf ears as Keith burst through the front door fifteen minutes later. "The bag's in the car" he shouted without realising how loud his voice was. Ruth just about jumped out her skin as she hadn't expected him home so soon never mind bursting through the door shouting about the bag.

"Calm down, Keith, I could be here for hours," she said as he flapped around. Keith was flushed and didn't quite know what to do with himself. "Either go back to work or go do something as I'm nowhere near ready to go to the hospital, Keith, and you flapping around is driving me crazy."

Keith looked hurt, however did as he was asked and went into the kitchen to make a cup of tea. Ruth had been preparing the babies room and decided she wanted to continue. She was in there for a good few hours, however, every time Keith popped his head around the door she gave him the look and he immediately knew to leave her alone. He called his mother to let her know what was happening and to ask her advice. "Leave her alone son, trust me, take her lead, she will let you know when she is ready to go to the hospital," she said as calmly as possible despite being super excited at the thought of her grandchild being born. Keith listened to his mother and left Ruth to get on with it knowing that she knew he was there if needed.

Keith had nodded off in front of the TV, Ruth walked into the living room startling him. "My waters have broken, Keith, and my contractions are getting stronger. I think it's time to head to the hospital."

Keith jumped up, "How far apart are they?" he asked.

Ruth burst out laughing, "every four or five minutes," she replied.

"I certainly didn't expect you to ask that!" she said giggling to herself. As they got ready to leave the contractions became much stronger and closer together. Keith helped Ruth into the car trying not to irritate her when a contraction came as she was clearly in a lot of pain. Soon they were on their way to the hospital about to become parents, they were both really excited at the prospect of seeing their child for the first time.

Ruth had been in labour for eight hours however she had still not dilated enough despite the contractions being pretty strong. She needed to be at least five cm before they would consider taking her to the labour suite but she was only four cm. Keith could see that Ruth was tired and felt helpless knowing there was nothing he could do to help. He had quickly learnt not to speak to her unless he wanted to be screamed at. He just rubbed her back and hoped that it was at least giving her some sort of comfort. After another hour Ruth was six cm dilated and ready to go to the labour suite. Keith followed the midwife as she pushed Ruth on the gurney into a small room that was one of the labour suites. He looked around and saw the tiny plastic box on wheels that was obviously for the baby. His stomach was in knots he was so nervous and excited at the same time. He felt guilty as he looked at Ruth lying on the gurney having contraction after contraction but nothing could take away his excitement at seeing his child being born even if it did mean seeing Ruth in so much pain.

The midwife quickly examined Ruth and said it would be another hour or so. By this time Ruth was exhausted and wasn't sure she had enough strength to carry on. "I want the baby out Keith, I can't keep doing this I'm in so much pain and I'm so tired."

Keith felt really sorry for his poor wife, just as he was about to say something Ruth screamed, "Emily please help me get the baby out. If you are there, help me, please." Suddenly Keith looked down and he could see the baby's head. "I need to push," said Ruth. Keith ran to the door shouting for the midwife. As the midwife entered the room, she could clearly see that ready or not this baby was being born. Keith stood with his mouth wide open he just couldn't believe what he was seeing. His child, their child, was entering the world in front of his eyes. He had never experienced anything like it, it was amazing how the head popped out and despite still being inside Ruth he could see his child's face with the eyes wide open.

"Oh my god, Ruth, our baby is looking at me," he shouted. Ruth gave one final almighty push and the baby was out. The midwife quickly put the baby on to Ruth's bare chest still covered in blood with the umbilical cord still attached. You have a beautiful baby girl she said as she turned to Keith and asked if he wanted to cut the cord. Keith was shaking and quickly declined cutting the cord for fear of doing it wrong and harming the baby.

"It's okay" said the midwife "You can't hurt the baby, or Ruth." She handed Keith the scissors and without taking any time to think about it he leaned forward and cut the cord.

The midwife took the baby from Ruth to clean her up and get measurements and weight for her records. Keith stood staring at the baby while the midwife did what she had to do. Finally, once the midwife was finished, she wrapped the baby in a blanket and handed her to her daddy. Their daughter was 8lb 2oz and 53cm long. She was just perfect, Keith had never seen such a beautiful baby and kept saying to Ruth, "She's perfect, she's beautiful, we have a little girl." Ruth was so happy and couldn't stop smiling, she was a mother. She looked at her child and promised her she would love her and cherish her for the rest of her life. She promised she would be the best mother possible and would never let her down. Keith suddenly looked at Ruth holding their daughter and said "What are we going to call her?" Ruth looked at the baby then up at Keith "Emily Amelia Vasillio, meet your daddy."

Keith bent down and kissed Emily on the forehead and then kissed his wife, "Thank you for giving me the most precious gift, our daughter, Emily Amelia Vasillio." He smiled at his wife "I love you, Ruth Vasillio." Ruth looked at her husband holding their daughter, she couldn't believe how happy she felt. At last, she had her very own family, a family to love. She thought for a second about her own mother, how could she have given birth and not fallen in love with her child. Ruth would never be able to understand that especially not now that she was a mother. She then thought about Emily and how much she had loved Amelia, that's the kind of mother I will be she thought to herself. Suddenly a thought sprung into Ruth's mind, "What if during labour, when I asked for Emily's help she had helped me in a way only she could, what if she had given herself back to me as I had her. She took baby Emily from Keith's arms and as she looked in her eyes she knew.

The End
(Or is it?)